For Mom & Dad

And in loving memory of Janice...

CHAPTER 1

I REMEMBER STANDING IN A CHECKOUT line at ShopRite when I was fifteen years old. I'd run in, exhausted from a full day of school plus two hours of basketball practice, to grab some milk and eggs for my mother while she waited in the car. In front of me in the self-service line was an older woman, maybe in her thirties or forties. She had shiny black hair and smelled of perfume. Clutched in her manicured hand was a fistful of coupons and ShopRite's yellow plastic basket piled with cosmetics and shampoo.

I sighed. I still had hours of homework to get through, a book report due at the end of the week, and apparently, I had pissed off my best friend, Lea, by not inviting her to a party I had no control over. I didn't even want to go that stupid party.

The woman must have felt my frustration or heard my heavy sigh because she gave me a great big smile. We ended up talking, and I'll never forget how the conversation ended. I asked her if life gets easier as you get older.

The woman looked at me with a kind smile. "Actually honey, it gets a bit harder." She walked up to the available kiosk.

I stared after her. *Please tell me you're lying.*

That was two years ago.

Tonight, my thick brown hair is tied back in a ponytail. My arms are slick with sweat as my polyester shirt clings to my over-heated body. My legs are exhausted, yet they keep moving. I glance up for a second, and I'm met with a gymnasium full of screaming faces. The crowd, mostly black teens and some rowdy adults, cheer as the girl I'm guarding bullies her way into the key. I'm our team's power forward, and at five-foot-five, I'm small for my position, especially compared to my opponent. She has tree trunks for legs, muscular UFC arms, and is at least two inches taller than me. I block a pass to her, and for that, I get an elbow in my rib cage. I hit the floor, and the foul goes uncalled.

"Call the foul, Ref! Call the foul!" Coach Prudenti yells, his size-thirteen dress shoes wearing out the sidelines.

I've been taking a beating all game. The referee doesn't seem to care or notice. We were supposed to get blown away in this game, but we are winning by one. I rise from the floor, and the bully shoots and misses. Sounds of disappointment echo. It's deafening in this small, sweltering gym. Lea, tall and beefy—she would kill me if she heard me say that— and having a remarkably solid game, bravely jumps into the fray as their Amazon center captures the ball like it's a small animal and easily lobs in a two-pointer.

The metal bleachers hum as a cluster of teens in baggy jeans and knit caps stomp their enthusiasm. Their rubber-soled sneakers pound the metal seats in sync. It's an impressive sound, a sound you won't find in our white, middle-class, suburban gym. This is Cantor High School East's home court, all black, except for the white, six-foot-two Amazon at center. They're ranked third in the state and usually our toughest game of the year. Tonight is especially difficult.

Our point guard fires the ball to me, and the bully claws her hand in for a steal. Her jagged nail catches the skin on my forearm. I ignore the pain and bring the ball in close. This girl is suffocating. I feel her hot breath on the back of my neck as I pivot to escape. She holds onto me, locking her arm into mine. I wait for a foul to be called. Again, the whistle is silent. *What's this referee's problem?*

Finally, I pull free, and the bully comes at me again from behind. The anger inside me boils, and without even thinking, I reel back with my elbow and connect hard with her nose. A whistle immediately sounds, and play is halted. The gymnasium erupts in noise. I ignore the shouts from the fans and watch as the stunned bully throws a hand to her nose. Drops of red fall through the cracks of her meaty fingers, sprinkling her jersey. I notice a small splatter of blood hitting the top of her white Nikes. Her teammates hold her still while a towel is rushed to her nose. Eventually, the bully is escorted off-court, and blood is wiped from the lacquered wood floor.

GIRL ON POINT

CHERYL GUERRIERO

Unlocking New Worlds

Girl on Point
Copyright © 2017 by Cheryl Guerriero All rights reserved.
First Print Edition: April 2017

Print ISBN-13: 978-1-940215-96-9
Print ISBN-10: 1-940215-96-X

Red Adept Publishing, LLC
104 Bugenfield Court
Garner, NC 27529
http://RedAdeptPublishing.com/

Cover and Formatting: Streetlight Graphics

The referee points to me. "Number 15! Unsportsmanlike conduct! Two shots!"

Coach Prudenti calls a time-out, and the crowd boos me as I walk off-court. It's not the first time I've been booed, but it's the first time I've been booed for making someone eat my elbow. Honestly, I don't feel bad for what I did. She played dirty the entire game. She elbowed me at least three times in the ribs, not to mention grabbing my shirt every chance she got. I had enough. If the ref wasn't going to protect me, I was going to end her.

"We don't play to their level! You got that, Alex?" Coach lays into me.

"Yes, sir." I bow my head and slouch my shoulders like a scolded child. Everyone knows I have a temper. Coach has been saying for years one day it's going to get me in trouble, but I don't think it's today, or rather tonight, because he keeps me in the game and takes out Amber.

"Jenny, you're in!" He points to my sister.

I throw my arm around my sister as she jumps into the pile. I love when Jenny comes off the bench, not just because she's my little sister and I want her to do well, but because she's hungry, dependable, and quick.

Coach draws a diagram. "Jenny, I want you to drive the girl to her weak hand. Lea, once she does, step up and double-team. We want her to pass. Alex, give your girl some room. Down below, keep on 'em tight! Got it? Twenty seconds! You can do this!" We all nod, pumped and excited. "Hands in! Hands in!"

We pile our hands on top of one another and scream, "DE-FENSE!"

Our team waits while their point guard takes her first of two free throws, compliments of my bad temper. She bounces the ball once, twice... then throws up a brick. Disappointment echoes. She makes her second shot, and the gymnasium explodes. They're winning by a point.

Seconds later, the ball is back in play. Jenny does exactly what Coach told her to do and forces the point guard to go weak. The girl dribbles like a caged squirrel, looking to waste the twenty seconds left on the clock. Lea helps out on a double team, and I ease off my girl in hopes of intercepting a bad pass. I see my two other teammates glued to their opponents. I'm jacked up on adrenaline as the clock ticks down from nineteen seconds... eighteen seconds... fifteen seconds... My heart is pounding. We need the ball! Just then, Jenny dives in for a steal like a little monkey. Her nubby fingers tip the leather and send the ball spiraling free.

7

Lea turns blindly and accidently blocks the point guard from recovering the ball. It bounces toward the sideline, and I sprint toward it. There is something about a loose ball that I absolutely love. At the very last moment, I pluck the ball from the sideline's edge and head down court. Jenny races to catch up. I hear Lea cheering me on. "You got this, Campbell!" The point guard is hot on my back, fueling me to go faster.

I have seven seconds to get down court. Seven seconds to hit the baseline and go in for a layup. I know the second I do, this chick is going to clobber me, so I go up strong, really strong. And she does exactly what I expect. She follows me in the air, her body pinned alongside mine, her sweat getting on my arms and shirt. I focus above her head and above her flailing arms. I zero in on a spot outlined in red and tucked in the upper right corner. I've done this a million times. The adrenaline is such a rush. It's such a high. I release the ball off my rolling fingers. It hits the spot and bounces back down—sinking the winning point!

My teammates' screaming, smiling, sweaty faces bombard me. Lea is so big she practically knocks me over. I grab Jenny and slap a wet kiss on her face. She hates when I do that but not tonight. Tonight, she is happy. Tonight, she screams so loudly my ears ring. Coach Prudenti and Coach Sheehan, a tall, good-looking dude barely out of college, meet us on the court, proud. Our excitement slowly dies. I wish it would never end.

"A'right girls, line up. Shake their hands," Coach tells us before he and Coach Sheehan walk off to do the same with the opposing coaches.

I watch as the crowd exits the bleachers in a hum of activity. Their team may have lost tonight, but we gave them a great show. As we line up to shake hands with the opposing team, the player whose nose I bloodied refuses to shake mine.

"Bitch! I'm gonna kick your ass!"

Fortunately, her coach reels her in and makes certain she keeps her hands to herself. I head off to the locker room with my teammates, thinking I'm going to get jumped, but nothing happens.

CHAPTER 2

OUR EUPHORIC MOOD CONTINUES IN the locker room, and I'm all hyped up.

"Making friends again, huh, Captain Campbell?" one girl says.

Jenny laughs.

"What are you laughing at? She was picking on me all game."

"Oh, my poor big sister," Jenny teases, hanging on me. "Wait till John finds out." She mocks Dad's voice.

"Hey—winning basket. Don't get all jelly and jam on me."

Jenny shoves me. "You're such an idiot."

"I'm just glad I didn't have to play against her," Lea says. "Jesus."

"I'm jus' stoked your cute little badonkadonk blocked that girl from gettin' the ball." I slap Lea's bare butt.

"Yeah, you're all welcome." Lea wiggles her butt before walking off to go put on clothes.

I pull off my uniform and step into a shower stall. Most of the girls don't shower after games, and I'm usually one of them, especially in this place. It's crawling with crud, but I have a date with Jay, so I quickly rinse off. When I step out, Jenny is waiting for me, rocking out to a song on her iPhone. She's such a dork but a fun dork. She always looks happy. I envy how comfortable Jenny is in her own skin. I've never felt comfortable in mine. I don't know why. Maybe it's my anger.

"Hurry up, ya big ho!" she yells at me.

"Hey, go get me a Dr. Pepper from that store." I dry off with a towel.

"What store?" She pulls the buds out of her ears.

"The one across from the school. When we pulled in. Amber just left with Cait. You can catch up to them."

"Go get it yourself, Miss Five-Finger-Discount." She side-eyes me.

"Hey!" I look around to make sure no one heard. "I haven't done that in a while."

"Yeah, right."

"It's true. C'mon… do it for your big sis? Pleasssse? I'd do it for you."

"Pfft. You would not."

"I would too. Here. You can get something for yourself." I bait her with a ten-dollar bill that I wave in front of her face. "C'mon, lil' squirrel… lil' squirrely rabbit. You can keep the change."

Jenny snatches the dough from my hand. "Fine! You're so slow!" She throws her ear buds into place and screams at me. "Take my bag!"

Her #2 sports bag rests at my feet. "Yeah, I got it. Now go!" I wave her away. She blasts the iPod and takes off. It sounds like Katy Perry.

"You two are so weird." Lea appears behind me. "Hey, have you seen my lucky hair band? I can't find it."

After a five-minute search for Lea's lucky hair band and then discovering it in her hand, we exit the locker room together. I'm in jeans and a sweater under my favorite puffy blue winter jacket. My hair is still wet, and I'm lugging both Jenny's #2 sports bag and my own as I listen to Lea yap about how Amber gets on her nerves.

By the time we enter the gymnasium, it's devoid of both people and noise. The emptiness and silence of this old, stale gym leaves me feeling like a scared, lost five-year-old girl. Even with Lea yapping at my side, it's as if I'm all by myself. It's a lonely, familiar feeling and one I hate. It usually gets triggered at the end of the summer when the weather changes, it gets darker earlier, and the "back to school" campaigns are all around. But every once in a while, like now, it hits me in the gut and has me vibrating with a terror that I am unloved, unwanted, and alone in this world.

We hear voices. Apparently, we're not alone because tucked in the corner of the bleachers is a group of teenagers hanging out. The white Amazon center is one of them. She's still in her uniform and is smiling as if she doesn't have a care in the world. She notices us, and her smile seems to grow.

"Hey, 15! Number 15!" a very dark-skinned teenage boy says, speaking to me. "My boy wants to know if you'd go out with him!"

"Yeah, Number 15! That shit was cool!" The boy stands up in excitement and imitates my elbow smashing backward. He's razor thin and not very attractive. His hair is wild and curly, and he looks like he's only five feet three. "I like how you play, girl!" He falls off the bleachers and struggles to stand, clearly wasted. His friends laugh. Lea stares at them as if they are circus freaks. She picks up her pace as we near the exit. I stare back at the center, wondering why she's still smiling.

We step into the cold night air, and a vicious wind slaps our faces. I pull my jacket close and lower my chin into it.

"Christ! It's freezing!" Lea clenches her teeth.

We hurry along the graffiti-tagged building. It's creepy and dark, and I don't exactly feel safe. A few students linger by their cars, but most are gone. It's too cold to stand outside. We fight our way against the wind and cold. I peek up from my jacket and see our bus. It's parked along the curb, less than fifty feet away, but in this weather, it feels like a million miles. From behind, I hear heavy bass. I turn and see a tricked-out car slowing down as it approaches. From inside, a group of male faces stare out at us, their heads covered by knit caps. My shoulders relax when the car speeds out of the parking lot. Another car chases after it. Each step toward our bus seems to take forever. *I should've worn a hat.*

A few feet ahead, a Honda with a dented bumper and a thick cloud of exhaust spewing from its tailpipe crawls to a stop in front of us. It takes me a moment before I realize the girl in the backseat is the bully whose nose I bloodied. And that's when the passenger door pops open, and a girl who looks exactly like the bully, but shorter, steps out. A second girl exits from the driver's side. They follow after us. Or rather, me.

"Hey, bitch! Where you going?"

I look toward our bus, hoping Coach will see us, but his back is facing us as he talks to someone I can't completely make out. Lea quickens her pace. She's never walked so fast in her life. If I'm scared, Lea's petrified.

The bully's sister catches up to me, and my heart begins to race.

"Gonna throw an elbow? Throw it now, bitch!"

She walks right alongside me, eyeballing me closely and waiting for me to do something. I fear any second, she is going to punch me in the face. But I keep walking, hiding my fear and trying to pretend this brute is not beside me.

"We don't want any trouble," Lea says, barely audible.

11

The ugly sister and her friend laugh.

"Hey, ladies!" a male voice calls. I look back and see Coach Sheehan running toward us.

"Thank God," Lea says.

Coach Sheehan is at our side within seconds. "Let it go, girls," he says to the bully's sister and her friend. "Game's over."

The bully's sister responds with a middle finger. "Fuck you!"

"Another time, a'right?" He places his arms around Lea and me and escorts us safely toward the bus.

The window of the car rolls down, and the bully, who no longer holds a towel to her nose, yells, "Bitch! Next time you're *dead*!"

My heart is still racing when we reach the bus.

"Thank God," Lea says. A burst of fog rolls out of her open mouth, and she thrusts down the zipper of her heavy coat. I know she secretly loved Coach Sheehan coming to our rescue. She is constantly telling me she thinks he's hot. Coach Prudenti, seeing what just happened, eyes the bully's departing car with concern as it vanishes down the road, leaving a wake of burning rubber.

"Everything okay?" Coach Prudenti asks.

"Yeah, it's fine," Sheehan says.

Coach turns to us. "Good game tonight, girls."

"Thanks." Lea happily boards the bus.

Coach puts a hand on my shoulder. "Watch those elbows. Okay, Alex?"

"Yes, sir." I look him straight in the eye this time. Then I enter the bus, grateful to be welcomed in by its warmth and loudness.

The lights are off, shrouding my rowdy teammates in shadows. I scan the seats for Jenny and sigh heavily when I can't find her. I'm jonesing for my Dr. Pepper. "Jenny!" I think I see her head in the back when Lea pulls me into a seat next to her. The windows are fogged from all the breathing. I drop Jenny's bag and zip out of my heavy jacket.

"Oh my God. We almost got killed!" Lea says, being her overly dramatic self.

"*¡Eres una reina del drama!*" I say.

"What? English, *por favor*."

"I said you're such a drama queen. *¡Ay, Dios mío!*" I throw my head back and place a hand over my heart.

12

"Well, I do like telenovelas." She blows a super large bubble in my face, and I pop it with my finger. "Hey!" She sucks it off her lips.

I laugh and glance around the bus for Jenny. She's certainly taking her time.

Amber sits across the aisle, eating pretzels. "Awesome playing tonight."

"You too," I say, lying. It wasn't one of her best games. "Hey, do you know where Jenny is?"

Amber points to the rear of the bus, where the noise is even louder. "I think she's back there."

I look, but I still don't see Jenny. Instead, my eyes land on a few sophomores who sit in the middle seats sharing potato chips and drinking sodas. I get lost watching them. This will be the last year I ride in this crazy, fun-filled bus. *Don't get sad,* I tell myself. A loud pop grabs my attention. It sounds like fireworks.

"Was that a gun shot?" someone asks.

All eyes turn toward the fogged windows. I wipe at the glass and see a shadow of a car speed away from the store. I wonder why its headlights are off.

"Quiet!" Coach Prudenti yells as he also looks out the window.

Lea asks me a question.

I don't hear her. I move into the aisle. "Where's Jenny?"

The bus driver enters from the outside. He exchanges a few words with Coach Sheehan. Again, my eyes frantically search the bus.

Lea watches me. "What's wrong?"

"Jenny… she's not on the bus." My hand pinches the leather seat, and with each face I look at that is not Jenny's, the air becomes harder and harder to breathe. I start to panic. "Has anyone seen my sister?"

I spin around, push to the front of the bus, and Coach Prudenti stops me from exiting. "Let go of me!" I fight like an animal until finally I'm able to break free of his grasp. I run out of the bus and sprint across the street, insane with fear. The store is a small brick building with a dirt parking lot.

"Alex! Alex!" Coach Prudenti chases after me.

I don't slow down. I burst open the heavy glass door. *Please, God! Please! Let Jenny be okay!* I scream inside my head. A male body, in jeans and a long-sleeved T-shirt, is face down on the floor, arms spread to the sides, a pool of blood spreading out from underneath his cocked head. Coach Prudenti enters behind me.

"Call 9-1-1!" I yell.

He tries to hold onto me. "Alex!"

I throw his hand aside. Cigarettes and candy litter the floor. I race down an aisle. "Jenny!" I scream. Boxes of household items surround and suffocate me. I beg Jenny to answer. *Please, God! Please!*

I turn the corner, and my heart stops. Jenny lies on the ground, looking right at me with a petrified stare. And that's when I see it—a blossoming circle of red on the front of her white jacket. I bolt toward her.

"I'm here! I got you!" I kneel down beside Jenny. She grips my arm, and her hands are covered in blood. "It's okay! I got you!" I gently remove the plugs of her iPod, which are still trapped in her ears. I hear Coach on his phone, yelling out our location. "Hurry!" I scream. Jenny's skin is pale and cold. She is clearly in shock. Coach hangs up the call and carefully opens Jenny's jacket. Her game shirt is drenched in blood.

"An ambulance is on the way. You're gonna be okay," he says in a shaky voice. He pulls off his sweatshirt and holds it over her wound. Jenny screams in pain and cries as Coach tries to keep the blood from escaping.

I hold her hands. "You're gonna be fine!" I promise her. But Jenny's frightened eyes make me doubt my words. She looks so small and scared.

"You're doing great, baby. Hang in there," Coach says.

Please, God. Help my sister!

"Alex..." she whispers, fighting to breathe.

I hold her eyes. "I'm here. You're gonna be okay. I promise." I force my lips into a smile and choke back my tears, trying to keep the fear from registering on my face. I start to babble, hoping it will keep Jenny calm. "You played so great tonight. We wouldn't have won if it weren't for you. It wasn't Lea's big ass that made me get that ball. It was you."

She almost laughs, and I see the faintest smile emerge on her lips.

"One of your best games. And next year... next year you're a starter... no doubt."

On the ground is a Dr. Pepper bottle, and I hate myself for it.

"You're doing great, Jenny," Coach repeats.

But she isn't. She looks like chalk. Like a ghost. Her clothes are covered in blood. I wonder where the hell the ambulance is. What is taking so long? But only a minute or two has passed. I kiss Jenny's head. "I love you."

Then Jenny shivers in pain and struggles to breathe. Her gaze holds onto mine.

I cry. "Jenny, you fight! You *fight*!"

She grips my hands, desperate. Her eyes beg me to do something, but there is nothing I can do. I feel so helpless. So fucking helpless!

"Jenny, please don't leave me! You fight... hang on." I cradle her in my arms like I did when she was two and I was four, pretending she was my own child. I kiss her cheek. "Love you, mean it..." I say those words over and over. "Love you, mean it..."

Tears drip from my eyes. Chin. Mouth. They drown me. I shake my head no. I pretend this is not happening. But Jenny's body remains still, and for what seems like forever, I stare into my sister's beautiful blue eyes. I feel Coach's hand on my back. A strangled cry rises from my throat. I scream a horrific "*No!*"

There will not be a next year.

CHAPTER 3

MY IPHONE ALARM GOES OFF, and I open my eyes, already dreading the day. I try to ignore the endlessly chirpy sound until, a minute later, I surrender and sit up in bed. I silence the alarm with a swipe of my finger. I hate mornings. Mornings are the absolute worst. I think mornings are the worst for anyone, but add a dead sister, and they become ruthlessly unbearable.

I squirm to the edge of my bed, and as soon as my bare feet touch the hardwood floor, I'm paralyzed. A tingle of icy air blows onto my unpolished toes from an open vent a few feet away. Whether it's fatigue or depression, I'm tired, so I take a moment to rest. I'm surrounded by purple, a color I regretted picking out as soon as the paint hit the walls. Above my head is a fish net. Other than that, my room is pretty bare. I stare at a photo of Jenny and me on a dresser. She's smiling as if to say, "You idiot." I sigh and remain in place until the thoughts in my head get so punishing that the only way to escape them is to move.

I push off the bed and get moving, but it does little to help me escape the feelings buried inside me: pain and sadness—two unwanted guests that follow me everywhere I go. To the bathroom. To school. To where I'm crowded by others. Or when I'm alone. They never leave, and I desperately want them to leave. I desperately want Jenny to be alive. But she is gone. And I am here. And here hurts.

It's been six months since Jenny died. She was shot with a .22 caliber gun. The store clerk was killed with a different gun. His name was Jose Gutierrez, and he was married and had two small children. Their deaths were ruled homicides during a robbery.

I grab a bottle of Zoloft off a dresser and pop open the lid. I've missed most of the second half of the school year and have been on antidepressants since Jenny's death. I swallow one of the little blue pills without water. I don't think these antidepressants help because each step I take feels like a thousand pounds.

I walk past my parents' closed bedroom door and step into the bathroom. Things are so much different than they used to be. Before, when I woke up, Jenny would already be in the shower, door locked, music blasting. I'd have to pound on the door for what felt like forever before she'd open up to let me in to pee. Our mother, who probably won't get out of bed any earlier than noon today, would've already had coffee with my dad, sent him off to catch his train into the city, and made our lunches for the day. Then ten minutes before Jenny and I needed to leave for school, Mom would start yelling up to us from the kitchen that we were going to be late. Now the house is painfully quiet without even the smell of coffee to keep me company.

I wash my face, brush my teeth, and in less than five minutes, I'm wearing my usual school uniform—jeans and a white tee. I head straight from my bedroom, down the stairs, and out the front door. It isn't until I'm driving away in my Jeep Wrangler that I realize I'm wearing two different Converse sneakers.

I arrive in the school's parking lot, and every spot is taken, except for a narrow one at the very end of the first row, facing the football field. It's too tight for anyone, except if you drive a Jeep, so I wheel over the curb and park halfway in the spot. I grab my backpack and head toward the entrance door closest to my first-period class.

Another kid running late tosses open the glass door, and I trail in behind him. I pass rows of lockers. Hanging above my head is a huge white banner with orange lettering, which reads Congratulations, Seniors—You've Made It! I turn the corner, and a herd of faces rushes past me. I'm surrounded by voices and laughter. A gym teacher smiles and asks me how I am.

"Good."

My token answer is always "good." I am anything but good.

A bell rings, and I'm seated in my Advanced Spanish class. The teachers have been taking it easy on me since Jenny's death. Sometimes I complete my homework, and sometimes I don't. They politely ask me to finish. But I never do, and they never ask again.

17

I pay mild attention as our Spanish teacher, Mr. Reddick, scribbles a bunch of numbers and words onto the blackboard in perfect alignment. He wears a bright-red button-down shirt with a tie and shiny loafers. Finished, he places the chalk on his desk and addresses the class. It's a semi-privileged bunch of seniors. Most own iPhones, iPads, and expensive handbags and drive cars that their parents paid for. Some have jobs, others don't, but everyone, with the exception of maybe me, is going away to college.

Jay is in this class with me. He's a big guy with broad shoulders, and he used to bargain shop at T.J.Maxx. It closed, and now he shops at Marshalls. He hates to pay full price, but mostly it's because, unlike every other spoiled kid in this class, Jay's parents don't pay for anything—car, phone, nothing. The poor guy even has to fork over his own dough to buy himself lunch. He rubs his kneecap and stretches out his ginormous leg. Jay was the starting shortstop of our high school baseball team until he tore his ACL. I see him watching me. He knows I'm depressed and wants to help. But he can't save me. No one can.

Mr. Reddick tells the class that the final exam will be in two weeks. "Chapters Eleven through Fifteen and everything from the first half of the year," he says in Spanish. Moans follow.

Tyler O'Connor, a ridiculously smart stoner with tats, speaks up from the back row in English. "Aw, come on, can't you give us a break?"

Mr. Reddick smiles. "No one's going to give you a break in college, now are they, Mr. O'Connor?"

Tyler responds with a roll of his eyes. You'd never know it by looking at Tyler, but he got into Yale.

Forty-five minutes later, the bell rings. The class rises and hurries to exit. I'm still sitting at my desk, slowly gathering my books. Jay waits for me by the door.

"Jay, you coming or what?" His best friend, Reed, a guy he's known since he was eight years old, yells at him.

I take my time, grateful when I see Jay follow Reed. Moments later, I walk out of the classroom and into a less-crowded hallway. Carly Williams, one of the more popular band geeks, hammers away on her iPhone, head down, while others I don't recognize scroll through Instagram and Twitter. The thought of going on either one makes my stomach turn.

I keep walking, and the hallway empties. A few pounding feet carry students into classrooms. I approach the room I'm supposed to be in—Advanced Chem. My teacher, Mrs. Cohen, stands outside the door. "How are you, Alex?"

"Good." I walk past her and take my seat.

I ditch school an hour early and speed out of the parking lot, dreading what awaits me at home. My mother has gotten drunk every day since Jenny's death. Her drinking was never unusual, but it was reserved for weekends. Now, I can't remember the last time my mother took a sober breath.

I drive down Monmouth Road, a pretty, tree-lined street, passing modest homes, a few white-steeple churches, and a quaint little post office. Middletown isn't a wealthy town, but it's a respectable place to live. My favorite part about it is that the nearest beach is only fifteen minutes away, and it only takes an hour to get into New York City by train. My mother used to say it's a place where you can leave your doors unlocked at night, even though we never did.

Most of the time growing up, I found Middletown boring. I suffered from what I like to call "anywhere but here" syndrome. I often fantasized about escaping Middletown by flying away on my bicycle and traveling through the clouds and landing somewhere exciting like the mountains of Alaska or on a horse ranch in Montana, someplace vastly different from this ordinary suburban town—unless, of course, I was playing sports. I never wanted to escape then, maybe because sports occupied my mind so well or maybe because they made me feel good about myself. Either way, if I really think about it, I'm not too sure Middletown was ever the problem.

I turn off Monmouth and onto Harmony Road. Soon, I am driving down our street. I'm grateful none of our neighbors are outside their homes as I pull into our driveway and park directly in front of the basketball pole. My dad put it up when I was in the sixth grade and Jenny was in fourth. It reminds me of Jenny, but then again, everything reminds me of her.

Our house is like all the others on our block: double-storied with three pillars. However, unlike most of our neighbors, we have an in-ground pool in the backyard, and our lawn is immaculate. There is not a weed to be found or a shrub untrimmed. My father is relentless in the yard. I think it's his way of escaping—to keep moving, to keep fixing things. The roof. The hedges. The lawn. The pool. Anything that keeps his mind occupied.

I enter the house and drop my keys in a ceramic bowl. Above the bowl are little wooden signs that read Welcome and Home is Where the Heart Is.

My mother likes country prints and potpourri in the bathrooms, everything I hate. My mother and I couldn't be more opposite in our tastes. She conceded to my father, Jenny, and me and allowed a large plasma screen TV in the living room. She called it her reading room. However, three against one won out, and the den became her reading room. As I pass through the living room, I try not to look at the walls covered with family photos.

I escape into the kitchen and pour myself a glass of tap water. Our kitchen is spacious and gets lots of sunlight. It's painted pale yellow and filled with gaudy country knickknacks. A large island takes up the center. It's cluttered with unopened mail and small prescription bottles—a mixture of painkillers, sleeping pills, and antidepressants—all labeled with my mother's name: Mary Campbell. My mother never so much as took three Advil in a day. Now, she is a middle-class suburban junkie.

As I drink the water, I wander toward the refrigerator. It's covered in papers, reminder notes, magnets, and more family photos. One of Jenny and me holds my attention, taken from last Halloween. We're dressed as pregnant nuns. Jenny wears a goofy smile, pretending to be drunk, while I hold a large makeshift joint in my hand and pretend to be stoned. I try not to slide deeper into depression as I stare at the picture. But it swallows me. The depression, the sadness, they drown me. My eyes land on a basketball schedule. Ws are marked all throughout. And one L. We lost against Manalapan High School. I was sick that day. There are check marks along the games we played. Toward the bottom, I see "Cantor High School East—Away." It is unmarked.

I want to rip the schedule off the refrigerator and tear it into a million pieces, but I don't dare. My mother would explode in a fit of rage. Nothing has been touched since Jenny's death. I hear the jingle of metal tags and see Duke heading my way. He must've been sleeping upstairs.

His big, handsome German-shepherd face makes me smile. I drop to the ground. "Hey, buddy. Hey, handsome." He mopes over to me, tail wagging. "How are you, my beautiful, handsome boy?" I cuddle up into his strong furry body and smother his snout with kisses. We got him at the pound when he was a little over a year old. How anyone could have abandoned him, I'll never know. He's the sweetest dog. "You're so handsome. Yes, you are." He plops down on the floor, his big paws sprawled across my legs. I run my hand across his soft, furry head. *God, I love this dog.*

For weeks after Jenny's death, Duke wandered aimlessly in and out of her bedroom. I felt so sad for him. How do you explain to a dog someone he loved died? He used to sleep in Jenny's bedroom, but after growing tired of searching for her, he started sleeping in mine. Last night, he was suspiciously missing. I think my mother forgot to let him back in after she let him out to pee.

"You wanna treat?" I move his big paws aside and stand up. I open a pantry closet, which seems very empty compared to how it once looked. The shelves used to be stocked with cans of green beans, corn, peas, tomato paste, tomato soup. You name the can, we had it. My mother, much like Jay, was a bargain shopper, and every time ShopRite had a "can-can" sale I had to go with her to lug several cases of cans into the back of her Lexus SUV. But now, the empty closet seems as hollow I am.

I grab a box of large Milk-Bones and walk back to Duke, who sits up. He knows the drill. "A'right, big dog... top dog. Gimme a paw." Duke obeys by throwing his massive paw into the palm of my hand. "Good boy, Duke!" I place two large milk-bones into his open mouth and quickly pull away my hand. He chomps down like Jaws, his tartar-stained teeth sending bits and pieces of Milk-Bones flying.

I walk over to the back door to see if his bowls are full. There's not a drop of water or a scrap of food in either bowl. I grab one off the floor and fill it to slopping over with water. I shut off the stainless steel faucet and hear another pair of footsteps in the kitchen. Before I even turn around, I feel my mother's intense energy behind me. I can also tell she's been drinking, or rather, I can smell she's been drinking. I turn and face her.

"Where's your father?" my mother asks without even a hello.

I shrug. "I don't know. I just got home."

"He was supposed to be home early."

"Yeah, well, you know Dad."

I place Duke's water bowl on the floor, and I notice mud caked onto the sides of my mother's white socks. I don't even want to know how that mud got there.

I stand back up and wonder if my mother's showered today. I doubt it.

She's wearing the same clothes she had on last night. And her hair, which never before had a single strand out of place, is greasy and unkempt. The roots on her otherwise blond, highlighted head are an inch deep, begging to be touched up. My mother used to look young for forty-six, but since Jenny's death, she looks remarkably older. The wrinkles around her mouth and eyes seem to have increased.

Duke licks a few remaining Milk-Bone crumbs off the floor and descends on the water, lapping it up with his big tongue and creating a small puddle on the floor.

"He needs a bath," my mother says and walks out.

I stand there, feeling even more alone and depressed.

An hour later, I'm slumped into the living room couch watching some mind-numbing TV show with Duke sprawled beside me, his big paws hanging over the edge. That's usually a no-no with my mother, but I doubt she'll even care or notice, unless of course, she's looking to take her anger out on me. I hear my father's Audi pull into the driveway, and so does Duke. His ears perk up, and he jumps off the couch to greet him at the door.

A moment later, my father walks into the living room. Duke is at his hip, tail thrashing. "You ain't so tough." My father roughhouses with Duke, who barks relentlessly. He gives Duke a solid pat on his back, letting the dog know the game's over. He tosses his briefcase down on the table in front of me.

"Hey, kiddo." He kisses the top of my head. "How was school?"

"Usual. Sucked."

"Yeah. So did work."

"John, I thought you were getting home early?" My mother appears from upstairs. Her hair is no longer greasy, and the dark roots are less noticeable. She wears a navy-blue blouse and jeans. In her hand is her Coach purse.

"I got tied up," he says.

"We're late. Let's go. Please."

My father is barely allowed a visit to the bathroom before we are rushed out the door. I dread where we're going.

CHAPTER 4

WE LOAD INTO THE AUDI, and Dad clicks on the radio, setting the volume at a level just high enough to fill the silence. Twenty minutes into our ride, we arrive at the New Jersey Turnpike entrance and head south toward Cantor. My stomach drops like a barbell hitting the floor as the small white E-ZPass device that is stuck to the Audi's windshield is read, and an electronic sign flashes "Go!"

I stare out the window. *If only I had gotten my own damn soda.* I feel tears coming on. I force them back and beg God to take away my pain. But nothing happens. I'm convinced God has me on mute.

Almost two hours later, my parents and I sit on hard padded chairs in a cramped office. We're surrounded by cinder block walls as fading sunlight drifts into the room through dirty vinyl blinds. I look across at my mother. Her blue eyes are dull, drugged, and filled with tremendous pain. My heart hurts, knowing I caused this pain. We didn't always see eye to eye, my mother and I. In fact, most days, we didn't get along. Most days, we fought. Jenny was the one who made her smile. Jenny was her baby. My mother, I'm convinced, barely even liked me.

Initially, the girl whose nose I bloodied was suspected in the shootings. But aside from threatening me, she didn't kill anyone. Less than a mile from the high school, her sister's friend was stopped and ticketed for speeding. I know this because of Detective Thoms, a white middle-aged man with short black hair peppered with gray and arms much bigger than belong on his five-foot-eight frame. We're sitting in his small cluttered office. Trapped beneath his meaty fingers is my sister's case file, a thick, unbound manila folder, filled with pages of notes and photographs. I stare at the folder, desperately wanting to examine it myself.

We've visited Detective Thoms twice before, and upon my mother's insistence, we're here again. She wants the detective to see us. She wants Detective Thoms to know the pain and torture this causes our family, the injustice we suffer while those who are responsible for my sister's death are free and living. We're living, but we're not free.

Those who are responsible—or so we are told by Detective Thoms—are members of a local street gang, all female, and for fear of us or the store clerk's family going to the media, or evidence being tainted or someone taking justice into their own hands—something I've often fantasized about—he is unable or unwilling to disclose the gang's name. There are several gangs in the Cantor area, but one in particular that Detective Thoms suspects murdered my sister. He has arrested these girls before for loitering, breaking and entering, vandalism, possession of drugs with intent to sell, and assault and battery. Because of their ages, they were sent to juvy. Now, they're older. Eighteen, nineteen, twenty years old, except for the youngest who's seventeen. Detective Thoms believes this gang committed the crime, and there's evidence to back him up, but mostly, it's his gut, and his gut can't arrest these girls.

Detective Thoms was hoping the store's security tape would be recovered. It hasn't been, and he repeats what he's already told us. "Without the store tape, there's no solid evidence."

I see the veins in my mother's neck bulge. She raises her voice. "I don't understand. You have tire prints from a car. You said there was gun residue on a girl's hand. You should be able to do something!"

Before Thoms can answer, another plainclothes officer pokes his head into the room. His head is shaved bald, and his arms are covered in ink. He apologizes for interrupting and tells Thoms he needs to see him. Thoms nods. "Give me ten, Rawlings."

Rawlings disappears, and I can't help thinking this interruption was planned.

Thoms returns his attention to my mother. He looks at her, sympathetic. "Mrs. Campbell—"

"Mary. Not Mrs. Campbell."

Detective Thoms nods. She's done this to him before. He goes on to tell my mother what she already knows, what we already know. And that is on the evening of the murder, a police officer acted prematurely

24

when he brought one of the girls in for questioning. A swab residue test was administered on the girl's hands and clothes, but no warrant was ever obtained to perform the test. The officer didn't even read the girl her rights, making whatever results found from the test inadmissible in court. What hurts the most is that trace amounts of primer were found on the palm of the girl's left hand, indicating a gun had been fired. But when they searched her home, no gun was ever found.

My father remains silent, and I wonder what he is thinking as Detective Thoms explains, as he did on our last visit, that without the murder weapon and admissible gun-residue evidence, a defense attorney could easily create reasonable doubt. He also reminds us—not that he needs to—two guns were used in the shootings. The autopsy report showed the caliber bullet found in Jenny's body was different from the three slugs pulled from Mr. Gutierrez's body, indicating there were two shooters.

"What about the second gun?" my mother asks.

Detective Thoms sighs, and it's hard to tell if it's from his own frustration or lack of patience in dealing with my mother. "Mrs… Mary. Neither gun has been recovered, and unless prints or DNA were on the weapon, it wouldn't be convicting evidence that this particular girl shot your daughter."

"Murder," my mother corrects him. He nods, and she continues her interrogation. "But you know it's this gang?"

"I'm confident. Yes. The car helps, but still we can't arrest these girls. At least not yet."

As for the car, Detective Thoms doesn't need to retell its story. I know that inside that manila folder is a photograph of a charred 2009 Thunderbird. The screeching I heard and the tire tracks left on the roadway were from this type of automobile. Thoms knew by heart that the leader of this female gang drove a 2009 Thunderbird. Unlike the other police officer, Thoms did obtain a search warrant and went to her house. Unfortunately, nothing of substance was found, particularly not the gun used in Jenny's shooting. When Thoms brought the girl in for questioning, she claimed her car was stolen two days prior to the robbery. Yet she never reported it. Weeks later, it was found in Philadelphia. It had been stripped and set ablaze.

"We're keeping a close eye on these girls, and most likely, we'll be able to bring them in on some other charge."

25

My mother's eyes grow wide with rage. "I don't want them brought in on some other charge. I want them arrested for killing my daughter!"

Detective Thoms's hands move off the folder. "We're doing all we can."

I see a coffee stain on the folder, which contains the details of my sister's death. She was shot and killed. She was only fifteen. The folder has not even been kept clean. It was used as a coaster.

My mother stands to leave. She hurls obscenities laced with "incompetence" and "civil law suits." She is hysterical. She searches for her purse. It is right in front of her, but she doesn't see it. My father awkwardly hands it to her, and she leaves without us. An uncomfortable silence is left in her wake.

Detective Thoms barely flinches. He looks across his desk at my father. "I'm sorry. I can assure you, Mr. Campbell, these girls are being watched closely. Justice will be served."

I don't believe him. I picture Detective Thoms reclined in his chair, drinking his morning coffee. It hurts to see that stain on my sister's folder. I wonder if it was an accident, callousness, or slobbery. Whatever the cause, it's there. It makes me want to scream and punch my fists through the wall.

Detective Thoms stands to walk my father and me out the door. I take my time, stopping to tie my sneaker, and my backpack falls off my shoulder. I hear Detective Thoms's voice drift away as he and my father leave the room. Seconds later, I stand inches from Thoms's cluttered desk. I look down and see my sister's name on the folder's tab: Jenny Campbell.

I know inside that folder are the names and addresses of those responsible for my sister's death. My heart begins to race, and before I can think twice, I grab the manila folder off his desk and stuff it in my backpack.

CHAPTER 5

M Y MOTHER DOESN'T SAY A word as my father and I join her in the car. She sits in the passenger seat, staring out the window, her eyes red and swollen. I'm grateful she is silent. I click on my seat belt and rest my head on the leather, relieved to be out of that police station and tucked safely in the back of my dad's car.

"We'll get through this, Mary. We'll be okay." My father turns on the engine and looks at my mother.

I think he says it more to convince himself. The truth is, we won't be okay. We will never be the same.

We drive off, and the police station grows small in the distance. I wonder if Detective Thoms has noticed the folder is gone. And if he does, does he suspect I took it? I don't care if he does. How would he prove I took it? There weren't any cameras in his office, and he didn't see me take the folder, just like he didn't see those girls shoot and kill my sister. But he knows one of them did.

As we head toward the New Jersey Turnpike and back to our home, I stare out the window as a parade of poverty flashes before my eyes. Cantor is just one big cesspool, a suburban ghetto. The sidewalks are littered with trash. The stores are dirty, run-down, and tagged with graffiti. The skyline is a landscape of dilapidated and abandoned warehouses. There are homeless men and women on just about every corner, pushing shopping carts, riffling through garbage, or simply taking up residency along the buildings. I watch as one woman practically buries herself in filth searching for a can to add to her collection.

We turn onto another street, and suddenly, we are in a more residential area. But these homes look nothing like the ones in Middletown. They are two-story brick buildings, surrounded by chain-link fences and rotted brown lawns. Farther ahead, I see a tall stack of ugly apartment buildings clustered together. I notice at least two girls, no older than me, holding small children. Nobody appears to have a job.

Cantor, as I have discovered, thanks to Google, has one of the highest crime rates in the country and is one of the poorest cities. I stare angrily out the window. This is where people get by on food stamps and welfare checks. This is where statistics on single teenage mothers soar. This is where one out of every two adults is functionally illiterate. And this is where those responsible for killing my sister reside, in this neglected shit hole, centered in the good old Garden State.

Almost two hours later, my parents and I are in a different world. It's dark when we pull into our driveway and empty out of the car. Each of us is silent, lost in his or her own depression and grief. My mother looks like a zombie as she leads the way to the front door.

"You okay?" Dad moves alongside me and places a hand on my back.

"Yeah," I lie as we enter the house together.

I escape into my bedroom with Duke and lock the door behind me. Downstairs, I hear ice cubes hitting glass as my mother fixes herself a drink. Down the hall, Dad has retreated into his bedroom to change out of his suit and tie and probably wish this day were over. I wonder what he's thinking. Unlike my mother, he keeps his emotions a secret.

I zip open my backpack and yank out the folder. Colored photographs fall to the floor, some matte, some glossy. They're pictures of what I assume used to be a 2009 Thunderbird. The only thing that remains is a blackened frame and four knobs of burnt rubber. I come across photos of the convenience store and quickly put them aside. I don't have the stomach to look at those.

I rifle through the contents and pull out a mug shot of a girl whose hair is pulled back tight against her head. Her eyebrows are pencil thin, and she looks anything but friendly. Her eyes are cold, vacant, and accented with layers of dark makeup. She looks as if she is staring right at me. A cold shiver crawls up my spine. On the back of the photo, scribbled in pen, is her name.

Lori Silva. 22 Oak Street, Cantor, New Jersey. Gang
affiliation: Black Diamonds. Age: 20.

A report stapled to the photograph lets me know that she's the owner of the Thunderbird and also the leader of the Black Diamonds.

There are several pages of notes from different detectives, and what I read doesn't exactly surprise me. It's a criminal resume, heavy on violence. Lori Silva's first arrest was at the age of eleven when she stabbed a boy, almost fatally, with a pair of scissors. There are hints of abuse and neglect in her upbringing with no mention of a father and numerous stints in juvy. From there, it lists her association with the other Black Diamond members: Cynthia "Cracker" Down, Ronnie Rodriguez, Natice Gentry. Various male names are also listed: Vince Martinez, Tray Brown, George Lutz. *Gang bangers probably. Drug dealers.* My stomach grows nauseated as I read.

I move on and pull another stapled photograph from the folder. It's of an extremely beautiful black girl. Her nose is thin, and her cheekbones are high and defined, almost like a model's. She looks pissed off at having her picture taken. I flip up the photograph and read the name on the report paper: Natice Gentry. It lists several arrests for shoplifting and breaking and entering and one for an assault on a high school teacher.

I find a packet of information on Cynthia Down. She's the youngest of the group and apparently a high school dropout. Her skin is pasty white and speckled with dark freckles. Her hair is frizzy and an ugly bright red. She has thin lips and an elfish nose. Her narrowed green eyes smirk, as if to say, "Fuck you." I flip through the pages that follow, and I'm met with a long list of criminal activities.

There are no photographs of Ronnie Rodriguez, although her name is listed in a police report as being a member of the gang. I read the handwritten notes scrawled throughout the pages.

Lori Silva—at home from 7:45PM 'til midnight. Mother incarcerated at the time—prostitution, narcotics. Mark Silva— ordered pizza at 8PM. Large pie. Confirmed with shop. Lori Silva—claimed car was stolen two days prior—at home during time of shooting. Passed polygraph. Mark Silva—confirms Lori Silva's car missing. Stated Lori was at home residence, 22 Oak Street. Time coincides with time of shooting.

Gun residue—Down girl acted suspicious when officer stopped and questioned her. Interrogation—confirmed watching Game of Thrones at residence of Lori Silva. Officer acted premature in polyvinyl-alcohol (PVAL) collection of gun residue. Results: Positive. Trace amounts of primer found on left hand.

I feel as if I'm going to vomit. I take a moment before I read my account of what happened. I remember when they took it I was in a state of shock. I was covered in Jenny's blood.

Alexandra Campbell. Age: 17. Could not identify make or model of automobile. No identification of driver. No determination of male or female. No determination of number of occupants in car.

I remember trying. It was all a blur of darkness. I had no idea. I wasn't paying attention. I hate myself for it. *I hate myself for not getting my own fucking soda!*

The phone next to me rings. It's a plastic Wonder Woman phone. The receiver is cradled in her gold lasso. It's connected to our house landline. It was a gift from my parents when I turned thirteen. In Jenny's room is a Princess phone. She got it when she turned eleven. Wonder Woman rings a second and third time then goes silent.

When I finally emerge from my cave and head to the bathroom, my mother paces back and forth in front of her bed as my father tries to calm her down. Apparently, she's drunk and is going off about the police being overworked and understaffed and incompetent and that our governor is going to hear from her. But I can tell something else is bothering her.

She catches my eye.

"What's wrong?" I ask.

"Nothing." My father clearly does not want to get me involved.

"Detective Thoms thinks you stole the case folder." My mother holds my stare. "That was him on the phone."

I feel my face grow red and think for sure my mother knows it's true. Duke wanders into the hall, and I stop him from walking past and pet his head. The truth is, I've stolen a lot of things. And my mother knows this. It started out innocently enough. When I was in fifth grade, we were shopping in Target, and I picked out a pair of earrings that I liked. I shoved them in my pocket only because I was too lazy to carry them. When we got to the checkout counter, I totally forgot to give them to my mother. Later, she found them in my jeans. "I could've been arrested," she said. "Next time, give them to me to hold."

Later, when I got into middle school, my mother would sometimes find bottles of nail polish and brand-new lipsticks hidden in my room. She knew neither she nor I had paid for them, and I'd get grounded for a week. Sometimes, though, I'd feel so guilty on my own, I'd return the items to the store within a day. It was more for sport anyway. I never even used the nail polish. I gave those bottles to Jenny.

It was when I stole the soccer ball that Jenny caught on to my little klepto habit. It was stupidity, really. It had another girl's name written on it. I hadn't planned on keeping the ball. I simply wanted to borrow it for the long holiday weekend, but my mother found it and made me return the ball without ever saying I took it. My father, of course, wanted me to return it with an apology. But my mother overruled him. "What'll the girl's parents think of us?"

From that day on, every new item that came into my possession was thoroughly questioned and scrutinized. If I had to think about it, I'd say my stealing was the only time my mother paid any attention to me.

But this time, for whatever reason, my mother doesn't accuse me of stealing. Maybe it's because she so desperately wants to put the blame on Detective Thoms for failing to arrest those girls. Or perhaps it's just her level of denial. Whatever the reason, my mother doesn't wait for a response from me. She threatens to sue Detective Thoms and the rest of those "fucking assholes!"

My mother never used to curse.

"He's an idiot," I chime in, kicking at a piece of dust circling the hardwood floor.

My father watches me, and I wonder if he suspects it's true. He puts a hand on my shoulder and tells me to get some sleep. When I return to my bedroom with Duke, I hide the case folder between my mattress and box spring.

That night, not unlike many other nights since Jenny's death, I'm unable to sleep. Around three in the morning, I hear my mother visit Jenny's bedroom.

Why did Jenny have to die? And why do I have to be here without her?

31

CHAPTER 6

BEFORE JENNY'S DEATH, I NEVER understood suicide or why people attempted it. It's the pain. The reason for the pain doesn't really matter. You just want the pain to end so badly that you're willing to die.

I meet with Dr. Evans once a week. I truly love Dr. Evans, and the only relief I ever feel is when I'm sitting in his office. He's the most popular counselor and one of only three black people in our high school. It was recommended I go to a grievance group after Jenny's death. I refused. So here I am, sitting with Dr. Evans. The first couple of times I visited with him, I said nothing. So he told me stories about himself.

When Dr. Evans was eighteen years old, he was driving back from a Bruce Springsteen concert at the Meadowlands in East Rutherford, the home of the New York Giants. He said he was with a group of friends, and his younger brother was in the backseat. His brother had wanted to get home an hour earlier, but Dr. Evans had stopped to chat up a girl in the parking lot. He said it took him thirty minutes before the girl finally wrote her phone number on a piece of paper and gave it to him.

"Back then we didn't have cell phones."

He said they were a mile from their house when a drunk driver slammed into his car. His brother was killed instantly. Dr. Evans told me he wished he had gone straight home after the concert. He shared his guilt and the hatred he had for himself and for the drunk driver. He said every day he plotted to kill the guy and probably would have if the court had released him from jail. It was his fourth DUI in a year. Eventually, the man was convicted of manslaughter and sentenced to twenty years in prison.

Dr. Evans said when he returned to school, a teacher had told him, "Things happen for a reason." He told me he punched the teacher in the face and had to be pulled off him. For months after, he said, he was filled with hate and rage. He wanted to kill everyone, including himself.

That was how Dr. Evans got me to open up. We talk about my recent visit to the police station, minus my stealing the case folder. I voice my guilt, and Dr. Evans tells me, as he has a million times before, "It wasn't your fault, Alex."

I say nothing. I can't stop thinking that if I had not asked Jenny to go to the store, she'd still be alive.

"How would you treat Duke if he had sent Jenny into that store?"

"My dog?"

"Yup. It's Duke, right?"

I nod.

"Would you not feed him for weeks? Never give him water? Yell at him every day? Beat him with a leash?"

I know exactly where Dr. Evans is heading with this. "I don't know."

"Yes, you do. I want you to think about this as if it were Duke who sent Jenny into that store to grab him... say, Milk-Bones."

I crack a smile. This is ridiculous.

Dr. Evans stares at me hard, waiting for me to answer. "I'm not letting you out of this, Campbell. I want an answer. Would you hug him? Love him? Forgive him? Or would you regularly beat the shit out of him? Because that's what you're doing to yourself."

I sigh. "It's easy to love Duke. He's sweet."

"You're sweet."

"No, I'm not. Ask my mom."

"I'm not asking your mom. I'm asking you. You gotta put down that bat, slugger. Be kind. Be loving. I want you to treat you, Alex Campbell, just how you would treat Duke. Can you do that for me?"

I exhale a long breath. "I'll try."

"Pretend it's a sport, and the goal is to not beat yourself up every day. Okay?"

I nod my head. "Yeah."

We move on from my guilt, and Dr. Evans asks me if I'll be attending the University of Virginia in the fall. A few months before Jenny's death, I got an acceptance letter in the mail with a partial athletic scholarship.

I was planning to attend, but I changed my mind. Dr. Evans hoped I'd reconsider. I haven't.

"Your dad thought maybe you'd still go to basketball camp this summer." Dr. Evans speaks to my dad regularly. Dad's worried about me. He's got one daughter dead and me, who's alive but no longer living. "What do you think?"

"I can't."

"You can't, or you won't?"

"Both."

"So how are you sleeping?"

"Fine."

"Yeah? Why don't you tell me how you're really sleeping?"

I've been having nightmares ever since Jenny's death. Most of my nightmares are filled with blood, and I wake up screaming. But this most recent dream was much different. It happened the night after our last visit to the police station. I dreamt I was at the convenience store in Cantor, looking in through a cracked glass window. I saw a group of girls taunting the store clerk. I couldn't make out their faces, but they wore knit caps, jeans, and big winter coats. I entered the store, and when I looked down at my hand, I was holding a gun. The next thing I remember from my dream is waking up next to a ringing phone. I heard my mother's voice as she answered the line from her bedroom. It was Detective Thoms calling to apologize. He said he wouldn't be able to arrest the girls on some other charge. He said they had been murdered.

"In my dream, I shot and killed those girls from Cantor."

"How did that make you feel?"

"Relieved."

Our time expires, but I don't want to leave. The truth is, I never want to leave Dr. Evans's office. But I force myself to stand, and as I get to the doorway, Dr. Evans says, "Alex, you still have my number?"

"Yeah."

"You ever need to talk—middle of the night, early in the morning— you use it."

Dr. Evans is afraid I'm going to kill myself. The truth is, I would kill myself if I knew it wouldn't cause my parents further pain. Or destroy Duke. I would take a bottle of sleeping pills and never wake up.

Later, I head to my Jeep with Lea. She's frenetic, talking nonstop. She tells me her latest Amber-hating story, which has to do with Amber not paying her back for booze Lea bought. "The ho drank most of it." Lea rolls her eyes. I half listen, and when Lea finally stops flapping her gums, I ask her why she even hangs out with Amber if Amber annoys her so much. Her response is classic Lea. "Because we're friends. Duh."

We pass a group of girls, and Lea yells out to them to see if they're going to some party that week. The girls holler back that they'll be there. "Hell, yeah. For sure," one of them says, her perfect white smile glaring at us. They all look the same to me. They all have long, straight hair, and they all wear tiny shorts and sleeveless tops from stores like Forever 21 and American Eagle. They're the nonathletes Lea and I are friends with, and overall, they're okay. Lea often dragged me out to party with them. But I'm so disconnected from everyone today. I can't imagine ever hanging out with those girls again.

As we walk to my Jeep, I think about where we're going. Not only didn't I tell Dr. Evans that I jacked the case folder, but I also didn't tell him that I know where the Cantor girls live, and today, I'm doing a drive-by of Lori Silva's house. I made the mistake of telling Lea, and she blackmailed me into taking her. She said if I didn't, she'd tell my dad. I didn't want to take the chance that she'd actually do it. So I agreed.

We climb into my Jeep, and Lea asks me whether I think Reed likes her or not.

"Sure, he'll like you for a night."

She shoves me. "Thanks!"

I smile, and this causes Lea to do a double take. I don't smile much these days. We shut the doors to my Jeep, and suddenly, she's conscious of what we're about to do.

"You sure you want to do this?" Lea asks.

"I'll take you home if you don't want to go."

"No. I want to go."

"You sure?"

"Yes. Go!"

I hang on Lea's last word. It reminds me of what I said to Jenny right before she left that locker room. It reminds me of what I wish I hadn't done.

"I can't believe we're doing this." Lea stares at me as if we're both nuts.

35

Before I can chicken out or change my mind, I program the GPS on my iPhone to 22 Oak Street, Cantor.

"Aren't you afraid?" Lea holds onto the strap of her seat belt and shivers, despite the warmth.

"No." I don't care if I live or die. I really don't. I turn the ignition and head out of our high school's parking lot. The female voice on the GPS directs me to the New Jersey Turnpike entrance, even though I know how to get there by heart, and in less than fifteen minutes, we are en route to Lori Silva's house.

CHAPTER 7

Lea's lips haven't stopped moving the entire ride. She's no longer scared and is now worried she's getting fat. I refrain from commenting. Lea's a binge eater, perhaps even bulimic. I brought it up to her once before, and she didn't speak to me for a week. She goes on to tell me how lucky I am that I can eat anything I want, and I don't get fat. I wish I'd never agreed to take her. She's exhausting and self-absorbed. If I were a lucky person, my sister wouldn't be dead.

The female voice on the GPS is mostly silent until over an hour later when we arrive at the Cantor exit. I pay the six-dollar toll with cash, and the female voice directs me to "turn right" and then "turn left" as we journey back into this armpit of a town. Poverty, filth, and desperation linger on every corner. Lea grows nervous and promptly locks her door. I don't think it will do much good if someone really wants into this Jeep.

We stop at a traffic light, and I notice a group of teenagers hanging out on the corner. The guys wear baseball caps and low-hanging jeans. The girls are in microskirts and tops that show off their stomachs. I hear words spoken in a mixture of Spanish and English. One girl playfully pushes her friend as another guy laughs. Then they spot us, and one thing is for certain—two white girls in a blue Jeep Wrangler don't belong in this neighborhood.

"Baby, you lost? I think you lost," one guy yells out with a thick accent.

The girl who pushed her friend focuses on Lea. "What you lookin' at, Snow White?" She laughs.

Lea turns to me. "Alex, I don't think this is a good idea."

"It's fine. It's daylight," I say, even though I know it doesn't matter in this 'hood.

Another guy yells something at us in Spanish. I'm not quite sure what he said, but I stare at him, feeling nothing. No fear. No panic. Nothing. The light changes, and I drive off. In the rearview mirror, I see the guy face his friends. I turn off the main road and onto a less-populated street. We pass a car propped up on cinder blocks in a front yard. One more turn, and halfway down the block, the female voice says, "You've arrived at your destination."

I drive past a numberless house and park on the opposite side of the street. I keep the engine running as Lea and I stare at Lori Silva's house.

"Okay, we saw it. Let's go," Lea says, as if expecting us to be shot.

I keep staring at the house. Tall, mangy bushes obscure the first-floor windows. Patches of shingles are missing from the roof—a few lie on the weeded front lawn—and paint peels from all sides of the house. I notice a small backyard surrounded by a chain-link fence, and leading up to a warped wooden garage door is an empty, potholed driveway. The house looks abandoned.

It feels weird and slightly frightening to sit in front of Lori Silva's house, knowing that she had something to do with my sister's murder. I picture her inside, watching some crappy TV and laughing with her criminal friends. I think about Jenny being dead and her being alive, and I grow angry. I think if I owned a gun, I would walk up to that house right now. I would knock on that front door, and when Lori Silva answered, I'd kill her. I'd shoot her a hundred times over. And then I'd go to Cynthia Down's house and each one of these Black Diamond girls' homes, and I'd kill them. Just like Charles Bronson. Just like Angelina Jolie. Just like every other vigilante in any movie I have ever seen.

I think about all this, and for the first time in what feels like forever, I'm not sad or lonely or depressed. I have a reason to live.

Lea's voice wakes me from my rage-induced stupor. "*Alex*, can we *please* go home now?"

Almost two hours later, I drop Lea off at her house. She exits, thanking God. I say goodbye, and a short time later, I pull into my driveway. My father is already home. I know this because I can see his Audi parked inside our open garage.

I enter the house and go straight to the kitchen. Duke's face stares at me from outside the screen door, begging to be let in the house. I pop open the door, and he heads for his water dish. I hear my mother's shrill voice upstairs, and I know something is wrong.

I walk up the stairs, and as I approach my sister's bedroom, I see my mother inside. She is still in her pajamas and is manically pulling clothes from Jenny's closet and shoving them into a large plastic garbage bag. My father stands in his suit, helplessly watching.

The rest of Jenny's room is exactly how she left it. Her bed is unmade. Stuffed animals are tossed all about, along with some clothes, a hairbrush, several pink ribbons, and a bra. My sister was girly, but she was also a slob. Tacked to the walls are Polaroid photographs of her friends, posters of her latest boy obsessions, and pictures of a few favorite NBA players. Her desk is cluttered with more photographs, the Polaroid camera, and a Mac computer. On a nightstand is her Princess phone.

"Mary, let's go downstairs," my father pleads.

"*No!* Let's forget we had a daughter!"

"That's not what I meant. I just want us to try to move on with our lives."

"You move on with your life! Move out! That's what you want!"

"Mary, please—"

"Why didn't you say anything?"

"What? What are you talking about?"

"At the police station! You said nothing!"

"What could I have said, Mary? Tell me!"

"Nothing, like you always do. Just say nothing. Just fucking sit there!"

My mother turns and sees me standing in the doorway. Her face burns hot red. The whites of her eyes are doubled in size, full of rage and deep in wrinkles. She clenches her teeth, and every muscle in her face looks ready to explode. "Why did you have to send her in there? You're so *fucking selfish*!"

My father grabs my mother's wrist, and for a moment, I think he's going to hit her. His face is red. His eyes bulge. He shakes my mother violently. "*Enough!* Do you hear me? *Enough!*"

My mother pulls free and crumbles to the floor. A horrific sound emerges from her lungs. She weeps openly on the floor, and it's unbearable to witness. My father stands above her with tears in his eyes. He doesn't know what to do. He doesn't know what to say.

I stand frozen in the doorway, thinking I caused all of this. I have to leave. I have to get out of this house. Tears blind me as I race down the stairs. I bolt out the front door, escape into my Jeep, and drive away.

I speed through our beautiful neighborhood and down Monmouth Road. I focus on a tree, a car, a telephone pole—anything that will put an end to this pain. I want to crash head on into all of it. Up ahead, a traffic light changes from yellow to red. I think about not stopping and flooring the gas pedal, but a hint of sanity returns, and I slam on my brakes. My Jeep burns to a screeching halt. My seat belt slaps me back into the leather and back into a reality I desperately want to escape. The smell of burned rubber fills my nostrils. I sit there, wishing I were dead. And when the light changes to green, I am still sitting there.

Horns sound behind me. Cars drive past. Dirty looks are thrown my way. I do not move, and I do not care. The driver trapped behind me angrily blasts his horn. I hold his stare in my rearview mirror. *Give me a reason to hurt you, and I will. Give me a reason to step out of this car and kill you, and I will. If only I had a gun.*

Suddenly, my cell phone rings. It's Lea. But for a second, when I looked, I wished it were Jenny. I have wished it a million times before. The phone rings, and I check the screen, hoping to see my sister's smiling face. But her face no longer appears. It never will.

There is a loud knock on my window. It's the driver of the car trapped behind me. His eyebrows are furrowed in anger. He's about to yell at me when he sees my face. It's pained and streaked with tears. His eyes soften. "Are you okay?"

I pull away and drive around aimlessly for hours. My father calls several times, but I ignore the phone.

When I finally pick up, it's after nine o'clock at night, and my father immediately apologizes for my mother. "Honey, she didn't mean what she said. Your mother isn't well."

My father tells me that they're at Monmouth Medical Center, where my mother has been admitted to the psychiatric ward. He says that she won't be home for a while.

CHAPTER 8

WHEN I FINALLY VISIT MY mother in the hospital, she is barely conscious of the fact that I am even there. I hardly recognize her as the woman who raised me. She peers at me through lithium-fueled eyes. "My beautiful baby is in heaven. I'm going to write to the governor's office. Every day. I'll make sure he gets involved in your sister's case. That son of a bitch is going to do something! I refuse..." Every word that spews from my mother's angry lips has me drowning in sorrow. I listen, nod, and silently pray that she will stop talking. My own rage bubbles up inside me like bile rising in my throat. I want to scream, "Will you please stop talking!" But I remain quiet.

By the time I leave the hospital, I just want to fall asleep and never wake up. I pull into our driveway and shut off my Jeep. I have no idea how I even got home.

Lying in bed, I can't stop thinking about those girls who murdered my sister. My brain won't quit. "Lori Silva's car was set on fire..." Evidence. "She was at home watching TV." Evidence. "The gun was not located." Evidence. "The store tape has not been found." Evidence. "Her brother, Mark Silva..." Evidence. "Gun residue..." Evidence. "Some other charge..." Evidence. I can't help thinking about something my mother said. We rarely share the same opinion, but I don't want these girls arrested on some other charge. I want them in prison for killing my sister. Or I want them dead.

I reach under my mattress and pull out the case folder. I flip it open, and staring right at me is Lori Silva's mug shot. I don't have to find Cracker's or Natice Gentry's picture to be reminded of what they look like. Their faces are etched in my memory. I know exactly what these girls look like, and I know exactly where they live, including Ronnie Rodriguez. I wonder what they do during the day and how they spend their nights.

I grab my laptop, open it up, and do something I haven't been able to since Jenny's funeral. I click onto Facebook.

I type in "Lori Silva" and hit return.

It doesn't take me long to discover the Lori Silva I want dead has an account. It's marked private, but I'm at least able to view her profile picture. She looks just as mean as her mug shot, except in this photo, she's blowing a kiss to the camera while hugging on some extremely unattractive dude. I check to see who liked her picture and discover two out of the twenty-one people who liked it are Cracker—literally it's Cracker, not Cynthia Down—and Ronnie Rodriguez.

I click onto Cracker's profile pic, and it's a selfie of her flipping off the camera. Her account is also set to private, but I'm able to see a few cover photos. One that was updated right before last Thanksgiving is of her and a bunch of busted-looking guys who all look wasted. There's another one from three years ago that shows her lying on the ground surrounded by trash. Someone holds a sign above her head that reads, "White."

Ronnie Rodriguez's profile picture is of a cute baby girl, maybe a year old, wearing a polka-dot dress and a big, happy, toothless smile. I click on the photo, expecting Ronnie's page to also be private, but it's not. *It's public!* My heart races, and I go nuts stalking her page. I check out her most recent posts and find one or two photos with likes from Mark Silva. I click on his profile picture. It's a photo of a red Mustang. But sadly, his page is private.

I troll her page, extra careful not to accidently like any of Ronnie's photos or send her a friend request, something I did once while I was stalking one of Jay's ex-girlfriends.

In the last month, Ronnie's checked herself into a McDonald's, Wendy's, Popeyes, and a pizzeria. I click on a photo that I assume is of Ronnie, her arm slung around Cracker. Ronnie is a goofy-looking girl but strangely cute. She has a big smile, long curly hair, a round, full face, and towers over Cracker. Another pic shows her at a party, bent over laughing with Lori and Natice. It was posted only a week ago.

I keep scrolling back in time, expecting to see pictures of guns or violence. But I don't. I see a picture of what I suspect are Ronnie's parents and a younger brother and sister, along with the baby girl and a caption that reads *Keisha's 1st b-day!* The photo is liked by Lori and Cracker and over fifty other people. She's also checked herself into "Vince's Pad" and posted a photo of herself, alongside Lori, Cracker, Natice, and some very high-looking dudes. The only photo that reminds me these girls are criminals is one of Lori Silva holding her hand as if it were a gun. I screenshot it, zoom in close, and see a small black diamond tattoo by her thumb. Then I find a post—*G-O-T got game, by'atches!* It was posted the day after Jenny died.

It's three a.m. when my battery finally dies, and my computer goes dark. I close the lid, and the very first thought that enters my mind is one that has visited me a million times before, except this time there's a slight revision. *Can I really do it?* I ask myself before finally falling asleep.

CHAPTER 9

FOR WEEKS, LEA HAS BEEN bugging me to go out with her. I finally agree, and Saturday night, I pick her up in my Jeep, and we head over to a party at one of the baseball players' homes. It's one of the nicer houses in Middletown. I think his dad works for Goldman Sachs, and there's always tons of booze and pre-bought food from Chili's and usually cheesy pop music playing from built-in speakers throughout the house. I see a closed bathroom door. It opens, and a group of kids walk out, high from doing Molly. It's obvious to me with their stretched-out smiles and ginormous pupils. You wouldn't expect it in Middletown, but heroin and Molly run rampant. Both are cheap and easily accessible.

Lea and I share a look.

"Could her eyeballs be any bigger?" Lea says. She ditches me to go flirt with Reed, who's tapping a new keg.

I'm standing by myself, feeling completely out of place and wishing I hadn't agreed to come with her, when a girl from my chemistry class walks over to me.

"Hey, Alex! I'm so happy to see you!" Her words are slurred, and she tilts unsteadily on a pair of high heels, grabbing onto my arm to keep from wobbling over.

I smile and feel even more uncomfortable. "Good seeing you too," I lie.

"Sooo... you excited for summer? Got any fun plans?"

My sister was murdered. How excited could I be? What fun plans could I possibly have? "Yeah, I don't know." I spot Jay from across the room. He waves a red plastic cup in the air, motioning for me to join him. "I gotta go say hi to someone."

"Sure, sure! Go!"

Her last word is like a sledgehammer to my gut. I want to leave the party right then, but instead, I walk over to Jay, and he greets me with a warm smile and an enormous hug. "I can't believe you're here."

His huge arms surround my body, and just like old times, I melt into his chest. I breathe in the Tide from his shirt, and we stay like that for a while. And for a moment, everything disappears, including my pain. When I finally emerge from his biceps, I smell of his cologne. "Yeah, Lea dragged me out of my cave."

"I'm glad she did." His head bobs then stops, and his expression changes. "Hey, how's your mom by the way? I hope she's okay."

"Yeah, thanks. The same."

Word got around fast that my mother is in a loony bin, thanks to having Lea as a best friend. She has the biggest mouth in Middletown, next to Amber, who also loves to spread gossip. This is probably why Amber gets on Lea's nerves so much. "*If you hate a person, you hate something in him that is a part of yourself. What isn't a part of ourselves doesn't disturb us.*" Hermann Hesse. The only thing I paid attention to in English Lit this year.

"You're not drinking?" Jay asks.

"Nah."

"Hey, I know you're going to say no, but I'm having my graduation party in July. I really want you to come."

"I'm sure it'll be epic." I say, avoiding having to say no.

"You know my parties. Hopefully, Reed won't piss in the kitchen sink this time. Dude, he's such a tool sometimes."

"Dude, I know." I raise both eyebrows. Then I notice Jay's shirt. It's collared and not faded like all his other T-shirts. This one is actually nice. "New shirt?"

"Yup. Got it at Kohl's."

"Kohl's? Wow, steppin' up your game, player."

"Not really. My dad bought it for me. Graduation present."

At least his father bought him something. He's forgotten Jay's last two birthdays. And Jay's such a good guy. I don't think he has ever given either of his parents five minutes of trouble in his entire life. His father left Jay's mother for some woman he met in Alcoholics Anonymous. Now, he's a deadbeat dad who doesn't pay child support but spends loads of cash on his trampy girlfriend. "I'm sure it was expensive."

"Nah, probably on sale. Ya know my dad."

It was probably a re-gift, knowing his father. But I remain silent.

Jay brings the red plastic cup to his lips and pounds the beer. After that, we stand, eyeing the crowd without anything further to say to one another. It makes me wish Jenny were here. If she were alive, she'd be standing right next to us, probably teasing Jay for his fancy new shirt. The three of us used to hang out a lot, especially at parties. Jenny loved Jay. And it was mutual. Jay would always tell me to take it easy on her whenever I gave her too much shit about something, usually about basketball practice if I thought she wasn't playing hard enough or not giving one hundred percent. Maybe that's why I have such a difficult time being around Jay. He reminds me of Jenny.

I see Max Hemberger, a cute boy with curly blond hair. I hadn't noticed him until now. Jenny had a huge crush on Max, and for a while, they were best buds. He also holds a red plastic cup in his hand and is surrounded by Amber and a few girls from his sophomore class. I hear his cackling laugh even above the music. It's the thing Jenny liked the most about him—his laugh. He smiles and catches me staring at him. For a second, his smile fades, and he looks at me with what feels like enormous pity. He tosses a nod my way then returns his attention to the girls. And in an instant, I'm hit with the heartache of Jenny being dead.

I feel the tears coming. "I have to go, sorry."

He nods, his face turning serious. "I miss you, Alex. I really miss you."

I hold his stare and can't help feeling the same. I miss me too. I walk away with Jay staring after me, hurrying to find the front door, worried I'll burst into tears any second. I rush past faces that smile at me. I knew coming to this party was a bad idea.

"Alex! Hey!" Amber yells as I push behind Max without a hello.

Lea notices me leaving. "Alex, where you going?"

I race out of the house in tears.

I hop in my Jeep and drive away, crying. I knew I wouldn't be able to handle being around normal happy people feeling the way I do. I don't give a shit about parties or college or who's screwing who or Facebook or Instagram or Twitter—things I used to take pleasure in. I grab onto the steering wheel as tight as I can, white-knuckling it, wanting so desperately for things to be the way the used to be, wishing Jenny were alive and beside me. I punch the dashboard. "*Shit! Shit! Shit!*" I hit it harder and harder and harder until my fist is bleeding and throbbing.

I think about Jenny being dead and those girls from Cantor being alive. I think about my mother spending another night in a mental ward and my father being home alone. I think about Duke, his metal tags jingling, endlessly searching for someone who will never reappear. I think about my friends and wonder what we ever had in common. They're like strangers.

Then it hits me—the thought from the other night—the crazy idea that had me asking myself, *Can I really do it?* I'm filled with hate when I answer: *Yes. What more do I have to lose? Nothing.*

CHAPTER 10

WHILE MY FORMER CLASSMATES ARE out partying and hitting the beach, I study for the first time that year. I research hotels in the Cantor area. I research used car dealerships and trade-in values. I Google anything and everything that has to do with Cantor and street gangs. I learn things that I would never before have wanted to know. I can easily identify a .22 caliber gun, a Ruger 9mm semiautomatic, and a Smith & Wesson .38 revolver.

"What are you doing, Alex?" I say to my computer screen. Duke's ears perk up, and his big brown eyes shift to me without him ever taking his heavy head off his paws. I hold his stare until his eyes close then turn back to my computer. On the screen is a photograph of a gun collected at a drug bust in Chicago. *The same type of gun that was used to kill my sister.* The sad, ironic thing is I always said if anyone ever harmed my sister, bullied or beat up Jenny in school, I'd kill them.

I let out a miserable low laugh and continue studying, fully aware that what I'm doing is crazy. But my obsession for revenge is like some sick, twisted addiction that I can't quit or control. Nor do I want to.

I go onto Facebook and block Lori Silva, Cracker, Ronnie Rodriguez, and Mark Silva from my account. I also block a few Natice Gentry profiles, even though I don't think Natice has a Facebook page, since she's never liked or commented on anything on Ronnie's page, but I'd rather be safe than sorry. I leave my profile picture and cover photo, since neither show my face. Later, I'll deactivate my account, but for now, I leave it up for stalking purposes only.

I go onto Instagram, get rid of my account, and set up a new one. My new name: Ally Walker. I do a Google search and turn into a beast following all things Seattle: Pike Place Coffee, Adams Junior High, Highland Park High School, Seattle Seahawks—even though I hate the Seahawks—a few badass bands, an Amy Winehouse fan page, not because she ever had anything to do with Seattle, but because I still dig her voice and that style. I follow whoever will take me and post random shit: Nike Sneakers, McDonald's French fries, Seahawks Stadium, a thorny rose, photos of guys I think are hot. I hit +Follow on kids whose names I've ripped off websites of sports teams, bands, clubs, whatever I can find.

It's amazing how many teenagers will just accept you as a follower without even knowing you. By the time I'm done, I'm following close to three hundred people, I have twenty posts, and almost a hundred people are following me. It's a start.

I take a break and go down into the kitchen to get something to eat. Duke trails behind me, and I toss him the last rawhide bone from what used to be a full bag. He plops to the floor with it, trapping the bone between his paws and drilling down on it with his teeth. It hurts my heart, knowing I'll be leaving him. I try not to think about it.

My iPhone rings, and it's Lea. I hesitate in answering then pick it up on the fourth ring.

"What's going on?"

"Nothing," I say and grab a very brown banana off the counter.

"I haven't heard from you. I'm worried."

"I'm fine."

"I call bullshit, but whatever. Me, Amber, and a few girls from the team are going to the beach tomorrow. Why don't you come?"

"Nah, I can't."

"Why not?"

"Because."

"What do you do all day?" Lea asks.

I research gangs, pretend to be someone I'm not on-line. "I watch TV."

"You need to get out of that house. Come to the beach. You can pick me up, and we'll take the top off."

For a moment, I wonder if Lea only called me because she wants me to drive her. "I can't. I have to help my dad with the pool. He wants to uncover it."

"Bullshit again. And even if you did, that wouldn't take all day." Lea is persistent when she wants something.

"I just don't want to go, Lea, okay? I'm sorry."

"Fine! I'm just trying to help. I'm worried about you. I miss you. We all miss you."

I feel the tears coming. "Lea, I gotta go. But thanks for calling."

"Call me tomorrow."

"Okay. I will." I know I won't.

I hang up and toss the banana in the garbage, no longer hungry.

Minutes later, I hear my father's car pull into the driveway. It reminds me of what I still need to do, or rather what I need to ask. I bite down on my already gnawed thumbnail. My stomach churns, and my legs turn restless, like every time I ever wanted to go into the city to see a band I liked—back when those things mattered to me—and worried he'd say no. But right now, I'm more afraid of him saying yes because once he does, there is nothing else stopping me from leaving home, other than my fear, of course. I release my thumb and look down at Duke, weighing my decision.

"Hey, kiddo." My father walks into the kitchen, fresh from a workout. Duke doesn't bother to look up. He never does when a bone is involved.

"How was the gym?"

"Good."

Dad pours himself a glass of water, and neither of us mentions my mother. Instead, we make small talk about his workout, and then I get to it. "So, Dad, I was thinking about going away to basketball camp. What do you think?"

He stops the glass from meeting his lips. "Really? You want to go camp?"

"Yeah, I do. There's one in July at the University of Delaware that I can still get into. I called, and they have room."

He takes a sip of water. A huge smile forms on my father's face, and for the first time in a very long time, he actually looks happy. "I think it's a great idea, honey. I think it'll do you some good."

"Me too. But it's a sleep-away camp. So I'd be gone for a few weeks."

He shakes his head as if it's not a problem. "Alex, if you want to go, you should go."

"I do. Thanks, Dad." I give him a big hug.

That evening, my father happily hands me a deposit check, and I now have a legitimate excuse to leave home.

CHAPTER 11

A S SOON AS SCHOOL LETS out for the year, I make a point of saying goodbye to Dr. Evans. In our previous session, he had asked me if I was going to walk at graduation. I told him I hadn't decided yet. Both he and Dad thought I should. Prior to Jenny's death, my mother never would've allowed me to miss it, and I wouldn't have wanted to, but when my cap and gown arrived in the principal's office, I never bothered to pick them up. I think they're still there.

I pop my head into Dr. Evans's office and knock on his open door. He looks up, surprised to see me. "Hey, Alex, what's going on?" He puts aside his work, and I take a seat across from him. "You look happy."

"I do?"

He smiles. "Yes, you do."

I'm not sure I agree, but I nod. "I decided to go to basketball camp. I signed up for one at the University of Delaware."

"That's great! I'm glad to hear that." His excitement fills the room. He leans back in his chair, throws his arms behind his head, and stares intently at me. "So what made you change your mind?"

I think about telling Dr. Evans the truth, and in a way, I do. "I need a change of scenery."

"Well, you're going to love Delaware. They run a good camp there. I know one of the coaches. She's been doing it for years. You need anything, you call me." He looks at me sternly. He knows how I am. "I mean that. Anything."

I smile. "Yeah. No worries."

He rises from his desk, and I hug him. I have never hugged Dr. Evans before. Maybe I hug him now because I worry I may never see him again. Or maybe I just need a hug.

"See ya, Dr. Evans."

"Hey, Alex…"

I stop and look back at him.

"I'm proud of you."

I nod and walk out.

On my drive home, I call the University of Delaware's Basketball Camp Director to let him know I won't be attending the session I had enrolled in just weeks earlier. "I've got strep throat," I say, trying to sound like I actually do.

The camp director tells me he's sorry to hear that and apologizes for not being able to return my deposit money. "I'm sorry, but due to the late notice…"

"That's okay." I'm grateful. The last thing I want is my father receiving his deposit check back from a basketball camp I'm supposed to be attending. The director wishes me a fast recovery, and we hang up.

As far as my father knows, the session I enrolled in starts the second week in July. But camps run all summer long. If I wanted to, I could literally spend my entire summer attending sports camps. It's insane, and most players don't, but it isn't completely unheard of. And depending on what happens, I may need the extra time.

CHAPTER 12

MY MOTHER IS IN GOOD spirits, thanks to whatever drugs the hospital gave her two days ago when they released her. I stand next to her in the driveway, watching my father load my duffel bag into the back of my Jeep. He's wearing his weekend clothes: khaki shorts, faded college T-shirt, and cross-training sneakers. He slams the door closed and walks toward me to say goodbye. Much like Dr. Evans, Dad looks proud. My going away to summer camp means I'm ready to start living again. But I am not. I just can't live at home anymore.

"Love ya, kiddo." My dad hugs me tightly.

"Love you, too, Dad." I mean it.

Saying goodbye to my mother is a lot more difficult. I can't remember the last time my mother hugged me or even told me she loved me. We had been fighting pretty bad right up to Jenny's death.

"Love ya, Mom," I say, noticing how much weight she has lost. I can feel the bones in her back when I hug her.

"Call us when you get there," my mother says matter-of-factly.

I look back at Duke, who runs around the front lawn like a nut, chomping at the air, most likely chasing a bug or a fly. "Duke!" I yell. He halts in mid-gallop and races over to me. I bend to the ground and get slobbered by his big wet tongue. "I love ya, buddy. I'm gonna miss you." I kiss his dopey, handsome face and hug him for dear life, almost crying.

"Don't worry. I'll take care of him," Dad says.

I give Duke one more kiss and a great big hug, then I let go. He runs off to hunt the bug. I climb into my Jeep, and a pang of guilt hits me for leaving Duke.

My father puts his arm around my mother's waist. He smiles and waves.

For a moment, they look like a normal, happy couple. I drive away with that image in my head.

By the time I arrive at the Turnpike entrance, what I'm about to do becomes very real. I start taking in long, deep breaths. I suffered a panic attack—or what I thought was a panic attack—when I was in third grade. My mother had left Jenny and me in the car while she went into an Applebee's to grab dinner to take home. She was in there so long I thought she had been kidnapped or, worse, had left us. By the time she returned to the car I had both Jenny and me in hysterics. My mother saw our faces and worried something tragic had happened.

"I thought you'd left us," I said, crying.

My mother looked so sad for us. "No, of course not. It took forever. There was a long line inside," She rubbed my back until I calmed down. I remember Mom was especially sweet. She even popped open one of the Styrofoam containers and let us eat chicken wings in the car, something she never allowed. As we drove home she said, "Don't worry, girls. If anyone ever kidnapped your mother, they'd toss me back so fast you and your dad would never miss me."

I take in another deep breath. It's not too late to turn back and go home. But instead, I pay the toll, press down on the gas pedal, and keep heading south toward Cantor.

After an hour of driving, I exit the Turnpike and follow the directions on my GPS until I arrive at Tom's Used Car Lot. It looks exactly like it does online: small, with American flags flapping in the wind and a row of used cars facing the highway. A sign reads Trade-Ins Welcome! A pit forms in my stomach as I shut off my Jeep and step out onto the lot. I haven't even closed the door when Tom, an older man in a suit and tie, approaches me with a smile. I know it's Tom because of the dorky photos he posts of himself on his website.

"Hi. How can I help you?" His huge smile glares at me.

"I want to sell my Jeep." My voice cracks.

"Do you have the title and paperwork for it?"

"Yeah. I own it."

Tom examines my Jeep, and the pit in my stomach grows larger. A wave of memories hits me as I remember how much Jenny loved riding around in my Jeep, especially in the summer months when we would head to Sandy Hook Beach with the top down and the music blasting.

"It's in good shape. Are you looking for a trade-in? Or cash?"

"Both, but I want something older. Not as nice."

"Let me show you some of our cars, and what's your name?"

I stare at Tom, suddenly not wanting to follow. "Hold on. I'll be right back, I need to check something." I walk away and take out my iPhone, pretending to be texting someone when really, I'm trying to decide if I can go through with this. I don't think I can. Another overwhelming bout of anxiety bubbles up. This time, it's much worse, like I drank a whole case of Coca-Cola at the same time the oxygen decided to leave earth. *Can I really do this? Should I really do this?* Then finally, after leaving Tom standing alone for several minutes, I make a deal with myself. If I can't go through with my plan, I'll simply come back here, buy back my Jeep, and go home. *But what if Blue Beauty isn't here?* I try not to think of that as I walk back to Tom to sell what used to be my most prized possession.

Thirty minutes later, I'm sitting inside Tom's office watching him print out a bill of sale from an archaic computer. "Do you want the check written out to Alex or Alexandra?" Tom asks.

"Alexandra."

"You got it." He finishes writing out the check and neatly tucks the bill of sale along with a stack of paperwork into an envelope. He scribbles "Alexandra Campbell" on the front and hands both the check and envelope to me. "Here you go."

"Thanks." I feel nauseous about the transaction.

"Come on." Tom rises from his desk. He grabs a set of keys off the wall, and I follow him out the door.

The trade-in car is something an old person would drive.

"It's a gas guzzler, but it flies." Tom stops in front of a dark-blue Oldsmobile four-door sedan.

I open the heavy door and move behind the wheel. Unlike my Jeep where I used to sit up high, the cloth seats are much lower to the ground. There's a long scratch along the dash, and the carpeting is faded, but other than that, whoever owned this car kept it in pretty good shape. It has a standard AM/FM stereo system with a CD player. There's no built-in GPS system or Bluetooth. The only fancy thing about this car is its pop-out plastic cup holders.

I insert the key, turn the ignition, and the engine roars to life.

"You take care," Tom tells me.

I barely touch the gas pedal, and the car explodes forward. Driving away, I already miss my Jeep. But I am grateful for one thing: the Oldsmobile is fast, much faster than my Jeep.

I make one more stop before I get back on the Turnpike. It's a check-cashing store, and after a woman with long acrylic fingernails matches the signature on my driver's license to that on the back of the check I received for my Jeep, I walk out with almost four thousand dollars in cash.

Finally, after an exhausting drive, I reach the Cantor City exit on the Turnpike. That sinking feeling in my stomach returns, and I know what I'm doing is nuts and that I should turn around right now and go back home. But I don't. I take a breath, hand my ticket and money to the toll agent, and keep moving forward. Again, I tell myself, if I can't do this, I'll simply head home.

The motel I selected is less than ten minutes from Lori Silva's house. It's an efficiency motel on the edge of a highway that mostly serves welfare recipients. It's run-down and has maybe fifteen rooms. On the opposite side of the street are a twenty-four-hour Laundromat, a Burger King, and a liquor store. There's a liquor store on just about every corner in Cantor.

I park right in front of the office, next to one other car that occupies the motel's parking lot. The car is filthy and looks abandoned, with papers and trash piled high in the windows.

I enter the office, and a fan blows warm air in my face. An older man with sagging skin and tattooed arms sits on a stool watching TV. He brings a nub of a cigarette to his cracked lips. His face is lined with wrinkles, reddened around the cheeks, and slightly bloated. He laughs at the people on the TV. He's watching *Judge Judy*.

He sees me, rises from the bar stool, and stamps out his cigarette. "Can I help you?"

"I need a room with two double beds."

"How long?" He stares at me curiously.

The question makes me squirm. I look down at my Fossil watch that I wear religiously on my left wrist—big faced, sterling silver, leather band. It was a Christmas present from Jenny two years ago. My eyes follow the second hand as it crawls around the bolded numbers. My fingers fidget with the knob, turning it even though the time is perfectly set. I look up at the office manager, who raises his furry eyebrows at me, waiting for an answer. I consider telling him I made a mistake. But I don't. "Two weeks," I say in my most adult voice. I step closer to the counter, placing my hands on the worn wood and hesitantly adding, "It might be longer. I'll be staying here with my grandmother until I find her a nursing home. She's not doing well."

He nods, looking uninterested in my lie, then retrieves a small index card and places it in front of me. It's the hotel's registration form. I grab a chewed Bic pen off the counter and scribble. Name. Address. Phone number. None of it is real.

The room is forty-nine dollars a night. I pay in advance and walk out of the office with a key in hand. I stop to collect my duffel bag from the Oldsmobile and walk to my room. A few doors down from where I am heading, an elderly woman sits outside an open door fanning herself with a folded newspaper. Next to her is one of those four-wheeled shopping carts like you use at ShopRite. In fact, I think it *is* from ShopRite. Her skin is pale white, and she has varicose veins that look like little purple spiders running down her legs. She wears an oversized cotton dress that sticks to her large frame, and her eyes never leave me as I approach my room.

I unlock the door, expecting the worst, but aside from the dank smell, the room is clean. I let out a cough and drop my duffel bag on the bed closest to the door. There are two full-sized beds centered in the middle of the room. I place my hand on the thin red-and-yellow-patterned comforter and press down a couple times to check its firmness. Satisfied, I remove my hand and glance around the hot room. It's like a sauna in here. I don't see the air-conditioner, but there aren't too many places it could hide. There's a bedside table with a lamp and a small refrigerator in the corner. On a chest of drawers are a TV and a sign that reads Free HBO and Wi-Fi. I walk across the tired brown carpet toward a closed window and see a small white plastic box sticking out about an inch on the beige wall. I click the little red on button and press an arrow until sixty-seven degrees appears. A warm burst of air filters through the vents above my head, then gradually, the air turns cold.

My bladder presses against my jeans, and without further inspection, I head to the bathroom. I flick on the switch, and fluorescent light showers the room. The tub is nasty with long strands of black hair circling the drain, and the plastic shower curtain is mildewed. I kick up the lid of the toilet and cringe at what looks like an upchucked Burger King meal floating inside.

"Jesus." I flush with my sneaker and consider asking for a different room, but despite the nastiness of the toilet and tub, the room is clean, and the motel seems safe, so I tell myself I can do this for at least a day. But if I'm going to survive the night, there are a few things I need to do first.

I drive to a nearby drug store and purchase rubber gloves, bleach, disinfectant, trash bags, air fresheners, and scrub brushes. I move into the home beauty section and pick up a pair of scissors. At the checkout counter, I grab candy and several packs of gum.

When I return to my motel room, I slide on the rubber-gloves and go to work drenching the entire tub and toilet in a gallon of bleach.

An hour later, I'm determined to stay. I'm stripped down in my black bra and shorts scrubbing the bathroom floor. I'm manic, and the scrubbing keeps me from thinking. It's good for me not to think. *Scrub. Scrub. Scrub. Clean. Clean. Clean.* I have never scoured a bathroom so hard in my life. My mother wouldn't even recognize me right now. The tub is no longer grimy. The mirror is no longer dingy.

Finished, I stare at my reflection. Sweat drips from my forehead and down the sides of my face. My hair, tied back with a rubber band, looks greasy. I examine my face, and everything looks the same: dark-brown eyes, thick arched eyebrows, full lips, strong nose. I keep staring, wondering who the hell I am. I know I'm a female. I know I have two arms. Two legs. I know I used to be a basketball star. I know I used to laugh. I know I used to have friends. I know I used to have a sister. But I have no idea who I am.

I remove the rubber gloves and leave the mirror. When I return, I'm holding the pair of scissors. A million thoughts race through my mind. *How did I get here? What am I doing?*

Jenny enters my mind, and my moment of reprieve from missing her is gone. In its place is the familiar gut-wrenching pain and sadness. I think about Duke's dopey face. I think about driving back to that used-car dealership and reclaiming my Jeep. I think about leaving this shitty motel room and never returning. I think about going back home, but then I remember what home is like.

I remove the band from my hair, and a wave of brown cascades down past my shoulders. I grab a fistful of thick strands and cut it. I grab another fistful. I cut it. Another fist. I cut it. Slice it. Shred it. The floor is covered in clumps of what Jenny used to call my "gorgeous lion's mane." I look back in the mirror and stare at someone I no longer recognize. My hair isn't pixie short, but it's damn close. Around my ears and the top of my head, it's trimmed pretty tight. The longest pieces are maybe an inch and a half at most. I've never gone short before, mainly for fear that I'd look like a boy. But it's clear that I am still very much a girl. I run my hand through the chopped, seductive mess. Jenny would freak if she saw my hair. She would freak and ask me if I was stoned. I grab a bottle of peroxide.

CHAPTER 13

I t's ten o'clock at night when I go on Facebook to see if Ronnie has checked in anywhere. As I'm thinking how easy it is to stalk people, I discover Ronnie's profile pic has been changed to a selfie. She's making some weird face, and I can partially see Cracker's head behind her. I know it's Cracker only because I can see the bright-red hair. I click on the photo, and her page is no longer public. "Shit." I hit it again and again and again, trying to will it to be public, but still—friends only. Same with her Instagram. Now, I'm worried Ronnie knew I was stalking her page. *But how could she?* I don't know when someone's stalking my page.

It totally blows, but it doesn't change anything. So before I chicken out, I grab the keys to the Olds and head out of the room. I unlock the car door, slide behind the wheel, and catch my reflection in the rearview mirror. I barely recognize myself with my new bleached-blond short hair. Although, some pieces are a lot more yellow than they are blond. I'm a cheap version of Madonna from the eighties when she had short platinum-blond hair and dark eyebrows. I remember when Jenny and I found my mother's Madonna CD collection in the basement, and Mom played her favorite album for us: *You Can Dance.* She sang "Everybody" out of tune and twirled her butt in a way that sent Jenny and me running out of the basement, screaming, "Ewwwww!" and covering our eyes. Still, Mom gained some cool points for even owning a CD collection.

I try not to let any of this take up space in my head as I lock the doors, program the GPS on my phone to 22 Oak Street, and drive off. I used to love driving around at night when the world seemed quiet and chill. Jenny used to call me a nyctophiliac because I did it so often. But here in Cantor, I find the nighttime anything but chill or quiet. The streets are, for sure, more sketchy at night, and I'm grateful for the Olds. I certainly would have stood out in my blue Jeep. Several of the blocks are nothing more than decrepit brick buildings with few signs of human occupancy. Other streets teem with people, both young and old, of various ethnicities. Most simply hang out on the front porches of small, run-down houses, drinking beer out of quart bottles and listening to music on massive portable speakers. A few boys run in front of my car, causing me to slam on the brakes. They laugh and shout in Spanish to one another. They're playing a game of tag.

I arrive at Lori Silva's house, and right away, I see the red Mustang from Mark Silva's profile picture parked in the driveway. At least I know Mark lives here. I drive past the house and park on an adjacent street. A hint of yellow light peeks out through the blinds of an upstairs window, but other than that, I can't see anything. I shut off the engine and sit in the dark, hoping to see Lori exit the house.

Only ten minutes have passed when I check to make sure all the doors are still locked. "What are you doing, Alex?" I ask myself out loud.

A *bang* startles me.

I turn and see a large man dragging two steel garbage cans to the curb. I sigh with relief. "Relax, you're fine," I say, trying to convince myself that I am. I grab my iPhone and check Lori and Ronnie's page. Still private. Same with Cracker and Mark. Then I do something I haven't done in a very long time. I scroll through my feed.

Lea has just posted an update: *Partying at Michelle's! Yeah, baby!* Michelle is one of the nonathletic girls we're friends with. I scroll down, passing various profile updates. I see a one-word post from Jay: *Ouch.*

I scroll to Jenny's name and click onto her page, knowing I'm clicking onto pain. When it got out about her dying, just about every friend on her page—close to eight hundred people—posted comments on her wall.

I heart you forever!

Thanks for always being my friend!

You are, and always will be, the best!

Jenny's status update reads *They're probably defrosted!*

A week prior to the Cantor High School East game, I pulled a groin muscle during practice. That night, Jenny gave me a bag of frozen peas to ice it. We were watching one of those stupid reality shows when our mother walked into the living room.

"What are you doing to my peas?" she'd shrieked.

Jenny and I busted up laughing.

Our mother didn't find it funny.

"Gimme those peas! They're probably defrosted now!"

Jenny and I laughed so hard we both fell off the couch, our eyes filled with tears.

A moment later, Mom returned with a block of ice, the kind you put in a cooler. "Here, use this. Honestly, Alex." She stalked off, shaking her head.

That night, Jenny posted the comment, *They're probably defrosted!*

It's been there ever since.

Smiling, I reread a text Jenny sent me. I've reread it many times before: *Yo, hooker! Can u give me a ride home today?*

Walk, fat ass, I wrote back.

Ha! You wish.

Fine. But no blowing bubbles out ya ass.

There's a smiley face after that.

Yo—I had Mom's meatloaf for lunch. Can't promise.

Gross!

Another smiley face.

I know! Love ya. Mean it!

Jenny was programmed into my phone as *Little Ho*, and I was programmed into hers as *Big Ho*. It was a joke between us. We were both virgins.

I last two hours before I return to the motel room.

I crawl into bed, exhausted yet unable to close my eyes. I stare at my iPhone, which rests silently on the bedside table. I would do anything to see *Little Ho* show up on the screen right now. Tears fill my eyes, and I pray I fall asleep fast.

CHAPTER 14

I T'S ALREADY EIGHTY-FIVE DEGREES OUTSIDE, and it's only eleven a.m. The steering wheel burns my hand when I touch it. I lower the windows and blast the air conditioner. I make a mental note to park in the shade. But there's hardly any shade to be found. Cantor is like one big cement block.

I head back to Lori Silva's house to spy on her. When I turn onto her street, the red Mustang from the night before speeds down the opposite end of the block. I hit the gas pedal and chase after it. I have to blow through a red light before I'm able to catch the Mustang stopping in a gas station. A guy with short brown hair steps out from behind the wheel and disappears inside the office.

For the next half hour, I drive up and down the highway, wasting gas, until finally, my gauge falls below three quarters. I return to the station and pull up to the first pump. Moments later, the guy from the Mustang emerges from the office and walks toward my car. He looks about seventeen or eighteen years old, and his hair is messy, as if he has just woken up and hasn't bothered to brush it.

He takes his time, not exactly in a rush. When he finally comes around to my driver's-side window, he immediately checks me out. "What's up? What can I get you?" His eyes drift below my face.

"Ten dollars, regular."

"You got it." He gives me another glance before turning to fetch the nozzle.

If this is Mark Silva, he looks nothing like Lori. He's way hotter than any boy in my high school, including Jay, although I'd never call Jay hot. This guy has dark-brown eyes, a medium complexion, and his body is lean and muscled.

When the pump finishes, he returns to my window. I hand him a twenty, and he fishes for change. "Here ya go." He gives me a ten.

"Thanks." I hold his stare.

I've never been one to flirt or act stupid in front of guys. I've never understood why girls act dumber than they are or flirt so obviously they are practically throwing themselves at the guy. Amber has it down to a science. To me, it's embarrassing. But I have a purpose being here. So I act like Amber. "What's your name?"

"Mark."

So he *is* Mark Silva, Lori's younger brother. I suddenly hate him by association. It must show on my face.

"What's wrong?" he says.

"Nothing." I force a smile. "I'm Ally. Ally Walker."

"Ally Walker, huh?"

"Yeah. I figured you should know my last name before you forget it."

"I won't forget you." His smile reveals a dimple in his cheek. He looks at me in a way I've seen other guys look at me, but few back up that look. "Yo, you're beautiful."

"Thanks."

"So I've never seen you before, Ally."

"No, I just moved here."

"To Cantor? Yo, I'm sorry to hear that. Seriously."

He looks genuinely sorry, and something about Mark makes me feel at ease. Maybe it's his smile or that dimple. But whatever it is, I don't feel threatened or uncomfortable. I decide to leave without seeming desperate, even though I know I'll be back to visit him.

"See ya around." I start the engine.

"Yo, what's your number?" Mark grabs onto the window to stop me from leaving.

Unfortunately, I'm not prepared to give him my number. And if I were, how many other female customers has Mark Silva hit on today? I'm guessing this is his thing.

"Jus' so you know, I don't ask every girl for her number," Mark says, as if reading my mind.

"I doubt that, killer."

He laughs as if caught in a lie. "Yo, it's true!"

I wonder if Mark Silva is telling me the truth. "I know where to find you."

"Seriously, you ain't gonna give up your number?"

"Not today, handsome."

"Not today, huh?" he says with another laugh, enjoying my attention. "Yo, at least come back and visit me, a'right?"

"Maybe." I drive off, leaving him staring after me.

From there, I head straight to the nearest wireless store and purchase a used iPhone with a Cantor phone number. I wish I thought of this earlier because if I did, I would've gladly given Mark my number. I think about going back to the gas station, but again, I don't want to look desperate. So I decide to do a drive-by of Natice Gentry's house instead.

I type in her address and follow the directions into a neighborhood that seems even less safe than Lori and Mark's. I can't even count how many boarded-up homes I pass, not to mention piles of junk wasting away in open fields of dirt. The block Natice lives on is a one-way street facing a hill of weeded grass along a highway. There aren't any houses, only two-storied redbrick apartment buildings clustered together with air-conditioners sticking out from the windows. Each pothole in the road I hit makes the car rattle. It isn't until I reach the end of the block that I notice a mailbox fastened to a screen door with the name Gentry written in white paint. There's a driveway on the side of the apartment, but no car is in it.

I only stick around for a few minutes before the heat and a crazy-looking dude wearing a long coat makes me want to get out of that neighborhood. I grab some Burger King from across the street from my motel and take it back to my air-conditioned room. I kick off my shoes and plop down on the bed, spent. The Coca-Cola is extra syrupy, and the French fries are less than crunchy. I take a bite out of my cheeseburger and look across the bed at the TV, wanting to turn it on to drown out the silence. The remote sits next to it on the dresser, but I'm too lazy to get up. I pull a fry from the bag, and my mind wanders to Jenny. Anytime we ate McDonalds or Wendy's at home—we never got Burger King—we'd sit at the kitchen table, tossing fries to Duke. He'd be sitting perfectly still, his brown eyes trained on the fry with the precision of a sniper's scope, following it from the box to our mouths. As soon as we tossed one in the air, like Jaws, his teeth would clamp down on the fry, and he'd swallow it whole.

Occasionally, Jenny and I would get brave enough to let Duke take the fries straight from our fingers. "He's so fast!" Jenny would scream, yanking her hand away as fast as she could. We'd laugh hysterically. You'd lose your thumb if you didn't move quickly enough. Thinking about the memory, I push aside my burger and fries and ball up into a fetal position, pulling the pillow in close to me. I try taking a nap, but after closing my eyes then quickly reopening them and staring at the wall for twenty minutes, I give up and call my dad.

"Hey, kiddo. How's camp?" my father asks, his voice upbeat.

"It's good." I sit on the edge of my motel bed.

"How are the coaches?"

"They're tough. They make Coach Prudenti look like a kitten."

"They're not working you too hard in this heat?"

"Nah. We've mostly been playing inside."

"Well, make sure you drink lots of water. You don't want to get dehydrated."

"Don't worry. I am."

I hate myself for lying to my father. If he only knew I was in some crappy motel room in Cantor. Thank God, he doesn't ask me a million questions. "How's Duke?"

"He's good. Misses you. I've been letting him sleep in our room."

I feel even guiltier, as though I'm the worst person in the world for abandoning Duke, but at least he and my dad are keeping each other company. "Give him a kiss for me. Okay?"

"I will."

"How's Mom?" I finally ask.

There's a pause. "She's doing better."

I can tell by my father's tone that things are the same, and by the time I hang up the phone, I'm determined to stay in Cantor the full two weeks.

Around midnight, I end up back in Lori Silva's neighborhood, and everything looks exactly as it did the other night, including Mark's mustang in the driveway. I park in a different spot and watch, this time without going on Facebook. About an hour later, Mark exits the house with a blonde, and they drive off together in his car. He may not be a criminal, but he's obviously a player. Unfortunately, I don't see Lori, and after growing restless and tired, I quit spying for the day.

CHAPTER 15

After eating a Twix bar for breakfast, I go by the gas station in hopes of flirting with Mark and somehow using him. But I don't see his red Mustang, so I decide to check out Ronnie Rodriguez's home. The case folder doesn't include much on Ronnie, other than her and her mother's testimony as to where Ronnie was on the night of the shooting. They both claim Ronnie was at home having dinner with her brother and sister. Her mother even stated that Ronnie felt sick afterward and stayed in, going so far as to say she gave Ronnie aspirin for a headache at around eight o'clock that night. I wonder if this is true or if Mrs. Rodriguez would lie for her daughter. Her father, Carlos Rodriguez, was at work.

Thankfully, Ronnie lives in a neighborhood that is actually nice, even charming. There aren't any cars propped up on cinder blocks, or trash cluttering the front lawns, or clothes hanging out windows. The people here seem to care about their homes. Each one is crafted in an old Colonial style. They're small and all bunched together like most of the housing in Cantor, but they're well kept and painted in vibrant greens, reds, and yellows. I arrive at Ronnie's house, and there's a statue of the Virgin Mary prominently displayed in the front yard.

I'm barely there five minutes when the front door swings open and a woman in a loud, aqua-blue dress hurries out, shouting in Spanish. "¡Llegamos tarde! ¡Cierre la puerta! ¡Cierre la puerta!" She waves for the door to be closed.

Two teenagers I recognize from Ronnie's Facebook photos trail after the woman.

"Ronnie! Tell your father to hurry!" her mother yells, breaking into English.

Ronnie finally appears, and she does not look happy. "*Dad!* C'mon!" She tugs at the dress she is wearing. It fits snugly around her sides and belly.

"Leave it. It's pretty," her mother says in Spanish, swatting Ronnie's hand away and fixing her daughter's dress.

"Can I borrow the car tonight?" Ronnie asks.

"No," her mother says flatly, continuing in Spanish. "I'm not in the mood to fight, so don't start with me." She throws a hand in the air to emphasize her point.

Ronnie breaks into Spanish, raising her voice, arguing that she asked her mother two nights ago, and her mother said yes.

"I did not." Her mother shakes her head no.

"Yes, you did!" Ronnie insists, pointing to the car. She quickly reminds her mother that she even promised to put gas in the car, and her mother agreed.

Her mother wags a finger in the air, saying she only agreed to give Ronnie the car Friday night, and not tonight too.

"Fine." Ronnie kicks at the ground like an upset child. "Friday night, and don't forget."

Her mother gives Ronnie an exasperated look.

Their conversation makes me glad I studied Spanish for four years and not French.

The front door opens, and the mother looks up. "Oh my God! What took you so long?" she says, again in Spanish.

A thin man dressed in a suit that is too big for him walks out of the house, carrying the little girl from Ronnie's profile picture. "My *bebecita* had to go to the bathroom."

"Let's go! We're late." The mother gently takes the little girl from him and rushes them all into a maroon Toyota Camry parked in the street.

Ronnie shoves her siblings aside and enters the back. As the Camry pulls away from the curb, I see a bumper sticker that reads Jesus is Lord. Rosary beads hang from the rearview mirror. I keep close behind the Camry and end up following the Rodriguez family to Sunday mass at a nearby Church.

It takes me another day before I'm able to get my first glimpse of Cracker. She lives in one of the most depressing apartment complexes, in one of the worst sections of Cantor, positioned right behind a cluster of abandoned warehouses. I'm guessing this area is considered the projects, and before I can even reach the front of Cracker's apartment building, I see a woman with pale freckled skin and greasy red hair standing in the street, screaming at a fat shirtless man, who seems to mostly ignore her. She's drunk and wears a sheer top that shows her small, sagging breasts. I park behind a pickup truck and watch from inside my car. I know immediately this drunk screaming mess is Cracker's mother. She looks exactly like Cracker, but older.

"Shut the fuck up!" someone yells.

"Mind your own fuckin' business, Gerald! You fat fuckin' queer!" Cracker's mother yells in the direction of the voice.

I see two young white faces staring out from behind a bedsheet used as a curtain for a fourth-floor apartment window.

Finally, a cop car arrives, and a male and a female police officer step out. Cracker's mother slurs her words as she tells the officers an incoherent story about what happened.

"Fat fuck's dog barking all goddamn morning! Fuckin' crapped all over the fuckin' place!"

After growing impatient, the female police officer threatens to arrest Cracker's mother if she doesn't go back inside her home. A door bangs open, and I look up and see Cracker hauling ass out of the building. She grabs her mother's arm. "Ma! Let's go!"

Cracker is shorter than I expect. I'm guessing maybe five feet four, the same height as Carly, the band geek. She wears a faded orange T-shirt and cut-off jean shorts that hang low off her ass, with about two inches of white underwear showing.

"Ma! C'mon!"

Her mother continues to curse at the neighbor, even spitting in his direction, until finally, she pushes Cracker off her arm and stumbles drunkenly inside the apartment building.

"Don't you all have nothin' better to do?" Cracker says to the two officers with the cadence of a guy. "Instead of fuckin' arresting people for doin' nothin'?" She shares her opinion on what she thinks of their jobs, and every sentence is laced with a curse. "Get a real fuckin' job!" Cracker yells before storming off.

The neighbor shakes his head as if this is an everyday occurrence. "They're nuts!" he tells the police officers then wanders away.

The cops leave, and after that, it's quiet.

I head back to my motel room to escape the heat. I think about calling Jay, but I don't. It's selfish. It'd only be calling him to hear a familiar voice, and besides, he'll only ask me questions I can't answer, like why aren't we together. Why won't I let him help me? *If he only knew. If anyone only knew.*

CHAPTER 16

FOR THE NEXT COUPLE OF days, I pass by each one of these Black Diamond girls' homes. It isn't difficult to spy. The worst thing about it is the fear of getting caught. Online, you can creep around for days, and nobody ever knows you were trespassing. Out here, doing it live, I worry that one of their neighbors may start to wonder who I am or what I'm doing in the neighborhood. Or worse yet, Mark Silva will notice me parked outside his home and think that I'm some crazy stalker, which essentially, I am. But I'm careful about my stalking. I drive past their homes at different times of the day and only start to park when it's dark. Today, I'm wearing a baseball cap. Yesterday, I wore sunglasses. The humidity is brutal, but my obsession with these girls keeps me less concerned with the weather and more concerned with how I'm going to get close to them.

My plan is simple: to befriend Lori Silva and her Black Diamond friends and somehow find evidence linking them to my sister's murder. How I'm going to do this, I have no idea.

The clock is ticking, and I'm not any closer to becoming friends with these girls than when I first rolled into town. I keep checking Ronnie's Facebook page, hoping that she made it public, and I can see where she's checking in, but it's still private. I think about returning to the gas station first thing in the morning to flirt with Mark Silva, assuming he's working. But if he has a girlfriend, I'm sure this'll cause other problems.

I try not to let any of this discourage me as I turn onto Lori Siva's block and see the maroon Toyota Camry with the Jesus is Lord bumper sticker parked in her driveway. Ronnie's mother kept to her word. It's Friday night. I do a quick U-turn and park across the street without a second to spare as the front door flies open, and Ronnie Rodriquez barrels out. She's eating something when it drops out of her hands and hits the ground. "Dammit!" I hear her say before she picks it up, wipes the food clean, and takes another big bite.

"You're nasty!" Cracker emerges from the house.

Ronnie laughs and gets behind the wheel, taking another bite of her food.

Cracker is about to climb into the shotgun seat when someone yells, "Backseat, Cracker!"

I look to the front door and see Lori Silva. Her hair is worn in the same pulled-back style as in her mug shot. She has on jeans and a red-and-white-striped tank top that fits snugly against her body. She's a much thicker girl in person. Her arms are fit and muscular. Cracker promptly takes the backseat. Lori approaches the passenger side, takes hold of the door handle, then stops as if she has seen something. She's looking directly at my car.

I freeze, waiting to see what Lori will do, when my Middletown cell phone rings. *Shit!* I grab it off the seat and duck down to the floor. Of course, it's Lea. I hit Decline and send it to voice mail.

I glance up ever so slowly. Lori continues to stare in my direction as if trying to sharpen her vision. She says something to Cracker, or maybe Ronnie, then walks down the driveway. My pulse quickens as she takes another step and another. I shift the Olds into drive, ready to burn out of there, when all of a sudden, Lori stops and scoops up a pack of cigarettes.

She walks back to the car and ducks inside. I breathe again.

A moment later, Ronnie reverses out of the driveway and speeds away. I put my phone on silent and toss it aside. I wait until the Jesus-mobile reaches the end of the block before I hit the gas pedal. I almost lose them as Ronnie tears through the streets, but I manage to catch up and stay close, at least for another mile, when I see them pull off the highway and into a shopping center.

I watch as the Camry travels to the far end of the parking lot, where parked cars and teenagers are gathered in front of the only open store. It's a pizza shop with the words Pop's Pizzeria written across its front window in large red scripted letters. I keep a good distance away, parking alongside a store that's boarded up and has newspapers covering its windows. There's also a "We Buy Gold" and a discounted food store in the shopping center, but both are closed. From what I can see of the crowd, it's mostly guys drinking beer and smoking cigarettes. I hear their car stereos, heavy with bass, blasting hip-hop.

I search the crowd and immediately spot Lori in her red-and-white-striped shirt. She's standing alongside Cracker as one of the guys in the crowd hands her a beer. Moments later, Ronnie appears with a slice of pizza. She says something, causing Lori to spit out what she is drinking and bust up laughing with Cracker.

As I sit watching Lori and Cracker having a blast, I think about all the times I've ever hated someone before, like when one teammate's mother spread rumors about me stealing booze from her house because I started over her daughter, or when I was in tenth grade and a male teacher blatantly lied about sexual comments he had made to me, or when Jenny was bullied so badly in third grade she was afraid to go to school. But never once did any of it even remotely compare to what I feel right now toward these two. This is a whole new level of hate. This is a Super Bowl stadium full of hate. This is homicidal hate.

There don't seem to be any consequences for what these girls did only six months earlier. They drink. They party. They laugh. Not a care in the world. And just as I'm beginning to think justice will never be served, a black girl in a red T-shirt and jeans runs out from the pizzeria and joins them. She steals a sip from Lori's bottle, talks for a while, and runs back inside. I wonder if that's Natice Gentry.

I stare at the Open sign in the window, debating if I should go in, buy a slice of pizza, and see if it is Natice who works there. But then what? I need to be smart about how I'm going to befriend these girls. Then it hits me. *Well, maybe they're hiring?* I can't wait for morning to arrive.

CHAPTER 17

I LEAVE MY MOTEL ROOM IN a white blouse and shorts. The sun is especially hot this morning, and by the time I arrive at the pizzeria, my blouse is drenched in sweat. The air conditioner in the Olds stopped working last night.

The parking lot, unlike last night, is a ghost town, void of any cars or teenagers. A sign hangs on the pizzeria's front door that reads Open. I push through a glass door, and the place is completely empty, not a soul in it. It looks like any other pizza shop. There's a long glass counter that runs the length of the front room, and behind the counters are ovens. A large bay window faces the parking lot, and in the back room are tables, chairs, and a basketball toss machine.

"Hello?" I call out.

A man, somewhere in his fifties, with a full head of gray hair and a gut protruding from under a white apron, appears from the kitchen. He carries a stack of brown boxes labeled Dough.

"Are you hiring?" I try to sound friendly.

"No," he grumbles, barely acknowledging me.

"I'll work for tips. I don't need a salary." I follow him, determined to get a job.

"You'll go broke, kid." He slams the boxes on the counter.

"I can work weekdays or weekends. I'll wash dishes. I'm good at cleaning bathrooms."

"You don't want to work here. Trust me," he says to himself in Spanish.

"I do, and I'm not leaving until you at least interview me," I reply in Spanish.

He looks at me closely and sighs heavily. "Sit down. I'll be right back."

It takes him almost forty minutes before he is right back. His name is Pop, or at least that is the name he goes by. His armpits are stained in sweat and his apron splotched in water. I tell him I can work mornings, afternoons, and evenings. He waves a dismissive hand in the air.

"That ain't my concern. Stealin' is." He stares at me, wondering if he can trust me. "No handouts to friends."

"That's not a problem. I don't have any friends."

He hands me a red T-shirt with Pop's Pizza written in white letters. "Come back at four, and don't be late." He walks off, looking exhausted just from having hired me.

I drive back to the motel all hyped up and nervous like a kid who's had way too much candy and soda. I'm not quite sure how I am going to pass the time. At least the air conditioner in my motel room works, even if it only blows out semi-cool air. I click on the TV, hoping to find a distraction and calm my nerves. *Game of Thrones* is playing. I stare at the screen, and it triggers something I read in the case folder. *Lori said they were at home watching* Game of Thrones.

I am doing this. I am really doing this.

———————— • ··· • ————————

I arrive fifteen minutes early and full of anxiety. Pop stares at me strangely and checks his watch. Apparently, he isn't used to employees arriving early. He orders me to clean the back tables and disappears to the kitchen without any further direction. I pick up a smelly wet rag off the counter and head to the back room. There are five wooden tables in all, booth style, lining the sides of the room. The basketball toss game is tucked in the corner of the room, and part of its net is ripped and sagging. Next to it is one of those old Centipede machines. A Not Working sign is taped to its screen.

As I wipe dried tomato paste and soda rings off the tables, fear, my new best friend, creeps in. It's like an undertow pulling me further and further away from the shore. *What if someone recognizes me from the basketball game? What if they know I'm the sister of the girl who was shot and killed?* I pull at the collar of my red T-shirt and struggle to take air into my lungs at the exact moment the walls start swimming around me. I drop the rag from my clammy hand, and it dawns on me that I'm having a panic attack. It's something Amber would sometimes experience before games. *What is it that she used to tell herself to calm down?* I remember. *"It's okay. I'm okay. It's okay. I'm okay."*

I grab onto the ends of the table and close my eyes. "It's okay. I'm okay. It's okay. I'm okay." I do this for about a minute before I release the table and stand upright on a pair of wobbly legs. I glance around the room—tables, chairs, nothing to be scared about. I catch my reflection in the mirror of a Coca-Cola sign. It reminds me how much different I look with short bleached-blond hair. Slowly, my breathing returns to normal, and I calm down. I pick up the wet rag and move on to a new table. I focus my attention on cleaning, hoping it will keep my mind distracted. I lean in twice as hard on the worn tabletops. There are names and initials carved into the wood and words like "eat me" and "fuck you" and every other curse word imaginable. I move to the last table in the back. Carved into the wood is a small black diamond. Next to it are the initials: "L.S."

"Ally! Come here!" Pop yells from the front room.

I turn and see him standing alongside the counter, and facing him is Natice Gentry. She looks exactly like her mug shot, right down to her pissed-off expression. She's a little taller than I am and much thinner, like a model. Her skin is dark, without any blemishes.

"You get here at four—not four-thirty!" Pop says to Natice, who stands with attitude, her arms folded across her chest.

"I told you I couldn't get a damn ride!" she yells back at him.

I take my time walking toward them, hoping their argument will come to a quick end, but it doesn't. I reach Pop's side, and he points at me. "The new girl got here early! You're late again, you're fired!"

Natice's narrowed eyes shift to me. I wish I hadn't arrived early.

"Show her around then train her on the goddamn cash register," Pop says as a way of introduction then walks off, leaving the two of us standing alone.

"You full time?" Natice asks, her tone anything but friendly.

"I don't know. He didn't tell me."

"Well, if you are, don't get here on time. Got it?"

"No problem."

Natice grabs a dirty rag off the counter and heads toward the back.

"I already cleaned the tables."

76

She stops. "Did I say I was cleaning the damn tables?" She rolls her eyes, drops the rag, and walks off. "C'mon."

She opens a door, and I follow her down a set of wooden steps into a basement. And without a word to me, Natice fills her arms with a bunch of cardboard pizza boxes that are stored on a metal shelf. I do the same and head back up the stairs ahead of her. I feel her eyes burning into my head. I hear a snicker of a laugh.

We stack the pizza boxes under a stainless steel counter. "You know your hair is orange in the back?" Natice says.

I had forgotten about my bleached hair. "Oh. Yeah. I did it myself."

She looks at me as if I'm stupid. "Girl, next time pay someone."

Natice gives me a rushed tour of the kitchen. "Here's the dough. Pepperoni. Mushrooms. Everything. Fathead makes all the pies himself." We pass a sink filled with dirty dishes. "You'll probably be back here cleaning later. 'Cause someone's too damn cheap to hire a dish washer!" She yells it loud enough for Pop to hear through the closed office door.

We move back to the front counter, and Natice shows me how to work the cash register. It's a huge piece of outdated machinery. Natice talks fast, and I can hardly keep up with her as her right forefinger moves swiftly, hitting various buttons to demonstrate. That's when I see it. Between her thumb and forefinger is a small black diamond tattoo.

"You got it?" Natice asks.

I don't answer. My eyes are focused on the tattoo, trying to determine for certain if it is a diamond. Natice follows my stare, and a bolt of anxiety goes through me. I feel my face turn red, and I shift from one foot to the other, shoving a hand deep in my pocket. "That's cool," I say, nodding to her tattoo, trying to sound casual.

Natice looks at the tattoo and couldn't appear less impressed by it. "Yeah. Now you're trained."

She walks away from me and stares out the window. Natice hasn't done half of what Lori and Cracker have done, but there's still plenty on her resume that disturbs me. She spent at least a year in juvy for various fighting. One girl was hospitalized.

"Sorry about getting here early," I say.

Natice shrugs. Then she faces me, shoulders hunched as if feeling bad. "Look, I'm not trying to be a bitch. A'right? I'm jus' tired. I was up late studying. And I got my period. So the last place I want to be is here, workin' late, with Fathead's nasty-ass breath following me around like a dirty fart."

I almost laugh. Pop does have really horrible breath.

"I got Advil if you need it." I remove my hand from my pocket.

"Shit. I already took five."

I think about the comment Natice made seconds before I offered her Advil, wondering if perhaps I heard her wrong. "So what are you studying?"

"Economics."

The look of surprise must show on my face.

"What? You never seen a black girl study economics?"

I feel my face turn red again. "No. It's just... I've never seen anyone study economics." It's the truth, but it's more the fact that I didn't expect Natice Gentry or any other member of a street gang to be studying anything, let alone economics. "I'm Ally, by the way," I say, hoping to change the subject.

"Natice Gentry. Nice to meet you," she says sarcastically. "So where you from?"

It's obvious that I'm not from Cantor.

"Seattle. I moved here for the summer to take care of my grandmother. She's sick." I repeat the lie I told Pop earlier.

"That sucks," Natice says.

After that, we stand awkwardly with nothing more to say.

CHAPTER 18

I've already burned my hand once taking a large pie out of the oven using a peel, a long, shovel-like wooden paddle.

"Shit!" I scream for a second time.

Natice laughs. "Girl, don't get so close to the damn oven."

Later, I drop an entire pepperoni pie on the ground and get reamed out by Pop. Thankfully, the Advil has kicked in, and Natice is in a slightly better mood. Her attitude is gone, at least her attitude toward me. "Don't let Fathead speak to you like that. Tell him to fuck off," she says after Pop walks away.

Around eight o'clock, cars start to fill the parking lot. It's mostly guys and only a handful of girls who empty out of the cars. A couple of times, I practically jump out of my skin thinking I see the girl whose nose I bloodied in the East Cantor game, but then it ends up it's not her. And most of the chicks never come inside the pizzeria. They simply hang out in the parking lot, drinking beers and listening to music. Natice knows every guy and girl who walks through the door. Some of the kids in my high school try to act tough and talk "gangsta" and wear their jeans low. But these teenagers really are gangster. At one point, a fight breaks out in the parking lot. A kid is beaten so badly his friends have to rush him to the hospital.

Natice shakes her head. "Dumb-ass don't learn. He got his ass beat twice last week."

I'm still recovering from the image of the boy's face being stomped with a shoe when a black Mercedes rolls up to the front of the restaurant. It's followed by the familiar Toyota Camry with the Jesus is Lord bumper sticker. Sure enough, Ronnie Rodriguez, Lori Silva, and Cracker empty out of the Camry. My anxiety quadruples just seeing Lori Silva, who once again wears her hair tight against her head and looks cold and menacing.

A moment later, the unattractive dude from Lori's Facebook profile picture steps out from behind the wheel of the Mercedes.

"What up, Vince?" Natice waves.

Vince sees Natice and nods. He's tall, thin, and his long hair is held back with a black headband. He wears a white tank top and loose-fitting jeans that look like they might fall off his waist at any second. A bunch of guys gather around him, bumping fists, greeting one another. Lori appears right next to him. Vince leans against his Mercedes and pulls her between his legs. Lori cracks a smile and kisses his lips. I instantly wish she were dead.

Seconds later, the door opens, and a surge of noise enters, followed by Ronnie Rodriguez. She bounds up to the counter with the energy of a puppy, wearing a black spandex top that's too small for her oversized belly.

"What up, Natty, Nat, Nat!"

"What up, girl?" Natice swings her shoulders from side to side.

Ronnie takes a step back and poses in a sexy manner. "Yo, I'm on a diet."

Natice laughs. "A diet? Again?"

Ronnie rubs her belly. "Yeah I gotta trim down. I ain't seen my feet in a year."

Natice laughs at her.

"For real. I ain't kidding. I took a shower the other day and looked down…" Ronnie wags her head as if picturing it in that moment. "It ain't pretty, girl. It ain't pretty."

Ronnie notices me. "Who's this?"

"This is Ally. New girl," Natice says sarcastically.

"Pop hired someone new?"

"Uh-huhhhhh. If you can believe that."

"Another white girl." Ronnie shakes her head.

"Uh-hmmm."

"He don't learn," Ronnie says.

"Nope," Natice adds matter-of-factly.

They speak as if I'm not even standing there.

"How long you give her?" Ronnie asks.

"I don't know. I can't tell with her." Natice stares hard at my face, as if aware I'm hiding a secret.

I feel my face grow red again, worrying Natice knows who I am, then without any hint of recognition, Natice says, "Two days."

"Shit, I give her two hours!" Ronnie laughs as she starts dancing to a song playing on the radio. "New girl, hook me up with two pepperoni!"

I grab two slices and layer on the pepperoni. Ronnie leans up against the counter like a little kid. "Don't be skimpy. More... more..." I double up on the pepperoni, and Ronnie responds with a smile. "Nice."

"I thought you were on a diet?" Natice says.

"I am. I'm only getting two." Ronnie grins. Her left hand clings to the counter, and I notice the same black diamond tattoo between her thumb and forefinger. I place the slices into the oven, and I hear her laugh. "New girl, what the hell is wrong with your hair?"

"She did it herself." Natice raises an eyebrow.

Ronnie cracks up. "Hey, I can fix it. For real. Fifty bucks." I turn around and face her. "Seriously. You'll go from Ronald McDonald to..." Ronnie can't think of anyone. "Anyway, you need that head worked out, girlfriend."

She smiles at me, nodding her head yes, doing a dance.

Natice laughs at her. Clearly she is making fun of me.

"Your hair is orange back there!" Ronnie stops dancing and holds her crotch. "Oh shit. I gotta go!" She runs to the bathroom, and Natice laughs harder. Ronnie has just pissed herself.

The door opens again, and before I can give thought to what happened, Cracker walks in. Her pasty skin is red with sunburn. She's wearing a low-cut blouse and tight, feminine blue jeans, which seems incredibly odd in comparison to how she walks, like a guy. In her hand, she clutches a box of Cracker Jacks.

"Natty, Ronnie in here?" Cracker says, having just stuffed a handful of the candy-coated popcorn into her mouth.

Natice, I notice, is a lot less friendly toward Cracker. "She's in the bathroom."

Cracker's face twists into anger. "What the fuck! I been standin' outside waitin' for her fat ass for an hour!"

Cracker spots me, and right away, I sense trouble. Unlike Ronnie or Natice, there is something truly frightening about Cracker. Maybe it's how she speaks or the look in her eyes. Or maybe it's that out of all of these girls, excluding Lori, Cracker is the one most likely to have shot and killed my sister. Whatever it is, I don't like how Cracker is looking at me. I wonder if she's carrying a gun.

I busy myself checking on Ronnie's slices.

"Yo, hook me up with a sugar high." Cracker tosses her head at the soda machine.

Natice grabs a large Styrofoam cup and fills it with orange soda.

"How the hell you work in here? It's hotter than outside." Cracker tugs at her shirt, impatiently waiting for her drink. When I turn back around, she eyeballs me. Bravely—or stupidly—I hold Cracker's stare. She smirks as if to say I'm a joke and not worth her time and shoves a handful of Cracker Jacks into her thin, angry mouth. She chews with her mouth open. She's rough and hideous, and I hate her even more.

Natice interrupts our staring game by placing the large soda in front of Cracker, who then tosses down a dollar.

"Yo, fire down below. Where's the other one?" Natice waits for more money.

Cracker begrudgingly digs into her jeans and dumps another dollar on the counter. She uses her left hand, the same hand that gun residue had been found on.

"Yeah, tha's what I thought. Cheap ass."

Cracker smirks, and Natice releases the soda.

"Damn, y'all. I almost shit myself too!" Ronnie reemerges from the bathroom, looking relieved she hasn't.

Cracker shoves her from behind. "Ronnie, I was waiting outside for you!"

"So? Tha's your problem."

Cracker calls her a bitch and walks off to the basketball toss game.

I pull Ronnie's slices from the oven and place them on the counter. "Four seventy-five."

Ronnie scoops up one of the slices and bites into it, burning her mouth. "Ah! Mmmuckin' hot." She chews with her mouth open, trying to swallow the hot pieces.

"Girl, let it cool down first." Natice laughs.

"I'm mumgry," Ronnie mumbles and walks away without paying.

I stare after her as she joins Cracker at the basketball toss game. Natice walks next to me and offers some advice. "Get the money first, girlfriend. 'Cause this crowd ain't nothin' but a bunch of bottom-bitch hoes."

I have no idea what a "bottom-bitch hoe" is, other than I know it's not a "do nothin' hoe," but after that, Natice takes a break and joins Cracker and Ronnie. I stand at the counter, staring at the three of them playing the basketball game. For a moment, I can't feel any part of my body—arms, legs, nothing. I clench my fist and push the heel of my sneaker hard into the tiled floor. It's surreal being so close to these girls, knowing they had something to do with my sister's murder. Before, they were only names and photographs, criminal resumes on paper: Natice Gentry, Ronnie Rodriguez, Cynthia Down. But now they're live girls, standing only a few feet in front of me, talking, laughing, and playing a game. I twist the leather band on my watch. This is why I don't own a gun. I'd have used it by now.

As the night wears on, it doesn't take me long before I understand why Natice and Ronnie bet on how long I would last. Pop apparently has trouble keeping new girls around because of Cracker. And I'm no exception. Cracker makes comments about my hair, dumps her trash on the floor, then demands that I clean it up. I simply take the abuse and ignore Cracker as best I can. At one point, she flicks a lit cigarette butt at me. It takes everything I have not to end this bitch with a wooden peel to the back of her head.

I'm relieved when Natice comes to my rescue. "Cracker, cut the shit a'ready!"

"Keep your pointy noise in your own damn business, Natice!"

"Why don't you keep it for me!" Natice says.

"Yeah, a'right," Cracker mocks then stuffs a handful of Cracker Jacks into her mouth and walks away. There's definitely tension between Natice and Cracker. I wonder why. But after that, Cracker leaves me alone, except for one last remaining comment.

On my way to the bathroom, I walk past Ronnie as she nets a basket. "Nice shot."

"What are you, a fuckin' cheerleader?" Cracker comments.

Ronnie laughs and keeps shooting. "Thanks, cheerleader!"

I hear Cracker call me a dumb bitch as I escape into the bathroom.

I close the door behind me and suddenly wish that I could be back home. I'm exhausted, and between the random thug guys hitting on me and Cracker's abuse, I simply want to be out of this shit hole and back in Middletown. But then I remember what home is like. I remember Jenny is dead. I remember I'll never see my little sister again. The pain doubles me over. I take hold of the sink, strangling its porcelain sides, fingers white knuckled, teeth clenched, tears streaming down my face. I look in the mirror. "You got this, Campbell! You can do this!" I try to psych myself up. I think about all the times I've ever gone up against much bigger girls on the basketball court. *They didn't own you, Campbell. You owned them. You're tough. You're a winner.*

I tell myself I can do this. I tell myself I have a plan and a purpose. I tell myself I am not leaving Cantor until Lori, Cracker, Ronnie, and Natice pay for killing my sister. I wipe away the wetness, take a deep breath, and open the door.

My heart skips a beat as I run straight into Lori Silva.

She stares at me coldly and reeks of cigarette smoke. I step out of her way, and she walks past, without a word. The bathroom door slams closed. A wisp of air hits my back. I swallow hard and walk to the front counter to finish out the night.

CHAPTER 19

MY IPHONE RINGS AROUND NOON when I have just woken up. On the caller ID I see: *Dr. Evans*. I think about not answering, but I know why he is calling. I know he will call again. But mostly, I pick up the phone because I could really use a friend right now. My finger swipes right.

"Checking on me?"

It feels good to hear his voice. As expected, he's calling to see how I'm doing. He asks about basketball camp. I tell him my legs are sore, since they are always sore at the beginning of any camp. He asks me if I am making any new friends. "...or are you isolating?"

I tell him the truth. "I'm meeting new people."

"Any that you like?"

"There's one girl that doesn't annoy me."

He laughs. "One? That's progress."

We talk for a little bit about how hot the weather is and what they're feeding us at camp—I say hamburgers, pasta, and pizza—and then Dr. Evans asks how I'm sleeping. I tell him it's pretty much the same, without going into details about my last nightmare, and he gives me a breathing exercise that he thinks might help me fall asleep. "It's called four-seven-eight. You breathe through your nose for four seconds, then hold your breath for seven, then exhale out your mouth for eight. Do it for a minute, and keep practicing. It takes time to get used to it, but it might help." He no longer sounds worried about me harming myself, probably because he thinks I'm at basketball camp. If he only knew where I was, he'd probably be a lot more concerned, not only that I'd harm myself, but that others might do the job for me.

We hang up, and I close my eyes and inhale through my nose for four seconds then hold it for eight. Or was it seven? *Shit. I've already forgotten.*

Later that afternoon, I wait in my car, sweating my ass off, until Natice finally arrives fifteen minutes late when she is dropped off in a tinted-window Lexus by the good-looking black dude I recognize from Ronnie's Facebook photos.

I walk in right after Natice, wet with sweat and feeling five pounds lighter. As a form of punishment for us both being late, Pop orders me to mop the floors and tells Natice to clean the bathrooms. A short while later, he leaves the pizzeria to pick up some supplies, leaving Natice and me alone.

Natice waits until his van drives out of sight before grabbing her book bag from under the front counter. "I'm going downstairs to study. If Fathead comes back before I'm up, tell him I'm still cleaning. Okay?"

"Sure." I watch her disappear to the basement, still finding it difficult to believe that Natice Gentry, or any other member of a street gang, could be enrolled in college.

An hour later, Natice reemerges. She has just stuck her bag under the counter when Pop walks through the door carrying boxes. His eyes land on Natice, and he immediately knows she is up to something. "Were you in the cellar?"

"Does it look like I was in the damn cellar?"

Pop looks at me as if expecting to find the truth.

"She was in the bathroom, fixing the toilet," I say.

"What the hell did you do to the toilet?" he screams at Natice.

"She didn't. I dropped my Kotex in there. It wouldn't flush."

Pop stares at me as if I'm an idiot. "What the hell is wrong with you? Don't be puttin' your damn woman products in there! Use the goddamn trash can."

"Sorry." I play dumb. "It slipped, and it bombed the bowl."

He shakes his head as if there is something truly wrong with me then turns to Natice, who I now see is suppressing a smile. "And you study on your own time!"

"Was I studying? I pulled a bloody Kotex out the bowl!"

Pop makes a sour face and orders us to get the rest of the supplies out of the back of his truck. Natice and I walk out the door, laughing so hard we almost break a rib, and it is with the Kotex lie that Natice Gentry starts to become my friend.

Out of the five nights I work at the pizzeria, Natice and I work three of them together. My friendship with Natice is not fast and furious, and at times, it's hard to tell whether or not she even likes me. Some days, she barely talks to me. Other days, she is funny and friendly.

"So what's Seattle like?" Natice asks. It's a slow night, and we are both standing at the counter.

"It rains a lot. It's really green and pretty. But boring." I repeat what I have read online, adding the boring part. I assume wherever you grow up, you think it's boring.

"It's gotta be better than here." Natice tosses her nose up at the outside. "So where's your grandmother live?"

"The Shell Motel."

"Girl, your grandmother lives at the shitty Shell? That place is a dump."

"Yeah, I know. I killed a cockroach last night." It's true, and it almost had me packing my bags.

"Fowl." Natice scrunches up her face as if smelling something rotten. She takes a step back, bends over, and places the palms of her hands on the dirty floor.

"What the hell are you doin'?" Pop appears out of nowhere.

"What does it look like? I'm stretching." Natice looks up at him from under her armpit.

Pop mumbles a few undecipherable words and stalks off.

A minute later, I'm pulling Natice's arms up high behind her back into a stretch.

By us working together and me subtly asking questions, Natice slowly starts sharing information about herself, which is exactly what I've hoped for. I learn Natice has been working at the pizzeria on and off since she was fifteen years old, which partially explains her relationship with Pop. Pop always threatens to fire Natice, yet he never does, mainly because Natice is loyal to him. I never see her give away free food or soda. Everyone pays. I also learn Natice doesn't have a boyfriend. The good-looking dude who owns the Lexus is her cousin, Tray.

The biggest surprise, of course, is that Natice is taking classes at a nearby community college to get an associate's degree in economics. I learn pretty quickly that Natice Gentry is not what she appears to be. She is actually much smarter and, at times, kind and compassionate. One second, Natice will be cursing out a group of teenagers, sounding pure ghetto. The next, she'll be commenting on how pretty my eyes are. I even watch her work out a math problem that seems totally foreign to me and call it easy.

"They put me in advanced math classes when I was younger. But you ever see who's in those classes? Shit, I made them switch me back," Natice says as we're cleaning the back tables together.

"So did you go to high school around here?"

"Yeah, Cantor High School North. Home of the Eagles pride!" Natice cheers sarcastically.

"How was it?"

"It was a'right."

"You play any sports?"

"Ran track. Almost got a scholarship too. Would'a been out of this dump and not stuck going to community."

"What happened?"

"Some shit went down earlier in the year. The coach got wind of it and decided he didn't want me anymore."

"What type of shit? Must've been something big for them to take it away?" The time coincides with the store robbery.

"Yeah, it was. But I can't change it, so whatever." Natice turns quiet and doesn't offer anything else.

I decide to leave it alone for now.

In return for what Natice does tell me about herself, I continue to reveal only lies. I tell Natice I just broke up with my boyfriend back in Seattle and that my parents are divorced, and I'm an only child. Saying, "I'm an only child" brings on a wave of sadness that I have to fight back in order not to cry. I realize it isn't a lie. I no longer have a sister. Jenny is dead.

As it turns out, Lori, Cracker, and Ronnie spend a lot of time at the pizzeria. The back room is pretty much their second home. Ronnie is the only one of the three who is ever nice to me, partially because I give her free slices of pizza and partially because that's just who Ronnie is. Natice gives me shit about the free handouts, but I don't care. I want Ronnie to like me. I want them all to like me. I'm not quite sure how this is going to happen with Lori and Cracker. Even with my budding friendship with Natice, Lori never acknowledges me, which in a way, I'm grateful for. There is something truly evil about her, as if she would smile in my face like a close friend and then stab me in the back of the head with a ballpoint pen. At least with Cracker, if she were to attack me, I'd see it coming. With Lori, I feel as though it would be done quietly.

I am surprised I haven't seen Detective Thoms yet. If he is watching Lori and her friends closely, where is he? Other police officers, however, regularly visit the pizzeria, if only to harass Vince. One evening, I witness a cop pull Vince over in his Mercedes and search the car.

"They never find shit," Natice says. "Vince ain't stupid."

It's clear to me that Vince is a drug dealer. He drives a brand-new Mercedes, yet Natice says he works in a body shop.

Occasionally, Natice and I play the basketball toss game when Pop's not around. I make sure to keep my scoring to a minimum so as to not bring attention to myself. But once in a while, I'll crush Natice. Like I am now.

"Shit, girl, you're good today. You play in high school?" Natice says.

"Yeah. Two years. Then I got kicked off the team for fighting."

"So you're one of those, huh?" Natice eyes me closely.

"One of those, what?" I score another basket.

"You keep it all bottled up inside. And then pop!"

"Pretty much. I'm patient up to a point."

"Yeah? And when's that point?"

"When I've had enough," I answer honestly.

"Well, I can't wait until you've had enough of Cracker."

"What's her problem, anyway?"

"Shit, what isn't Cracker's problem? And trust me, if she doesn't have one, she'll find one. But look, it's probably best if you stay clear of her."

"I will, don't worry. Like poison ivy."

"Good. Now, gimme that!" Natice steals the ball from my hands and takes my shot. "Two points!"

I reach in to grab the ball, and she playfully pushes me away and shoots another basket.

"Winner!" Natice shouts, smiling.

She's in a good mood, and I want to ask her then and there if Cracker has ever killed anyone. She nails another basket, and as I hold my tongue, waiting for the right moment, an unsettling feeling washes over me, like being home alone, middle of the night, and someone knocks on your front door. You know not to open it. I shift uncomfortably in my sneakers and shove my twitchy hands deep into my pockets. I decide to wait. The last thing I want to do is raise any suspicions when she's beginning to trust me. Besides, even if Natice were to answer the question right now, I'd have no way of recording it. I've forgotten my iPhone back at the motel. So instead, I offer to give her a ride home.

"I don't live far." Natice slides into the passenger seat next to me. She can barely keep her eyes open she's so tired. I'm exhausted too, but I think it's the excitement of having Natice Gentry in my car that keeps me awake. I've been stalking her for weeks, and now I'm giving her a ride home. If this isn't the biggest game of Catfish, I don't know what is. I reach Natice's street and almost turn before she tells me to.

"Make a left here. It's the last one on the end." She points. The driveway is empty, so I pull in and park.

"Thank God." Natice eyes the dark apartment.

"For what?"

"My asshole step-dad isn't home." She steps out of the car and slams the door.

Her back is to me as I watch her through the open window. I reach down and lift something up off the floor. "Gentry!" Natice turns and faces me. I'm holding up her book bag. "I think you'll need this."

She wags her head. "Damn, that would'a sucked."

I hand her the bag through the open window. "Good luck on your test. I hope you kill it."

"Thanks. I'm dead if I don't. You know how to get to home from here?"

"Yeah, I'm good. If I get lost, I'll jus' ask someone for directions." I see Natice's face change and say, "That was a joke. I'll map it."

"Shit, girl. I was 'bout to say, 'Don't ask in this 'hood.' Well, thanks for the ride."

"Any time. See ya."

Natice walks to her front door, throwing me a quick wave before disappearing inside. I promptly roll up her window, lock the passenger door, and speed away. I drive back to the motel, thinking about how different

Natice is from how I imagined her. I'm glad I was wrong about her. I only hope I'll be able to get Natice to tell me the truth about what happened to my sister.

"Just be patient..." I tell myself. "You're winning her over."

CHAPTER 20

THE PHONE RINGS TWICE BEFORE my father's secretary answers the line.

"Good afternoon. John Campbell's office."

"Hi, Linda. It's Alex. Is my dad there?"

"Hi, Alex. Of course. Let me get him for you."

As I wait for my father to pick up, I pace back and forth across my motel room's carpeted floor, trying to pretend I am actually at basketball camp. My stomach growls from not having eaten all day, but I just want to get this call over with, especially since my dad is expecting me home tomorrow. I'm at least confident my next story will give me more time than any basketball camp.

"Hey, kiddo, how's it going?" my father says.

"Good."

"So how's the rest of camp? The coaches take it any easier on you girls?"

"No. They ran us twice as hard." I sound exhausted.

"I guess they got you in shape, then?"

"Yeah, for sure. So, Dad, a girl here at camp just invited me to her summerhouse in Ocean City, Maryland. It's right on the beach and sounds awesome. I'd really love to go. Do you care?"

There's a pause on the other end of the line, followed by what I imagine to be my father smiling. I haven't shown any interest or excitement in anything since Jenny's death, except of course, for wanting to go away to basketball camp. "I wish I had a friend with a summerhouse," my father says, sounding happy for me. "Of course you can go. What's your friend's name?"

"Natalie. And really, you don't mind?"

"As long as her parents don't mind, it's fine with me."

"They don't. She already asked them. They have plenty of room."

"That's great. How long you going for? A few days?"

"I don't know. Maybe a week? I guess it depends on how much fun I'm having."

This time I do hear my father smile, probably because we both know I haven't had fun in a long time.

"That's great, honey. Well, tell Natalie's parents thank you. And you're leaving tomorrow afternoon?"

"Yup, right after camp." I keep up my enthusiasm.

"Okay, kiddo. Just make sure you call me as soon as you get to her house. I'll let
your mother know."

"I will. Thanks, Dad." I don't bother to ask how my mother is doing simply because I don't want to spoil my father's good mood.

"Drive safe. Love you, honey."

"Love you too. Bye, Dad."

I hang up the phone and plop down on the bed, ten pounds lighter. I stretch out my body, tapping my feet on the bed, relieved my father didn't ask to speak with my new friend's mother. I think any other parent from Middletown probably would have, but considering all that I have been through and my father's own state of mind, he probably feels that being away from home is doing me good. After all, I sound much better than I have in a long time.

Later, I pay for an additional two weeks at the motel.

It's my day off from the pizzeria when my Cantor cell phone rings. I know immediately who it is. It's the only person I have given that number to. I pick up the phone, curious to know why she is calling. "What up?"

"Hey, can you pick me up?" Natice asks in a rushed voice. "I need a ride to work."

I drive over to Natice's house, and she's waiting outside.

"Thanks, girl!" Natice hops in the car. "Tray was supposed to pick me up, but that fool got stuck in Philly. Calls me at the last minute. 'Sorry, cuz, ain't gonna make it.' I'm like, you could've given me more than five minutes."

"It's no big deal. I wasn't doing anything, just watching TV with my grandmother."

"You're not working?"

"Nope, I'm off today."

"And you came to pick me up? You're all right, Cheerleader."

"No big deal. Tomorrow, I'm gonna ask Pop for another night. My grandmother keeps torturing me with *Judge Judy* on my days off, and I could use the extra dough."

"Well, I hope he gives it to you 'cause I hate working with him alone. The other day, I was doin' homework, and he freaks out on me. Starts yelling and shit, right in my face. And lemme tell you, his breath was somethin' awful."

I laugh.

"It's true, girl."

"Dude, I know. And he's a close talker too. I'm always backing up, and he's always creeping in. I don't know how his wife deals. His breath can knock flies off a shit truck." I roll my eyes, thinking about it. Strangely, I feel more myself around Natice.

Natice laughs. "Shit, she's a nurse. Maybe she wears a mask around the house."

A few minutes later, I speed through the pizzeria's parking lot, slamming into just about every pothole in the ground, before pulling up to the door.

"Girl, you're the worst driver."

"I've been told. Tell your lover I said hi," I say, referring to Pop.

"Thanks. I will, and I owe you!" Natice jumps out of the car.

I watch as she walks into the pizzeria on time—thanks to me.

CHAPTER 21

THE NEXT DAY I BUG Pop for another night. I'm expecting him to say no since he's a bit cheap, but surprisingly, he gives it to me. In fact, he's actually nice about it, patting me on the back and telling me it's good to see a teenager who wants to work and isn't so goddamn lazy. So now out of the six nights I work at the pizzeria, Natice and I share four. It makes going in a heck of a lot easier, but the one thing that is really starting to bother me is getting hit on by thugs. One guy won't take no for an answer, and it makes me want to call in sick every day, especially when he starts sitting in the back room, staring at me all night. He won't even order food. He'll simply sit and stare. It's creepy. When he brings me flowers, I decide to take another approach.

"Yeah, no. I'm gay."

"You gay?"

"Yeah, I have a girlfriend in Seattle. Sorry."

"Damn. I don't mind." He smiles, and I see a gold tooth in the back. Thankfully, Natice steps in.

"Hey, Cotton Mouth, illiterate dumb motherfucker, the girl said no! You deaf? Or just stupid?"

"What the fuck you say, Natice?" he mumbles as if his mouth is stuffed with cotton.

"Oh, you hear me now? Your hearing's okay, then?"

"You lucky you Tray's cousin."

"You're lucky you're ugly. 'Cause when he beats your ugly dumb ass, nobody will notice." Finally, the guy walks off. Natice turns to me, her perfectly unblemished face angry. She chucks an empty can of soda hard into the trash. "Damn, these brothers are stupid. Don't even leave ya alone when you tell 'em you're gay."

Later that night, Lori, Ronnie, and Cracker roll into the pizzeria. Their bloodshot eyes and obnoxious voices let me know they're both high and drunk. "What up, Cheerleader?" Lori says with a huge smile on her face as she walks past with Cracker.

It's the first time Lori's acknowledged me since I started working there. Cracker, however, ignores me as usual.

"Yo, Cheerleader. Give me two pepperoni and a Coke." Ronnie stops at the counter.

A moment later, I hand off the pizza and soda.

"What up, Pop?" Ronnie asks.

He shoots her a look and waits until she pays before walking away. Apparently, Pop knows Ronnie well.

As soon as Ronnie and Cracker sit down, Natice goes on break to go hang out with them in the back room. I'm alone at the counter when the glass door swings open and a rough-looking group of girls enter the pizzeria. I can tell they do not play well with others.

"Gimme a large pie to go," says a girl wearing a purple bandana around her neck. Underneath that is a thick gold necklace with an iced-out "T" dangling from it. She's the prettiest out of the bunch and has an exceptionally large ass. She sparks a cigarette and stares back at Lori. But by now, Lori and the others have already noticed her.

"What the fuck is this ho doin' in here?" Lori yells.

"It's on!" Cracker says.

Within seconds, Lori, Cracker, Ronnie, and Natice are in the front of the pizzeria.

"You must be stupid," Lori says.

"Nah, just hungry," Tonya replies.

"You better take your fat ass to Popeyes, 'cause you ain't getting shit to eat here!" Cracker says.

"Cracker, you need to get a fucking tan, ya ugly-ass corpse," says another girl.

"You need to brush your rotten teeth, you ol' snaggletooth!" Natice says.

"You really are stupid." Lori gets in Tonya's face.

"Silva, you need to lay off the booze," Tonya replies.

They stand eye to eye, and I think for sure a fight is going to break out, when Pop emerges from the kitchen.

"In two seconds, I call the cops!" Pop yells to Tonya and her crew. "Get the hell outta here! *Now!*"

Tonya hesitates then glares at Lori. "You'll be seein' me again, Silva."

"You know where I am." Lori holds her stare.

Tonya smirks then pushes through the glass door. Her crew of girls follows her out like a pack of mutts.

"That's right. Popeyes, bitch!" Ronnie yells after them.

"Let's go kick their asses!" Cracker says.

"What the hell is wrong with you? You're ladies! Act like it!" Pop screams.

"Pop, no one says ladies," Cracker tells him.

"Yeah, we women! Sexy bitches, baby!" Ronnie does a dance and runs her hands over her body.

Cracker and Lori laugh.

"Funny. Always funny." Pop storms off.

"C'mon, Pop. Don't be mad! They low-rent. You don't want them skanky asses in your store!" Ronnie yells.

Things settle down, and Lori, Cracker, and Ronnie return to the back room.

I look out the window and see Tonya and her friends drive off in what looks like a brand-new car. Natice peers over my shoulder.

"Who are they?" I ask.

"Locust Park."

"What's their deal?"

"They're in the wrong neighborhood, and they ain't lost," Natice says before walking away.

I stand at the window, wondering if Detective Thoms could be wrong. What if it wasn't Lori or Cracker who shot Jenny? What if it was another group of girls?

The next night is my only night off from the pizzeria, and I'm lying on my bed staring at a shirtless Channing Tatum dancing on screen. I've started leaving the TV on even when I'm not here because I never want to walk into my room and have it be silent. Right now, I'm trying to focus on Channing so as to drown out the noise in my head. It's a daily, if not a minute-by-minute battle, fighting what goes on between my ears. And what

I tell myself is never kind. I'm usually defenseless against the first thought. I don't even know it's there, but then I'm fanning the flames, encouraging other unkind thoughts. By the time I'm done, I'm drowning in a cesspool of feelings that usually bring me to one last remaining thought—if I kill myself, all this pain would end.

I change the channel on Channing, and after clicking through several other TV shows that make me yawn, I chuck the remote onto the pillow and pop off the bed. "Fuck it." I grab my car keys, stuff my iPhone in my jeans, and head out the door. Ten minutes later, I'm doing a drive-by of Lori's house. It's not the brightest idea now that Lori knows what I look like. How the hell would I explain sitting in my car, stalking her house? *I was just driving past, and my car died.* Yeah, that'll work. Despite my brainlessness, I loop Lori's block and find a new spot to stalk.

Mark's Mustang is parked in the driveway, and about twenty minutes later, he comes out of the house with the same blonde I saw him with a few days earlier. The two climb into his Mustang and drive off. Not too long after that, I hear a blast of loud music as Ronnie and Cracker show up in the Jesus-mobile to pick up Lori.

Ronnie honks the horn several times before Lori finally emerges from the house. She climbs into the car, and they drive off, leaving behind a wake of loud music. Ronnie drives like a maniac, and I almost lose sight of them until the last second when I catch the Jesus-mobile pulling into a liquor store. I circle around the block, and when I come back, I see Lori and Cracker go in the store, while Ronnie remains in the car. I wait to see if a cop will show up, or anyone else for that matter. But no one does. Clearly, they are not being watched closely by Detective Thoms. They're all underage.

I pull up alongside Ronnie's car, and when I step out of the Olds, she's too busy texting to see me enter the store. A bell on the door rings, and an older white man looks up from his newspaper. His bloodshot eyes stare after me as I pass the counter.

"Just pick something!" I hear Cracker say as I turn down the first aisle. She and Lori are facing an open refrigerator, trying to decide what type of beer to get. Inside are the forty-ounce bottles of beers I've never seen before, like Country Club, Olde English 800, Wildcat, King Cobra, and Hurricane.

Cracker sees me and immediately stops what she is doing. "What the hell, Cheerleader? You following us?"

Lori turns and stares at me as if it is true.

My face turns red. *Play it cool,* I tell myself. *They have no idea who you are.* "Yeah, Cracker, I am. I was hoping you and I could share a Bud Light together." I keep walking.

"Shit. I bet you do. Bitch, Diet Coke's over there!" Cracker yells after me. Lori laughs, and they return to arguing over what to get.

I walk to the end of the aisle where the soda is, feeling stupid. What did I think I was going to accomplish by coming in here? Just then, I notice a man in his fifties, thinning hair, eyeglasses, tall and lanky, and looking like a total pedophile, in a button-down shirt and dirty dress pants. Something about the way he is eye-raping Lori and Cracker bothers me. Lori catches it too.

"What the hell you looking at?" Lori says to the man.

"Just admiring you ladies."

"Ladies? What the fuck is with everyone sayin' ladies?" Cracker says.

"Well, stop staring. You creepin' me out," Lori says.

Lori and Cracker open the fridge and pull out two large Country Club bottles.

"You need help buying that?" The man walks closer to them.

"You a cop?" Lori responds.

"No."

"Then fuck off."

"What's your name?" He smiles, unfazed. And I wonder if he's mental.

"Lollita Bollita Senorita," Cracker says in an oddly accented voice.

The man's eyes explore Lori's body. "Do you like to party?"

Lori stops as if she has heard him wrong. "What'd you say?"

"How much?" He pulls out a wallet.

Lori takes her hand off the bottle she is holding and faces him. "Do I look like a fucking whore to you?"

The man takes a step back. "Sorry. My mistake."

He's about to walk away when Cracker snatches the wallet from his hand.

"Hey! Gimme that!" The man reaches for his wallet.

Cracker stuffs it down into her bra. "Nah. Mine now."

Lori and Cracker laugh and turn to leave.

The man reaches out and grabs Cracker's arm with his bony hand. "Where you going?"

"Get the fuck off me!" Cracker yells.

It all happens in seconds.

Cracker smashes the bottle she is holding across the back of the man's head. The bottle shatters on the ground. Glass and malt liquor spill across the aisle. The man stumbles forward and hits the floor on both knees. He doesn't completely fall over until Lori kicks him in the face. His glasses go skidding across the floor, and the man lands hard on his side, trapped against a shelf. Lori and Cracker kick him mercilessly. I hear the thumps of their shoes against his face and body. The man pathetically holds up his hands, but it does little to help. Blood pours from his nose.

"Get out! Get out of the store! I'll call the police!" the clerk yells. He picks up the phone to dial, but he doesn't do anything with it except hold it in his hand.

Finally, Cracker gives the man one last vicious kick between his legs before walking away with Lori, who stops in front of me, breathing heavily. "You didn't see nothing. Right, Cheerleader?"

I hold Lori's crazed stare and simply nod, too scared to speak.

"Get out!" the clerk yells.

Lori walks away from me and drops money on the counter. "You didn't see nothin'. Right?" She holds the clerk's stare, and something tells me he knows full well who she is. I look around and don't see any cameras.

He pushes the money aside. "*Get out!*"

"Sorry about the mess!" Cracker laughs as Lori hustles her out of the store.

I walk over to the man, who is now balled up on the floor, clutching his groin. There's a gash on his forehead, and his face is full of blood. I stare down at the man, and my heart aches for him, but then I also think he asked for this, treating them like whores. I step closer, and his eyes plead for help. I reach over his body and pick up something that's wedged under the shelf.

The clerk stares after me, expressionlessly, as I leave the store with the man's wallet in my hand.

CHAPTER 22

THE PIZZERIA IS EMPTY EXCEPT for Cracker and Ronnie, who play the basketball toss game, and Lori, who sits at her usual back table with Vince and another friend of his, smoking cigarettes and drinking beer. It's pouring rain outside, and only a handful of kids have come in tonight.

Pop has a few rules, and one is no drinking. He doesn't carry a liquor license, so if he gets caught with alcohol in the pizzeria, it can cost him a fine. But Pop allows it for Vince.

Pop even comes out from the kitchen to say hello.

"Pop, what's goin' on?" Vince smiles.

"I got a large pie for you." Pop slaps Vince on the back like a son.

"The Towering Inferno?" Vince tugs at his stubbled jaw with his tattooed hand and leans deep into his seat, legs stretched out in front of him.

"What else? No one eats that ass-burning shit but you."

"A'right." Vince brings his hands together in a heavy clap.

Lori and Vince's friend laugh. The Towering Inferno has five different types of cheese with three types of jalapenos.

"Everything good? You need anything?" Vince asks.

"I need to win the goddamn lottery," Pop growls as he wanders back to the kitchen.

Unlike the other stores in the area that have been robbed or vandalized, Pop's Pizza never is, mainly because of Vince. As Natice puts it, "People know if they fuck with Pop, they fuckin' with Vince. And nobody fucks with Vince."

Everyone is afraid of Vince, including me. But Vince looks after Pop as if the man was his own father, and in return Pop, who is only really nice to Vince, protects Vince from the police. The cops routinely stop in and ask questions about Vince, and Pop blatantly lies, saying he hasn't seen Vince in weeks. Then he'll offer the cops free pizza and soda.

The need for a bathroom always becomes very urgent every time a cop car pulls up in front of the shop because I always expect Detective Thoms to walk through the door. But so far, he's yet to appear.

Vince stamps out his cigarette in a plate, kisses Lori goodbye, and walks off with his friend, leaving Lori alone to chain-smoke.

"Pop, thanks for the Towering Inferno!" Vince yells, picking up a large boxed pie off the front counter, then heads out into the pouring rain.

Lori is still sitting at the table when I go over and clear off the empty beer bottles. I feel her eyes on me the entire time, and being so close to her makes my skin crawl. I keep waiting for her to say something about the liquor store beating, but she doesn't. Neither she nor Cracker has said a word to me since they entered the pizzeria. Cracker went straight to the basketball toss game and hasn't left it since.

"You suck. You suck. You suck," Ronnie says, heckling Cracker as she plays.

"Go away! You're so annoying!" Cracker shoves Ronnie.

Ronnie laughs, finishing off her fourth slice of pizza and tossing the crust onto a nearby plate. I walk past and head to the bathroom to wash my hands. I don't bother to close the door, and I'm only in there a minute when I hear a familiar voice.

"Cracker-barrel, you and me, girl! I got next game."

I peek out from behind the door, and walking in, soaking wet from the rain, is Mark Silva.

"All right, you wanna go first?" Cracker's face softens, and her voice sounds feminine for the very first time.

"Nah. You got it, girl."

"You wanna go first?" Ronnie mocks Cracker's feminine voice.

"Shut up!" Cracker's entire face burns beet red.

It's also the first time I see Cracker look embarrassed.

Mark wipes the wetness out of his hair and acknowledges his sister with a nod.

"What up, sis?" His rain-soaked T-shirt sticks to his body, showing off his well-muscled chest.

"What up, Romeo?" Lori says.

Mark smiles and heads straight to the bathroom. I prepare to act surprised, but Mark beats me to it. "Hey!" He stops at the sight of me. His dimples deepen high into his cheeks. Then he notices my red Pop's Pizza T-shirt. "You work here?"

"Yeah. I begged Pop to hire me." I tell the truth for the first time.

"Yo, that's crazy." He laughs. "So what happened to you? You never came back."

"I got busy," I say with a bit of flirtation.

"Oh really? You got busy?"

"Yeah. I got a job."

"Yes, you did. Pop's got taste," he says.

"Mark, you playing or what?" Cracker yells, her hateful tone returning.

"Hold on." Mark says without taking his eyes off me. "It's Ally Walker, right?"

"You remembered? Surprise." I smile.

He laughs again. "That's right! I told ya, I don't ask every girl for her number. So how long you been workin' here?"

I don't get the chance to respond.

"Mark, don't be messing with Cheerleader. Bitch has work to do." Cracker flings Ronnie's plate of crusts onto the floor. "Come on, Cheerleader. Clean it up!"

"Dammit, Cracker. I was gonna eat those!" Ronnie stares down at the crusts like a sad kindergartner.

I knew it was only a matter of time before Cracker picked a fight with me. *Why the hell did I have to flirt with Mark Silva right in front of her?*

"Do it, Cheerleader! Now!"

"C'mon, Cracker. Don't be such a punk," Mark says.

"Shut up, Mark! You fuckin' pussy!" she yells.

"Sorry, I'm on break," I say.

Cracker drops the basketball and heads right toward me. "What'd you say?" She gets in my face.

Her hot breath reeks of booze, and even though she is several inches shorter than me, she is downright scary. Her psychotic stare makes my mother's crazed look seem tame in comparison, and I won't have to worry about my fucked-up orange hair anymore because she'll probably tear it out in clumps. Then I see her fingernails—long and dirty. I can already feel the damage they'll do across my face.

"Cracker, c'mon, be nice." Mark places a hand on her arm.

Cracker shoves it away. "Well, what you got to say?"

"I'm not fighting you. If I fight, I'm fired. No thanks."

"Oh, Cheerleader's scared." Cracker smirks and becomes even uglier.

"Fuck's goin' on?" Natice shows up from having been down in the basement. "Cheerleader's gonna do a split!" Ronnie says.

She and Natice still have their bet going on when I'll quit. So far, I've lasted longer than either of them expected.

"Go clean my shit up. I ain't playin' with you!" Cracker shoves me.

My heart does summersaults. I really wish Pop would come out from the kitchen. If I pick up Cracker's trash, I'm her bitch, and she'll never leave me alone. And if I don't, we're going to get into it. Neither appeals to me. I see Ronnie juggling the ball, waiting to see what I will do.

"Fine. You wanna play a game. Let's play." I walk past Cracker and stop in front of Ronnie.

"What up, Cheerleader?" Ronnie asks.

I grab the ball from Ronnie's hands and face Cracker, who hasn't moved. "Fifty bucks I beat your ass in a game. If I win by ten, you also pick up the trash. And clean the shitter."

"Oh no she didn't!" Ronnie yells.

"Oh yes she did!" Natice slaps Ronnie's hand.

"You scared?" I cradle the ball.

"Nah. Cracker's too cheap," Natice says.

Lori looks amused but doesn't say a word. She takes a drag off her cigarette and waits to see what Cracker will do.

"C'mon, Cracker-barrel! Put your money where your mouth is!" Mark chimes in.

"Shit, I'll take her money." Cracker walks up to me.

"You wanna go first?"

"Drop the quarters, Cheerleader. You're gonna pay twice."

"A'right. It's on." I pull four quarters from my jeans and drop them into the machine. "You're up. Light it up if you can." I step aside, and Cracker takes the ball from my hands.

"Shit. You better have the fifty," Cracker threatens.

"I have it, but I won't need it."

"Oooo, I like Cheerleader!" Ronnie says.

Mark moves to my side, and we watch together. Cracker hits the red button and starts out strong, sinking three perfect shots in a row before she begins to miss and words like "whore," "bitch," and "cunt" fly out of her mouth. By the time Cracker's turn ends, she has a total of fifty-five points. It's a decent score but beatable.

"Wanna make it a hundred?" I step up to the machine.

"Hell yeah," Cracker responds.

"Fire down below, you ain't got no hundred," Natice says.

"Call me that again, Natice, and see what happens!"

Natice strikes a pose. "Well, it's true, ain't it?"

Ronnie nods her head in confirmation. "Ten bucks on Cheerleader!" she yells.

Cracker shoves her. "Ho."

I step up, hit the start button, and the scoreboard rises.

"Go, Cheerleader! Go, Cheerleader!" Ronnie sings, dancing alongside Natice.

I drop in one ball after the next. I miss the last two throws, but I crush with sixty-eight points.

"Ooooo. You got showed up, Cracker!" Natice howls.

"You owe me a hundred," I say.

"Fuck you," Cracker replies.

"That'll cost more," I answer. It's followed by laughter.

"You want your money, come collect." Cracker says.

I knew if I won Cracker would never pay me. I dig a wallet out of my back pocket and toss it at Cracker. She snatches it from the air, knowing at once where it came from.

"Where'd you get this?" Cracker says.

"You left it behind. It dropped out of your bra."

"That's cause she got itty-bitty titties. Shit just drops straight down," Ronnie jokes.

Cracker opens the wallet. "It's empty?"

"No shit. There was a hundred in there. Now we're even."

"Oh snap, crackle, pop!" Natice says.

"Cheerleader is wacked!" Ronnie laughs.

Cracker chucks the wallet onto the floor.

"Cracker, bathroom's waiting. Go to it. Quick, quick, girl." Natice snaps her fingers.

"I ain't cleanin' up nothin'!" Cracker says.

"Pick it up, Cracker!" Lori rises from the back table and heads toward us. Cracker stands there, not moving. "All of it. You lost. Do it." She holds Cracker's eyes, demanding her to collect the pizza crusts off the ground.

"Why? Ronnie'll jus' eat 'em later," Cracker says.

"No, I won't. I ain't hungry no more," Ronnie answers.

"That's a first," Cracker says then begrudgingly picks up the trash and dumps it in a nearby garbage can.

"Bathroom's waiting, Cracker," Natice says.

"Fuck you." Cracker jabs a middle finger at Natice.

Cracker doesn't clean the bathroom, but I don't care. I'm just happy to have avoided a fight with her.

I write my number on a napkin and hand it to Mark. "Call me."

"Old school." He smiles and tucks it into his jeans.

"So do you have a girlfriend?"

"Why you wanna know?"

"'Cause I don't date other girls' boyfriends, especially in Jersey. It could get my ass kicked."

He laughs. "That's true."

"So? Is there anyone else?"

"Nope. Nobody."

I hold Mark's stare and instantly think about the blonde I saw exiting his house. Mark has just lied to me. And he did it easily. "Great." I smile.

Later, I drive Natice home and tell her my version of what happened in the liquor store.

Natice shakes her head, picturing the beating. "Shit, the last thing you wanna do is call Lori a whore."

"Yeah, it was pretty brutal. Cracker kicked the guy in the nuts."

"Shit." Natice grits her teeth.

We both laugh, even though, at the time, it was anything but funny.

"Poor bastard." Natice smiles, then she looks over at me, impressed. "That was a hella cool move, though, giving Cracker an empty wallet."

"If she wasn't such a twat, I would've given her the money."

Natice laughs. But the truth is, there was never any money in the wallet, not even a driver's license. The wallet was stuffed with coupons.

"It's kinda crazy, though, you being in that same store when it happened," Natice says.

"I was jus' looking to buy beer," I say casually.

Natice nods, tapping her hands on her thighs. Then she side-eyes me, and in a voice that sounds oddly suspicious asks, "Why didn't you go to the store across from the Shell?"

Her question stops me. *Why is Natice asking me this? And how does she even know there is a liquor store across from my motel?* I grow paranoid, thinking Natice knows I've been following them this entire time. "I tried going into that store a few times, but they carded me. I just happened to find the one Lori was in. Lucky for me. Not so lucky for that guy," I say nervously.

Natice takes in my answer, and it's hard to tell what she is thinking. "Shit. Tha's for sure. We know he won't be going in *there* again."

I smile. "Not unless he's stupid." I pull into Natice's driveway, ready for her to be out of my car and for the questions to come to an end. "A'right, see ya later."

"Hold on, girl. Geez, what's the rush?"

"I gotta pee." I bounce in my seat as if I really do need a bathroom.

"Whaddya doin' Sunday morning?" Natice says, not looking the least bit in a hurry.

"Nothing, why?" I say in a rushed voice.

"You wanna play basketball with us?"

I stop fidgeting, and my body comes to an immediate halt. I don't have to think twice about it. "Yeah, sure," I say in a high-pitched voice, startled by my own excitement.

"A'right, cool." Natice drum rolls on her thighs. "We play every other Sunday down at these courts on the other side of town. It's run by the city as a way to give back to the community, which is bullshit, since all those mothafuckers are crooked. But whatever. They pay for officials. Water. It gets a pretty good turnout. It's rough, so you can't be fragile."

"Do I look fragile?" I say.

"No. So you in?"

"I'm in!"

"Well, a'right. You can pick my sexy ass up at eleven." Natice holds up the palm of her right hand, and I give it a high-five.

"You got it, Fathead."

Natice wags her head and reaches for the door handle. "You're funny. You know that, Ally?"

I stare after Natice, thinking I genuinely like her. Then I quickly remind myself she's friends with Lori and Cracker, and she's their alibi. So whatever happened to Jenny, she's equally guilty. Then I think about what I agreed to do—play basketball.

I realize I haven't played since Jenny's death.

CHAPTER 23

IT'S A SUNNY DAY, BUT not nearly as hot as it has been, when Natice and I arrive at the park. There are two basketball courts side by side, separated by graffiti-covered bleachers and surrounded by trees and rotted grass. A young crowd, mostly female, is gathered in the bleachers, watching a serious game of men's hoops that is already in progress on one court. I watch as a monstrous man impressively grabs a rebound and dunks it. A group of girls scream, and the bleachers ring with excitement.

Natice leads me toward Lori and Cracker at the end of the second court. Along the way, we spot Ronnie making a quick exchange with a kid who barely looks fifteen years old. The kid pockets a small bag, and in return, Ronnie strolls off with his money. But what is interesting about the exchange is that Ronnie is holding the little girl from her profile picture in her arms.

"Ronnie got knocked up by some dope-head friend of Vince's," Natice says. "But that baby is adorable."

We are halfway down the court when a skinny teenage boy with curly hair runs up to Natice. He wears a dirty tank top, and I can see his bones under his skin.

"Yo, Natty! My girl, Natice Gentry."

"Sweetie, I have no money for you," Natice says as we keep walking.

"Oh, come on, baby. Where's the love? Gimme some love today. You know you my favorite diamond. And diamonds are a man's best friend!" He laughs. He is cracked out, and his teeth are slightly yellowed. He turns to me. "What about you? Hey, pretty girl, what's your name? What about you?"

Natice introduces him. "This is Glendon. And don't give him any money."

"Ah, dogged! Baby, where is the love? You harsh today. Very harsh, my beautiful black diamond."

I stare at the boy's face, thinking I know him from somewhere. I assume it's from the pizzeria or maybe from one of Ronnie's posts. Until he says, "Yo, Natty, when you gonna be my girlfriend? When you gonna go out with me?" Then it hits me—he's the boy from the East Cantor basketball game, the one who fell off the bleachers and whose friend yelled out to me, "Number 15, my boy wants to go out with you!"

"Yo, pretty brown-eyed girl, what's your name?" Glendon stares right at me.

Without even looking, I pull money from my pocket. "Here. Happy Birthday."

It's a five-dollar bill, and he snatches it greedily. "I'll be your boyfriend for ten! It's a one-time offer!" He laughs then runs away, happy.

"Why the hell you give him money?" Natice asks.

"Dude, he stunk. I wanted him to leave," I say, heart pounding.

Natice laughs. "Yeah, he does smell. But, uh, hate to tell you, giving Glendon money has the opposite effect on him. Now his stank ass is always gonna be buggin' you."

"Great." I follow after Natice with the weight of a thousand stares bearing down on my back. Each step I take is like walking on very thin ice. *What if someone else from the East Cantor game is here? What if that brute or her sister is watching?* I swallow hard, thinking any second this ice is going to crack, and I'm going to plummet into an icy cold death. Once again, I have to remind myself how drastically different I look with blond hair. But still, what if someone recognizes my face? I search the crowds for anyone who might be staring at me with recognition. I tell myself if the brute or her sister is here, what could they possibly do or say? "*Hey, that's that dead girl's sister!*" "*The one who was shot and murdered!*" "*The one from Middletown!*" They may not even know a girl from our team was shot that night or that she was my sister. And if they did start to think it was me out here playing basketball, they'd probably think themselves crazy for it. I mean, why would I be in Cantor?

"What the fuck is she doin' here?" Cracker greets me with her usual charm.

"Shut up, Cracker! I told Natty to bring her." Lori smacks Cracker on the back of her head.

"Oww! What the fuck?"

Natice laughs. "Girl, you should just keep your mouth shut."

"Fuck you, Natty." Cracker walks away, holding her head.

"You ready to play?" Lori asks me.

"Hell yeah, she's ready." Natice slings her arm around me.

"I haven't played in a while," I say nervously.

Lori looks at me as if I have lied to her. "You shoot like you have."

"I was lucky."

"Get lucky today, Cheerleader. We play for money."

A moment later, Ronnie arrives, lugging her daughter, who sucks on a princess pacifier in her mouth.

"Look how you're holding her. Gimme Keisha." Natice takes the child from Ronnie. "How you doing, baby girl?" Natice playfully bounces Keisha in her arms. Keisha smiles at Natice, and the pacifier drops out of her mouth. Ronnie picks it up and begins playing a game of peekaboo with her.

"Boo!" Ronnie says. "Boo!"

Keisha smiles and giggles. It's an odd juxtaposition: two gang members playing a game of peekaboo with a child.

A whistle sounds. "Five minutes!" a ref yells.

"Everyone, come here! Listen up!" Lori waves us closer together. I join the girls, stealing another paranoid glance at the bleachers. I don't see anyone I recognize, except for Vince, manspreading amongst his usual crew, who prepare to get day hazed as they light up a fat joint. His presence unnerves me, but it always does.

"A'right, this is how we're gonna play," Lori says. "I got center. Natice and Cracker are guards. Ronnie, you're forward. Cheerleader's gonna take point. Hands in! Hands in!" Lori places her hand in first.

We movie into a huddle and drop our hands on top of one another in a pile. Each hand has the same small black diamond tattoo. Except for mine. I think any second, these girls are going to realize who I am.

"On three, we yell 'diamonds,' bitches," Lori says. "One, two, three..."

I catch Cracker staring at me. I hold her eyes as we yell... *Diamonds!*

A group of five other girls from a neighboring town square off next to us. As I walk onto the court, I clear my throat and try to ignore my nausea. I stop and stretch, holding onto my calves, mainly to catch my breath. My eyes land on a scuff mark on the top of my white high-top sneakers. I take in a long breath of air then stand, and before I can give it any more thought, a whistle sounds. Natice dishes the ball into me and heads down court. I look into the crowd and see Glendon watching me. I dribble with a weak hand, and the ball is quickly stolen out from under me. My opponent, a small black girl, blows past me and easily scores on a layup. I catch the ball as it drops from the net.

"What the fuck, Cheerleader?" Cracker yells.

I look into the crowd, and once more, Glendon's eyes are fixed solely on me. I carry the ball up-court, wishing I had never agreed to play. I'm jacked up on fear and rush getting rid of the ball, making a flimsy pass to Natice, and the same girl who picked it off before does it again and scores for a second time in a row. The opposing girls celebrate as we move back into an offensive position.

Cracker chucks the ball at me, hard. "Try not to give it away!"

I dribble nervously and try to focus. Natice works to get free. My mind is all screwed up. I am out of breath and out of shape. Ronnie has just gotten herself open. She is surprisingly quick for a big girl. I fire the ball down to her. She jumps and dumps in two points.

"Finally!" Cracker high-fives Ronnie.

I move back on defense, and Natice slaps my ass. "Nice job, Cheerleader."

Glendon's attention, thankfully, is no longer on me or the game. His skin and bones shuffle down the bleachers toward the street, most likely to score his next high. My paranoia temporarily subsides.

On the next drive, I go in hard for a layup and score. In time, I slowly ease back into the game I used to love. Natice and I work together as if we've played for years. I block for Lori, forgetting she may have killed my sister. I pass the ball to Cracker, forgetting that I hate her.

At the break, we are winning by ten. Lori offers me water and congratulates my play. And just like that, I'm a part of their crew. I'm included. *I have deceived everyone, including myself.*

I make a point not too score too much during the game. I don't want to bring attention to myself. I feed the ball to Cracker as much as I can, hoping she'll ease up on me and that it might even make her my friend. As the game wears on, a succession of great plays unfolds. My mind grows silent, and for the next thirty minutes, I remember why I love this game so much.

CHAPTER 24

AFTER THE GAME, I DRIVE Natice back to Lori's house to celebrate our win. The maroon Toyota Camry is already in the driveway when we arrive. I park in the street and kill the engine. I stare at Lori Silva's house as I have so many other times before. But this time, I am about to enter. Invited.

"Are her parents home?" I ask Natice as we step out of the car together. I already know, thanks to the case folder, that Lori doesn't have a father, and on the night of the shooting, her mother was in jail. But I have no idea where her mother is anymore. I've yet to see the woman.

"Lori don't have a dad. And her mother's never home."

"A house to herself. Nice. So what's her mom like?"

Natice shakes her head. "Drug addict. A fuckin' mess. She never should'a had kids. Aborted at least four babies. And those are only the ones Lori knows about."

"Fuck." I'm honestly blown away.

"Yeah, you can say that. Vince basically pays for everything. Otherwise, this house would be gone." We reach the front door, and Natice turns to me. "But look, don't mention it. Lori's kinda sensitive 'bout it."

"Yeah, no worries. It's not exactly a conversation starter."

"Just don't forget." Natice opens the unlocked front door, and I follow after her. My entire body tenses up the moment I step inside Lori Silva's home.

The best way to describe Lori's home, if you can even call it that, would be to say it looks like a fraternity house, or what I imagine a college frat house looks like. It's dark and depressing. Tattered drapes barely let in any light. I stay close to Natice like a shadow. The carpet is so gross I'd probably catch a disease just by lying on it. There are at least three holes punched into the walls. Natice flicks her painted fingernail at a cardboard skeleton that's missing part of its leg. It hangs as a decoration tacked to a closed door. "In case you haven't noticed, Halloween is twelve months outta the year around here."

We walk past a sectional sofa that faces the only nice thing in the room: a large plasma TV. In front of the sofa is a glass table that seems to collect rings from soda cans. Several Diet Coke cans litter the grimy surface. On the floor is a small white bowl that overflows with cigarette butts and ashes.

Natice heads to the kitchen, and I'm right at her hip. The kitchen is small and cramped and as run-down as the living room, but thanks to a few open windows, there's a lot more sunlight, making it slightly less depressing.

Cracker sits at a table, stuffing Cracker Jacks into her mouth and arguing with Ronnie about how many points she scored.

"You had twelve, Cracker." Ronnie holds Keisha like a rag doll as she rummages for food. There are dirty dishes stacked in the sink, and the refrigerator is covered in grease stains. Lori's home couldn't be more different from mine. I suddenly appreciate my mom.

"I had sixteen! You can't count!" Cracker tells her.

"Yo, Lori, you ever clean this shit hole?" Natice says.

Lori cracks open a forty-ounce bottle and hands it to Natice. "The maid comes next week," Lori says sarcastically then pulls another large bottle from the refrigerator and hands it to me. "Drink up, Cheerleader."

It's a Colt 45, a brand of malt liquor I've never seen before. "Sweet." I take a huge gulp and hope the effects hit me quickly. Despite Lori's friendliness, I'm far from relaxed being in her home. On court was different, but now, standing beside Lori in her own kitchen and knowing why I am here—to send these girls to prison for the murder of my sister—every nerve in my body is as sharp as a razor's edge. I take another sip of my beer and try to at least appear normal.

"Ronnie, gimme that child," Natice says. "She ain't some rag doll."

Ronnie hands Keisha off, and Natice sits down in a chair and tickles Keisha's toes. "Mmmm. This is what I wanna eat!"

Keisha giggles. I stare at her blissfully innocent face, and it helps to calm me down. She really is a cute kid.

114

Ronnie opens a cabinet and looks inside. "Damn, Lori, there's never shit to eat in this house." She slams the door closed and heads to the refrigerator.

The front door opens, and Mark swaggers into the living room, tossing a magazine down on the grimy table.

"Watcha doin', Romeo? Come have a drink with us!" Natice bounces Keisha on her lap.

"Nah, another time." Mark disappears upstairs without seeing me.

I take another quick sip of beer, trying to hold onto the bottle with one hand.

"Girl, slow down. It ain't going anywhere," Natice says.

I pull back on the bottle with both hands, almost spitting it out.

Natice laughs and smiles at Keisha. "Cheerleader's funny, ain't she?"

Cracker leans over the table and holds out a handful of Cracker Jacks for Keisha. "Here you go. You can be a lil' crackerjack head."

Natice slaps Cracker's hand away. "Girl, don't be feeding her that junk."

"Oww! Fuck you, Natice!" Cracker massages her hand.

"And don't be cursin'! Child's gonna know nothing but swear words!"

"Fuck you!" Cracker says, louder.

"Don't try me, girl," Natice threatens.

Ronnie puts her arm lovingly around Cracker. "Oh, Cracker's just trying to be nice, Natty." She dips her chubby hand into the Cracker Jack box and pulls out a handful. "Right, Cracker?" Ronnie stuffs the candy popcorn into her mouth.

Cracker pulls the box away. "Hope you washed your hands."

Lori's cell phone rings, and she heads outside to answer the call.

"Where's the bathroom?" I ask.

"Upstairs," Natice answers.

I breeze through the living room and head toward the carpeted stairs I saw Mark run up. I feel as though I'm back in the third grade when I invited a boy I liked to my birthday party, and he said he'd come, but then the day of my party, he never showed up. However, right now, I have a lot more riding on this than hurt feelings.

Upstairs is just as dirty and depressing as the rest of the house. The bathroom is at the far end of the hall, and there are three bedrooms in all. One bedroom door is wide open, another is closed, and the third is cracked open with music flowing around it. I pass the first bedroom and look in.

There's an unmade bed with sheets crumpled on the floor, a dresser, and not much more.

I move to the door that is ajar and peek inside. I see Mark facing a desktop computer. I knock, and when he doesn't look up, I knock louder, and the door pushes open.

"What?" Mark sounds annoyed. He turns and sees me standing in the doorway.

I'm not sure what to expect from him. He didn't call me after I gave him my number.

He smiles. "Yo. What, are you stalkin' me?"

"You wish." I step into his room. "I was playing basketball with your sister. I thought I'd say hi."

"Really? You're hangin' with my sister?" I note a hint of disapproval in his voice.

"Just for the day. We won." I casually inspect his room.

"Cool," Mark says, not seeming to mind my nosiness.

"Who's this?" I ask, liking the song that's playing.

Mark raises the volume. "Goldfish. They're a South African band."

"Cool, I like it." I notice Mark has the full collector's edition of *Rocky*. I pick the box off the shelf. "*Rocky?*"

"Yo. It's my favorite movie," Mark says with a cute laugh.

I put the box back on the shelf and continue my inspection. There's a TV, Xbox, and tons of Blu-rays and DVDs of action and horror films. Nothing unusual. It's just like any other seventeen-year-old boy's bedroom.

"You still have my number?"

"Yeah, I got it."

"You ever gonna use it?"

"Don't worry. I know where to find you," he says, using my line.

"Oh really?" I give him a flirtatious look. "Then I'll see ya around."

"You can bet on that."

We share a smile, and I walk out of Mark's bedroom, feeling good about my visit. I give the wall a little tap with my fingers and head toward the stairs. I still have a plan to use him. After all, he corroborated Lori's story about her being home the night of the shooting.

The girls are in the backyard when I drop back down the creaky stairs. I hear Lori and Ronnie arguing.

"I can't get the damn car. How many times I gotta tell you all?" Ronnie says.

"Damn, Ronnie! I need the money," Natice says.

I watch unnoticed from inside the kitchen until I see Cracker has spotted me. I make myself busy by filling a glass with water. I take a few quick sips before I step outside and join the girls. Keisha scurries around me on the dirty ground, and I try to keep from tripping over her as Lori angrily walks past.

"I told Vince we were cool for a delivery!" Lori shouts.

"Whaddya want me to do? My mother's got church on Sunday nights!" Ronnie says.

"And Wednesday nights. And Thursday nights," Cracker mocks.

"Your momma's freaky on Jesus," Natice adds.

"I got a car. I can drive," I say.

"Who gives a fuck? No one's talking to you!"

Apparently, it doesn't matter how many times I pass the ball to Cracker.

"Yeah! Let Cheerleader drive! She got a car." Ronnie is more than happy to volunteer my services.

"I could use the extra cash." I ignore Cracker.

"What fuckin' extra cash? Go the fuck back to Seattle! Why is she even here?" Cracker says.

"No, hold on," Lori says. "I think we could use Cheerleader."

"If she's in, I'm out!" Cracker responds.

"Cracker, shut the fuck up! You're in if I say you're in!" Lori turns to Natice, who hasn't said a word. "Natty, whadda you think? Cheerleader cool to drive?"

"I guess. If she wants to." Natice looks at me.

"This is bullshit! We don't even know her!" Cracker yells and storms off inside the house.

Lori laughs and walks over to me. "Forget her. So what do you say, Ally? You feel like doing a lil' convenience store shopping?"

"Sure. What is it?" I ask.

"That part's a surprise. But if you wanna earn extra cash, jus' come back here at nine, and you'll find out," Lori says.

Natice walks me to my car.

"Will anyone get hurt?"

"No," she says.

"But I'm guessing it's illegal?"

"You guessin' right." Natice waits to see if I'll change my mind.

"Cool."

Natice laughs. "Shit. Well, I'm glad you don't have a problem with illegal activity."

"So what is it that we're doing?"

"You really want to know?"

"Yeah."

"All I'll say is that it can be fun. But if we get caught, it's serious."

"That narrows it down. Are we robbing a store?"

"No."

"Will guns be involved?"

"Definitely not."

I'm relieved. Another question pops into my head, and I'm very curious to hear Natice's answer. "So why don't any of you have cars?"

"I don't know how to drive. Cracker's too cheap to buy a car. And Lori had a car, but she don't anymore."

I purposely hold off on asking about Lori's car. Instead, I say, "You don't know how to drive?" I smile as if finding it funny even though I couldn't care less.

"Nope."

"You're serious?"

"Yeah."

"Well, if you ever want to learn, let me know."

"A'right, I will." Natice smiles.

"So what happened to Lori's car?" I finally ask.

"Nothing. It was stolen."

"That blows. Where'd it get stolen?"

Natice points to the driveway. "Right here."

"In front of her house?"

"Yup."

"Come on! Someone stole it out of her driveway? Bullshit!" I say with a laugh.

"Well, that's the story she told me." Natice raises an eyebrow without giving anything away. "Look, I'll see ya later."

"Do you need me to pick you up?"

"Nah, I'll be here." Natice starts to walk away then stops and looks back at me as if troubled by something. "Ally, you sure you wanna do this?"

"Sure. Long as no one's gonna die."

Natice stares at me strangely, and for a moment, I fear I've said too much. Then I see something in her eyes that wasn't there earlier, a hint of sadness.

"You all right?"

She nods and forces a smile. "Yeah. I'll see ya later, Ally." She walks away.

"Yeah. See ya." I know I've hit a nerve.

When I return to my motel room, I shower and change my clothes, all hyped up. Natice might not have confessed the truth, but it was written all over her face. I know in my gut that these girls had something to do with Jenny's shooting and that Lori's stolen car story is bullshit, just as Detective Thoms suspected.

I click on the TV and search for something to keep me calm. I check the clock at least fifty times before nine o'clock nears, and as I'm about to head out the door, my Cantor cell phone rings. It's Natice.

"Hey, what's up?" I ask, afraid they no longer want me to drive.

"Change of plans. Pick us up in the schoolyard behind Lori's house. We're here in the parking lot."

"A'right." I don't ask why.

I hang up the phone and catch my reflection in the mirror. It dawns on me that once I leave this motel room, I will be committing my first crime. I stare at myself. *I used to be an honor student. I used to have friends. I used to have a sister.* Before I change my mind, I grab the car keys and head out the door.

CHAPTER 25

WHEN I ARRIVE AT THE schoolyard, everyone is there. Cracker stands next to Ronnie, who appears to be dealing drugs to a bunch of teenagers in a beat-up Honda. She dangles a small baggie of what I'm guessing is either coke or heroin between her thumb and forefinger.

"Yo, I got fifty. Fifty's good," the teenager behind the wheel says.

"This ain't no Best Buy! Get the fuck outta here!" Ronnie says, about to walk away.

"A'right, sixty's cool!" The teenager turns to his girlfriend in the passenger seat. "Bitch, gimme the money!"

Ronnie sees me and smiles. "What up, Cheerleader?"

"Hey." I nod, expecting Cracker to say something nasty or erupt in a fit of anger, but she remains silent. If anything, Cracker looks happy to see me. And right away, my gut gives me a big hard kick in the ribs, letting me know something is not right.

"I told you. I told you. You always bitchin' about how you gonna fail." Lori takes a hit off a joint.

"Shit, I thought I did fail," Natice says. "What up, Ally?"

"What'd you fail?" I try to act normal, but inside, I feel like a ball of aluminum foil that's been thrown into a microwave set on high.

"Nothing. I scored an eighty-eight on my trig exam," Natice says.

"Nice job." If ever there was a girl I wanted to kiss, it would be Natice, simply for the fact she puts me at ease.

"Thanks, girl." She slaps my hand.

"So you ready to make a delivery?" Lori asks.

"Sure. Let's do it."

"That's what I like to hear. Let's do it!" Lori offers me the joint. "Here, Cheerleader, have some."

I've only smoked weed once before and hated it. All it did was make me feel tired, hungry, and paranoid. I basically hid in a closet all night eating an entire bag of Salt and Vinegar potato chips. I woke up the next morning, still in the closet and feeling like shit. My mouth was so dry it hurt to talk.

I take the joint from Lori to keep things friendly. I inhale too hard and cough uncontrollably. My lungs feel like they're on fire. Ronnie and Cracker arrive in time to witness my coughing fit.

"Dumb ass," Cracker says.

Ronnie laughs. "Cheerleader's like me. She can't hold her smoke!"

Lori grabs the joint back. "Let's get rolling!" She heads toward my car.

"Old man give you a hard time for calling out sick?" Natice asks.

"He fired me," I say with another cough.

"Shit. He fired me three times last month." Natice laughs.

I slide behind the wheel with one last, lingering cough.

"Turn on the fucking AC! It's hot as hell in here!" Cracker yells from the backseat.

"It doesn't work," I tell her.

"You're kidding me?"

Lori doesn't seem to mind as she directs me out of the schoolyard. "Make a left then straight out to the highway. About two miles up, you're gonna hit the Turnpike. Take it south, Cheerleader."

"Lori, turn on the radio!" Ronnie reaches up from the backseat, finds a station she likes, and blasts the music.

"Get the hell outta here!" Lori pushes Ronnie's big body back and lowers the volume.

"Your grandmother needs a new car." Lori looks around the front seat. She pops open the glove compartment and picks through it.

And that's when it hits me—the envelope with all the paperwork for the car is in there. And my name, Alexandra Campbell, is scribbled on the front.

"Yeah, she does." I take my eyes off the road and plant them firmly on Lori at the exact moment she pulls out the envelope. "Look, my grandmother hates when I go through her stuff." I sound a lot more nervous than I probably should.

"Relax, Cheerleader." Lori holds the envelope in her hand, while tossing out old candy wrappers. "You need to clean this shit out." She continues to rifle through the contents.

Panic sets in as I see my name poking out from between her fingers. I think any second she is going to notice it too.

"Look who's talkin'," Natice says. "When's the last time you cleaned your house?"

Lori finds a Tootsie Roll lollipop and without bothering to look at the envelope, tosses it back inside the glove compartment and slams it closed, keeping the lollipop for herself.

I relax slightly and hope Lori doesn't open the glove compartment again. I make a mental note to destroy that envelope first chance I get.

"Turn that up!" Natice hollers as Beyonce's "Drunk in Love" comes over the radio. Lori cranks up the volume, and Natice and Ronnie burst out singing.

"So Cheerleader, where'd you meet Romeo?" Lori asks, having no idea how close she just came to discovering who I am.

"The gas station," I answer, still on edge.

She unwraps the lollipop and sticks it into her mouth. "Really? The gas station." Her tone sounds suspicious as if she knows I'm lying.

"Yup." I keep my eyes on the road.

Lori leans in close. "You high, ain't you?"

"Yeah. What the fuck was in that joint?" Whatever was in it has made me doubly paranoid. Then again, the envelope scare did not help.

Lori laughs. "Just follow the white lines, Cheerleader. We don't want to get pulled over."

CHAPTER 26

WE GET OFF THE TURNPIKE and take Route 34 until we reach Edgewood Gardens. It's a nice middle-class suburb that looks exactly like Middletown. Its highway is littered with the same fast-food restaurants: Chili's, Applebee's, and Friday's. There's even a movie theater and a Barnes and Noble.

"Slow down. Pull in here." Lori points to a bank on the right. It's next to a flower shop, and the parking lot is dark, except for the bank's well-lit ATM.

"Lori, what are you doing?" Natice leans up from the backseat.

"I'm making a withdrawal, Natice. What does it look like?"

"If you're doing what I think you're doing, don't!"

"Natice, how 'bout you don't fucking tell me what I'm doing?" Lori snaps. She looks over at me again. "Park away from the ATM. There." She points to a spot parallel to the bank but in the shadows.

"Lori, you said we were doing a delivery!" Natice hollers.

"Shut the fuck up, Natice!" Lori yells.

I park and turn off the engine. "Now what?"

"Now it's time for a withdrawal." Lori pulls out a gun from under her shirt and holds it out for me.

Viewing guns on a computer screen doesn't compare to this. I feel as if I'm inches away from death. I hold Lori's stare, this time unable to hide my fear. "Last time I checked, I only needed a debit card for a withdrawal."

"Exactly," Natice says.

"Not when it's other people's money," Lori says.

"Yeah, people need motivation," Cracker says with a laugh.

Now I know why Cracker looked so happy when she first saw me. She obviously knew Lori was going to do this.

Ronnie buries her face in her hands and tries to keep from laughing.

Lori waits for me to take the gun. "What do you say, Cheerleader? All you gotta do is hop in the backseat and say hello with your little friend." She smiles and shakes the gun as if she is holding a Coca-Cola bottle.

"Fifty bucks Cheerleader shoots herself," Cracker says.

"Ally, you don't have to do this," Natice says.

"Shut the fuck up, Natice! I swear to God!" Lori threatens.

"You said we were doing a delivery! I need the fuckin' money!" Natice yells.

"You'll get your fucking money! She wants to be a driver. Earn it! I don't fucking know her!" Lori screams.

"Damn straight," Cracker says.

"Let me outta the car!" Natice reaches for the door handle.

"Natice, where you gonna go?" Lori grabs her arm.

"Fucking girl scout," Cracker says.

"Fuck you, Cracker!" Natice yells back.

"Shit, I'll go," Ronnie pipes in.

"*No!* I'll do it!"

Everyone turns and looks at me. And before I can remind myself I am not Charles Bronson or Angelina Jolie and this is not a movie—this is a real gun—I take the pistol from Lori's hand. It is cold and heavy. I feel sick to my stomach.

"A'right, Cheerleader!" Lori claps.

"She still has to do it," Cracker adds.

"Let's hope she doesn't," Natice says.

"Jesus, Natice! Next time we'll leave your ass at home. A'right?" Lori says.

"*Yes*, do me the favor!"

Lori tells me to wait until a car pulls in front of the ATM. There have to be at least two people in the vehicle. One of the passengers has to be female, or both passengers have to be old. Lastly, she warns me that if there are two or more guys in the car, I hold off.

"Lori!" Natice says. "C'mon, this is bullshit! Don't make her do this!"

"Shut up, Natice!" Lori turns back to me. "Put the gun on whoever's in the passenger seat and tell the driver as soon as you get the money you'll be gone. You ain't gonna shoot anyone. And make sure you take their phones before you leave the car."

Ronnie hands me a stocking. "Here, Cheerleader. It's my mom's. Hanes Her Way."

"Yeah, extra large," Cracker says.

"Hey, my momma's big-boned."

"Big-boned is another word for fat!"

I tighten my abdominal muscles and clench my jaw, fighting to keep the food I ate hours earlier from dislodging. I look at Natice in the rearview mirror. She holds my eyes and shakes her head, warning me. I consider handing the gun back to Lori, and as if reading my mind, Lori says, "You don't have to do this if you don't want to, Cheerleader. No one's holding a gun to your head." She laughs, and I hate her even more.

There is no longer any doubt Lori, Cracker, Ronnie, and maybe even Natice were involved in that store robbery and my sister's death. It is more than a gut feeling. I have proof Lori commits crimes and owns a gun. *I am holding it in my hand.*

I say nothing as we sit in the dark, waiting for a car to arrive. Lori mentions Vince having a party that night. Ronnie yawns. Cracker complains about how hot it is in my car. I wonder if this is what went on before they entered that store and shot my sister to death.

Lori shouts, "Show time!"

A car pulls off the highway and heads toward the bank's ATM. My heart is beating so fast I feel like it is going to explode out of my chest like an alien baby.

"We got a couple of blue hairs tonight!" Ronnie yells, laughing.

I look closer and see somebody's grandparents inside the car. I wonder where Detective Thoms is. How is he going to bring them in on some other charge when he is not even around? Is he even watching them? How is it that they are still committing crimes? Then it hits me—they're *not*. I'm the one who is about to commit a crime.

"Get ready, Cheerleader." Lori says.

The car's brake lights go on. I don't think I can do this.

"*Now!*" Lori shouts.

I fly out of the car like a racehorse whose gate has been opened and sprint toward the car, holding the gun firmly in my hand and praying nobody will get hurt. I see the old man waiting for his wife to pull something out of her purse. Neither of them sees me as I grab the back door handle and jump inside. The last thought I have before I enter their car is, *I cannot believe I am doing this.*

I slam the door closed behind me, and the elderly couple jumps, startled by my presence. "There's a group of girls, and they have guns!" I say, panicked.

The old woman's eyes frantically search the dark parking lot.

"They want money. Please, just go to the ATM. Take out money, and everything will be okay." I keep the gun pressed against the seat. I have no intention of using it.

The old woman looks at me in a way I have never seen before. It's a look filled with terror and hate. "Leave this car now, young woman!"

"Please, just go to the ATM and get money. They have guns!"

"Get out of this car!" the husband screams at me with bulging eyes.

The woman reaches into her handbag for her cell phone, and I quickly grab her wrist. It feels weak and brittle in my grasp. "Please, don't!"

Her husband grabs hold of my arm. "Let go of her!" He punches me in the face, awkwardly, but I hold onto his wife, desperate to stop her from making a call.

Her hand fights to open the phone.

"Please! I don't want to hurt you!" I let go of the gun and grab the old woman with both hands.

The phone falls to the floor.

"Get out!" Her husband strikes me again in the face. I know I should leave the car, but I don't. And that's when the door next to me flies open.

A nylon stocking covers a face. I know immediately it's Cracker. "Go to the fucking ATM! *Now!* Or I blow a hole in her!" A gun is aimed directly at his wife's head.

"Walter!" the old woman cries.

"Now, old man! Fucking *do it!*"

"*Please!*" I beg him.

Perhaps it's the desperate look in my eyes or the gun pressed to his wife's head. Whatever the reason, the old man finally exits the car. The old woman begs for Cracker to lower the gun, but this only makes Cracker angrier. "*Shut up!* Shut the fuck up!"

I hate Cracker even more. The old woman is shaking. I think she is going to drop dead of a heart attack. *Please, God, help this woman!* I scream inside my head. I want to do something, but there is nothing I can do.

The old man approaches the ATM. His hand trembles as he slides his card into the machine and hits a few numbers. No money disperses.

"What the fuck is he doing!" Cracker says.

The old man's panicked eyes stare back at us. He doesn't know his PIN number. He must have forgotten it. His wife quietly sobs. I look at the gun being held to her head. I want to take it. I want to get the hell out of that car. I reach down by my foot and pick Lori's gun up off the floor. I think about holding it up to Cracker and demanding that she let go of this woman. But I don't. I am too scared. The old man tries again. My stiffened muscles relax some as I see money emerge from the slot.

A moment later, the old man is back inside the car. He holds out a wad of twenties to Cracker in his shaking fist. "Take it!"

Cracker grabs the cash and bolts out the door, leaving me behind. I sit there watching the old man comfort his crying wife.

"I'm sorry." I jump out of the car.

———————

Ronnie speeds down a back road, and a second later, we merge onto the highway. Cracker rips off the stocking.

"I told you! I fucking told you!" Natice keeps repeating.

"What the hell took you so long?" Lori yells.

"He forgot his pin number!" Cracker says.

Ronnie laughs. "Damn, Cracker, those old folks probably shit their Depends!"

I still have Lori's gun in my hand. I think about shooting Cracker in the head. I hate her with every ounce of my body. I want her to see how it feels to have a gun shoved in her face. I want her dead. But before I can do anything, Natice takes the gun from my trembling hand.

"You guys are assholes. You know that?" Natice says.

"Relax, Natty, we were just having fun. Right, Cheerleader?" Lori smiles at me.

Natice shoots Lori a dark stare. "I needed the money from a delivery, not some fuckin' ATM robbery, okay?"

"Cracker, give Natice my share," Lori says.

Cracker is about to hand Natice a stack of twenties.

"I don't want it!" Natice shoves the money away.

"Natty has principles," Ronnie says.

"Don't worry. We're gonna make a delivery. Just needed to make sure Cheerleader wasn't no girl scout, if you know what I mean." Lori eyes me.

"Really? A fucking cop? Next time, just ask the fucking girl. Ally, you a cop?" Natice asks.

I look at Natice as if she is joking and remain silent.

"She didn't say it," Cracker says.

"I'm not a fucking cop." I notice I'm still trembling.

CHAPTER 27

FOR THE REMAINDER OF THE drive back to Cantor, Natice and I don't say a word while Lori, Cracker, and Ronnie laugh about the robbery and joke as if this is a normal Saturday night. When we reach Vince's house, cars line the street, and music roars from inside.

"Shit, I'm ready to party!" Ronnie hops out of the car with Cracker.

"Natty, you coming?" Lori says.

Natice doesn't answer.

"Oh, don't be mad, Natty. Come have a fuckin' drink."

"Gimme a fuckin' minute," Natice tells her.

"No hard feelings, Cheerleader." Lori looks at me over her shoulder. "Hell, why don't you come in too? You could use a drink." She smiles then gets out of the car and catches up with Cracker and Ronnie. I stare after Lori, wishing she and Cracker were dead.

"Ally, if I had known Lori was gonna do that, I swear to God I would'a told you. I never would've gone," Natice says.

"I know."

"You a'right?"

I think I am anything but all right. But I now know Lori and Cracker own guns. More than anything, I want inside Vince's house. "Let's go in."

"You sure?" Natice asks.

"Yeah. Lori's right. I need a drink."

Natice hesitates. "A'right. Let's do it." She pops open the door, and we step out of the car. When we reach Vince's front door, Natice stops me. "You sure you're up for this?"

"Yeah, I'm fine. I always wanted to hold a gun." I force a smile.

"Shit." Natice wags her head. "I need a fuckin' drink too."

Natice pushes open the front door, and the smell of marijuana and cigarette smoke hit me before I even step inside. Rap music blasts, and the entire downstairs is filled with thuggish guys and girls dressed in short skirts, high heels, and tops that barely cover their breasts.

As I follow Natice in search of alcohol, I keep thinking about the old woman. I can't get the image of her crying out of my head.

"Hold up." Natice stops and directs us toward a sofa, where a group of guys in baseball caps and football jerseys are sitting.

"What up, fellas?" Natice says, getting into party mode.

One dark-skinned guy smiles. "What up, my beautiful black diamond?" He puts a hand on her ass. Then he notices me. "Damn, lullaby. What crib you crawl out'a?"

Natice pushes him away. "Go fishin' somewhere else. She ain't interested in you."

Another guy looks up from a plate. "Yeah, she wants a real man. Twelve inches." He grabs his cock then snorts two thick lines of white powder.

Natice sits down next to him. "Don't be stingy. Share the wealth."

The dark-skinned guy offers her a small square dish with a row of white lines. "Hell, baby. Jus' call me Willy Wonka 'cause I got your golden ticket."

Natice bends over a line, places a finger over one nostril, and makes the line disappear up the other.

"Magic," one of the guys says. As he laughs, the whites of his eyes double in size, and his extremely dark, dilated pupils focus on me. "What about you, lullaby? Want some candy?" He offers me the plate.

"I'm good."

He grins, a gold tooth showing. "Yeah, you are." Then he greedily snorts it himself.

I look up and see Lori, Cracker, and Ronnie at a dining room table with Vince and a few other guys, including Natice's good-looking cousin, Tray. They're playing cards and drinking beer. "Your cousin's here," I say to Natice, wanting to be sitting at that table. "Wanna join them?"

Natice looks over at the table and sees Tray, along with Lori and the others. "Sure."

We grab some beers and head toward them.

When we arrive at the table, Lori whispers something in Vince's ear. Their eyes are fixed on me, and I suddenly wish I were invisible.

"Move it," Natice says to Tray, motioning his arm out of the way so she can sit down.

"Oww. Shit, Natice! Your bony black ass hurts," Tray hollers, sliding over to give her room on the chair.

Natice slaps his head. "Shut up. Ally, sit here."

I take the empty seat next to Natice and quickly guzzle some beer.

"What up?" Natice says to the group, sampling a fry from Tray's plate.

Vince looks over at me and takes a drag from his cigarette. "It's Cheerleader, right?"

It is the first time Vince has spoken directly to me. "Yeah." My voice cracks.

"I heard you had a lil' fun tonight." He scratches his shoulder.

"Yeah. I made an old lady shit her Depends." I take another sip of my beer.

"You didn't make anyone do shit!" Cracker yells. "Fuckin' welfare bitch wants in the game but can't step up to the plate!"

Vince laughs. "Don't let these bitches scare you. They just rotten."

Lori leans over and kisses Vince's lips. "Rotten to the core."

"You a hell of a ball player, though. Where you learn to play like that?" Vince asks me, dealing a hand of cards to the guys.

"Summer camp."

"Is that right? Shit, I never could afford no summer ball. What about you, Tray? Your folks send you to camp?"

Tray stares at his cards, not bothering to look up. "Nah, man."

"And now you want to be a driver?" Vince smiles at me.

"I could use the cash."

"Hell yeah. We can all use cash. But who the fuck are you?" His eyes bulge with anger. Then he laughs, aware he has scared me. "Don't worry, baby. I'm jus' messin' with you."

"Jesus, what the fuck is with you all tonight?" Natice slams a hand on the table. "Leave the damn girl alone. Christ!"

"Oh, Natty, the Tin Man got nothin' on you, does he?" Vince says.

Natice displays her middle finger.

"Cheerleader better hope those old folks didn't get a good look at her face," Cracker says. "Po Po be lookin' for you!" She and Lori laugh.

"See, Ally? They rotten to the core." Vince shuffles the cards. "Who up for a game?"

"I got a game we can play," I say.

"We ain't interested in your fuckin' game," Cracker says.

"No. You'll like it, Cracker. It involves a gun. Anyone have one I can borrow?"

Tray holds up two. *Probably 9mm.* "Shit, which one you want, baby?"

I look across at Cracker, knowing she's holding. "Neither. I want Cracker's .38."

Tray looks at me curiously. "Shit… a'right." He tucks his gun away.

"Fuck off," Cracker says.

Vince looks amused. "Nah. Giv'er your shit."

Cracker reluctantly hands me her revolver.

All eyes are on me. And maybe it's the booze, or the weed, or that ever since Jenny's death, I have struggled to want to live, but I feel nothing, only hate, as I empty all the bullets, except for one. "You wanna go first?" I spin the chamber and lock it.

"This girl ain't playing. Where'd you get her, Lori?" Vince asks. But Lori remains silent. A few of the guys laugh. They think I'm joking, but I'm not. I hardly notice them. My attention is on Cracker.

"Fine. I'll go first," I say.

"Yeah, right," Cracker spits back.

"Yo, Ally, this ain't cool," Natice says.

Vince waves Natice away. "Yes, it is. This shit's very cool! Let the girls play!"

"Bullshit. She ain't gonna do it," Cracker says as if I am bluffing.

I look her dead in the eyes and with every ounce of hatred pumping through me I say, "If I do it, you do it?"

"A'right. You go first."

I place the gun to my temple.

"Ally, put the gun down!!" Natice yells.

Cracker holds my stare. "She ain't gonna do it."

The others watch with amusement. The guys continue to make noise. Ronnie throws a hand over her face. "Cheerleader is wacked!"

Natice reaches for the gun. But she's too late.

I pull the trigger, and there's a *click.*

The guys erupt in laughter.

"Oh, *shit!*" Vince bangs the table with his fists. "Fuck! I like Cheerleader!"

Ronnie uncovers her face. "No, she didn't! No, she didn't! This snatch is wacked!"

I hold out the gun to Cracker. "Your turn."

"She thinks we're stupid. How much you wanna bet there ain't no bullet in there?" Cracker says.

I open the chamber. One bullet rests inside. "Your turn." I wait for Cracker to take the gun.

Vince rubs his hands together as if he is about to enjoy a good meal. "Come on, Cracker! You up, girl. You up! Now serving!" He drum rolls the table.

"Yo, this is not cool." Natice's eyes dart nervously around the table.

Lori takes a pull off her cigarette. "Don't worry, Cracker ain't gonna do it. She's too chicken."

Cracker angrily responds by taking the gun from my hand. "Fuck you. Gimme it." She gives the barrel a spin and jokingly places it under her chin.

"Cracker, put the gun down!" Lori yells.

Vince pushes Lori's hand away. "Nah. Let Cracker play!"

Ronnie stuffs her face with food. "Cracker, no one wants to see your ugly pale ass splattered across the wall!" Ronnie rises to take the gun, and Cracker slaps her hand away.

"This is stupid," Natice yells. "Cracker! Put the fuckin' gun down!"

Cracker looks across the table at me.

"Do it," I say.

And that's when I see it in her eyes. She is a coward.

"Fuck this. I'm too pretty to die." Cracker drops the revolver on the table.

"Ooooooooooo! Cracker got showed up!" Tray yells.

"Fuck you. I ain't stupid!"

"Gimme that shit." Vince picks up the gun. "We about to find out." He aims it at the window. "Place ya bets!"

He pulls the trigger, and *boom*! Glass shatters.

The room erupts. Ronnie pulls up her shirt and nervously rubs her belly. "Crazy! This shit's crazy!"

"Cracker, you one lucky bitch." Tray takes a sip of his forty.

Lori seems unaffected. She rolls her eyes and rises from the table. "Shit. Who's got the Bud?"

CHAPTER 28

I SIT BEHIND THE WHEEL, WAITING for Natice. She is talking to Tray on the steps of Vince's front porch. A moment later, she joins me in the car.

"This was one fucked up night," Natice says. "So is that the kinda games you play in Seattle?"

I reach to turn the ignition, and Natice stops me. When I look at her, I have tears in my eyes. I don't want to cry in front of Natice, but I can't help myself. I can't hold back the pain. Natice doesn't say a word. She watches me sob uncontrollably, then she does something unexpected. She reaches over and holds me.

"It's okay, Ally. Whatever it is. It's okay."

Twenty minutes later, I pull into Natice's driveway. She tries to convince me to sleep over, but I refuse to. Even though I've worked so hard to get this close to her, I need to be alone.

"You sure you don't want to sleep over?"

"Yeah, I'm fine."

"A'right." Natice observes me carefully. "Promise you'll call me in the morning?"

I nod. "Promise."

She gives me one last hug and exits the car.

The sun is beginning to rise when I arrive back at the Shell Motel. I sit staring at my room door, unable to get out of the car. I think about driving home to Middletown. I think about Jenny being dead and the things I did tonight. I watched Cracker shove a gun in an old woman's face. I watched her husband, unable to protect her, tremble with fear. I put a loaded gun to my head and pulled the trigger. I begin to cry. *I really am alone.*

CHAPTER 29

I WAKE UP, HAVING DREAMT THE gun in my hand had gone off. Moments later, my Cantor cell phone rings. "Hello?"

"Good. You didn't kill yourself," Natice says. "Pick my ass up in an hour. We're going to the aquarium."

Natice won't take no for an answer, and an hour later, I step outside of my motel room and into the sweltering morning. It must be a hundred degrees outside. As I walk to the Oldsmobile, my thoughts travel back to last night. *I played Russian roulette and lived.* My only regret this morning is that Cracker did not pull the trigger.

A loud squeak grabs my attention, and the old woman from a few doors down appears from the curb, pushing her grocery cart. She stops in front of her room, and I watch as her frail hands, ravaged by arthritis, insert a key into the lock and turn the knob. But the door doesn't open. I suspect the heat has made the wood frame expand. The old woman pushes again and again. Her ill health and brittle body work against her. I stand there, watching.

I pick up Natice at her house, and she directs me to the waterfront, where the aquarium is located. I remember having been there once when I was in elementary school. All the grammar schools in the Middletown area routinely take field trips there. I remember it being nice.

"So how you doin'?" Natice asks.

"Good."

"Uh-huh. Why is it I get the feelin' there's something you ain't telling me?" She holds my stare.

"Probably because there's something I'm not telling you."

"Yeah. Then what is it? What's going on?" Natice sounds genuinely concerned.

I laugh.

"Why the hell you laughing?"

"I don't know." But that's not true. Any time I'm asked a direct question I don't feel comfortable answering or I'm simply not quick enough to make up a lie for, I become nervous and laugh.

"You're not right in the head, you know that, Ally?"

I laugh harder.

"It's a'right. You keep cackling over there. We all got our secrets." Natice fans herself. She's sweating. "Damn, girl, you need to get that AC fixed."

"Yeah it's on my to-do list, right after 'play Russian roulette with Cracker.'" I look over at Natice and crack a smile.

"Like I said, you ain't right in the head."

We arrive at the aquarium, and it's as nice as I remember it. Natice and I pay our twenty-six-dollar admission fee and enter, grateful to be in cold air conditioning.

We hit the Shark Realm exhibit first, walking through a mind-blowing glass tunnel with three-hundred-and-sixty-degree views. We are literally surrounded by dozens of sharks, whose eyes seem to watch our every move. Natice grows reflective as she watches a tiger shark swim directly above our heads. "I haven't been here in forever."

I almost say, "Me too," but I quickly catch myself. We walk up to the glass and touch it.

"This is my favorite. The sharks. I mean, look at those eyes on that mean motherfucker. He's like, 'Don't fuck with me, bitches.'"

"He looks like Cracker. 'What the fuck she doin' here? What the fuck, Natty! This is my fuckin' tank! What's Ally doin' here?'"

Natice laughs at my spot-on imitation of Cracker.

"We should've invited her."

"Shit. Cracker may be scared of you now."

"Good. Maybe Dirty Jersey will back off."

Natice smiles, and we keep walking.

"So how often you come here?" I ask.

"Shoot. I've only been here twice since my mom died. When I was little, she used to take me here all the time. She loved the sharks too."

I look at Natice, surprised to hear that. I had just assumed her mother was like Lori's, off doing drugs, or in jail, or had just plain abandoned her. "I'm sorry."

"It's a'right. It's been awhile."

"When did she die?"

"Right before I turned eleven. She had cancer. She fought it for a couple years, then it jus' got really bad, and she was gone in a month."

"That really sucks. I'm sorry, Natice." I pause, reflecting on my own pain. "It's probably the worst pain in the world. One day, someone you love is here, and the next... gone. And there's nothin' you can do about it."

Natice nods. "I miss her every damn day." She looks over at me and forces a smile. As if sensing something, she asks, "You ever have anyone close to you die?"

I want to tell Natice the truth, but I shake my head. "No."

From there, we visit a few other exhibits—Touch-a-Shark, Seal Shores, Secrets of Africa—before ending up at Penguin Island. Natice and I find a spot on a bench and sit down to take a break. Families shuffle by, and the place empties out, leaving us alone to observe a few dozen penguins enjoying what looks like an easy life behind a plate-glass wall. A couple of adventurous ones dive into a tank of water and swim around, while most simply sit on a huge rock, doing nothing but looking adorable in their little tuxedo-suit bodies.

"Look at that little dude." Natice points to a penguin whose back is to us. "His butt is all fuzzy."

"Fuzz-butt!" I nickname him, and we laugh hysterically, enjoying his tiny wedge-shaped tail waddling around. I take notice of another cute fella. "I like that one over there, though, with the little belly."

"Shit, there ain't nothing little about his belly. He's plump. Getting fat on fish."

We nickname a few other penguins then sit in silence, watching them. Natice's cell phone rings, interrupting our moment. She pulls it from her pocket and sees it's Lori. "Ignore," she says, and sends the call to voice mail with a press of her finger.

"Did Lori say anything about last night?"

Natice looks at me. "Other than thinking you're crazy, no."

"So do Lori and Cracker always carry guns and rob ATMs?"

"They were just fucking with you last night, Ally. That's all. Just forget it. It was stupid, what they did. And it was stupid, what you did."

"Have they done it before?"

"What do you think? Of course."

"Have they ever shot anyone?"

Natice is silent for a moment then looks at me, serious. "You carry a gun around long enough, sooner or later, it'll go off." She rises from the bench. "Come on. Let's go see the fuckin' seals."

I sit there a moment longer, making sure Natice doesn't look back. When I am certain she is gone, I open my hands, grateful to see the emblem of a tape recorder on the face of my iPhone. The app continues to voice record until I hit Stop.

"Ally, you coming?" Natice yells from the other room.

"Yeah." I tuck the phone in my back pocket and chase after her.

Despite the tense moment of me asking if Lori or Cracker ever shot anyone and my disappointment at Natice's vague answer, Natice and I leave the aquarium exhausted by a good time together. The truth is, I like Natice. She's a lot easier to spend the day with than Lea ever was. "Thanks for today," I say to Natice as we arrive at her house. "I'm glad you called."

"You liked the aquarium, huh?"

"I loved it. If I could, I would've smuggled Little Belly and Fuzz-butt home with me."

Natice smiles. "Cool. See ya tomorrow." She gives me a big hug before leaving the car.

I watch Natice disappear inside her house and wonder if I will ever get her to tell me the truth about Lori and Cracker. I remind myself I just need to be patient.

When I arrive back at my motel room, I hit Play on the recorder to make certain it worked. I hear a crackling sound followed by my voice. "Have they ever shot anyone?"

After a few seconds of silence, Natice's voice comes in loud and clear. "You carry a gun around long enough, sooner or later it'll go off."

CHAPTER 30

I ARRIVE AT THE PIZZERIA THE next day and learn from Pop that Natice has called in sick. Later that night, I receive a text from Natice: *Not in the mood for Fathead. See ya on Fri. xo Natty.*

None of the girls come in that night, and I'm pretty sure whatever they are up to is not good. I only wish I knew what it was or that I was included. The following day is Friday, and both Natice and I are scheduled to work. We each show up ten minutes late.

"So what'd you do last night?" I ask as we wash and dry dishes in the kitchen. It's our punishment for arriving late.

"Nothin'. Jus' stayed in."

I know Natice is lying because she doesn't look me in the eyes. I'm starting to know her better. I try to coax the truth out of her by making a joke. "You sure you and the girls weren't doin' a lil' convenience store shopping?" I still have no idea what "convenience store shopping" means, but I am determined to find out.

Natice raises an eyebrow. By now, she's getting to know me better too. "Crazy, I ain't gonna tell you what it is. And the answer is no."

"No what?"

"No, you ain't joining us when we do."

"Why not? Dude, I could use the money. Trust me. My phone's about to be shut off 'cause I can't pay it." I raise my voice.

"Well, that ain't my fuckin' problem, now is it?" Natice storms off.

Natice can be mean when she wants to be, and she's still moody at times, but I feel more myself around her and less on edge. Even working at the pizzeria is becoming more comfortable. I'm learning Pop is all bark and no bite, and even some of the guys who used to scare me don't bother me as much. After the Russian roulette routine, they act more like fans than guys who want to date me, which is a huge relief.

Later, when we're tossing bags of garbage in the dumpsters out back I make one last attempt at being included in Lori's criminal activities. "Look, if you guys can't get the Jesus-mobile, just let me know, and I'll drive."

"What's the Jesus-mobile?"

"Ronnie's mother's car."

Natice cracks up. "Shit, that's funny. I gotta tell Lori that one." She starts to walk away, but this time I follow her.

"Natice, can you at least talk to Lori about including me?"

"Girl, didn't you learn your lesson the last time?" Natice snaps. "And why you gotta be so pushy about it?"

"Lemme see. Not only is my phone about to be shut off, I'm also sweating my ass off in that fuckin' piece of shit car 'cause the AC needs to be fixed, and I don't have the money." Then, preying on Natice's sympathy, I add, "I know it's not your fuckin' problem, but my grandmother's medicals bills are insane, and she's gonna get kicked out of that shit-shack Shell motel because we're two months behind. I'm sorry I asked." I walk back inside.

"Hold up. Jesus," Natice says.

I stop and look back at her.

"Let me think about it, okay? I'll feel guilty if something happens to you. A'right?"

"What could happen?"

"We get caught."

"You haven't so far, have you?"

"Ally, I'll let you know. Just quit fuckin' askin' me."

I stop asking and begin to lose hope that I will ever get the evidence needed to send these girls to prison. I'm in the basement cleaning and restocking the shelves when Natice confronts me. "Are you serious about making extra money?"

"As long as it isn't an ATM robbery."

"Don't worry. It won't be."

"So does that mean Lori said yes?"

"What the fuck do you think it means?" Natice disappears up the stairs.

"Thanks, Natty!" I yell, smiling.

CHAPTER 31

"You see this?" Cracker shoves her left hand into my face, showing off her black diamond tattoo.

It's Sunday night, and this is the first thing Cracker says to me when I arrive at Lori's house.

"What's that, a beauty mark?" I'm no longer afraid of Cracker.

"You're just the fucking chauffeur. That's it." She climbs into the backseat of my car.

"Come on. Let's go! Chop, chop, hookers!" Natice yells to Lori and Ronnie, who walk at a leisurely pace to the car.

Ronnie holds a fork and eats something out of a plastic container.

"What the hell is that?" Natice asks.

"Dinner." Ronnie slides into the backseat next to Cracker.

Lori swaggers up to me with a smile. "You ready to do a lil' convenience store shopping?"

"Hell yeah." I plaster a big, happy smile on my face and hope my phoniness isn't as transparent as it feels. True happiness would be seeing Lori dead.

Lori laughs. "See? That's why I like Cheerleader. Girl says yes to anything, even when she don't know what the fuck it is."

We're the last to climb into the car.

Lori looks over at me from the passenger seat. "Jus', uh, no guns to the head tonight, a'right, Cheerleader?"

"Can't promise. I didn't take my meds this morning." I pull out of the driveway, and Ronnie's food spills onto Natice's leg.

"Ronnie, put that shit away!" Natice flicks a piece of meat off her leg. It hits Cracker.

"Hey! What the fuck!" Cracker yells.

"What the hell is that, anyway? It stinks!" Natice says.

Ronnie shovels something unrecognizable into her mouth. "My momma made this. Besides, that smell's just Cracker's upper lip."

They laugh.

"Fuck you all!" Cracker waves her middle finger.

During the drive, Lori whines about how Vince is being an asshole, Natice worries out loud about a test she has just taken, and Ronnie complains about how she thinks she is gaining weight.

"Look what the hell you're eating," Natice says.

Forty minutes into the ride, we arrive in Cherry Hill, a white upper-middle-class suburb in New Jersey. I spot at least three Mercedes on the road, and with each sparkling chrome wheel we pass, I tug at my jeans and at the collar of my white V-neck shirt. Both are suffocating me. We must stick out like a sore thumb, although no one else in this car seems the least bit concerned.

"There's one little farther up," Natice says.

A few minutes later, a 7-Eleven store appears on the right-hand side of the road. Across the street from it are a hardware store and a bank. Both are closed.

"Park near the hardware store, next to that van," Lori says.

I make a quick left and pull up alongside the van with a view of the 7-Eleven.

"Shut off the headlights," Lori tells me.

I switch them off. "Now what?"

"Now we wait, Cheerleader." Lori smiles at me.

"Shit, she's scared." Cracker watches me in the rearview mirror.

She's right. I am scared. My hands are clenched around the steering wheel like a drowning swimmer grips a buoy. I get a bad feeling about what will happen next, wondering if Cracker or Lori has brought along a gun. Even though Natice and I were promised that they wouldn't, who's to say they kept their word? Especially Cracker. I mean, everything feels exactly like the other night except that Natice is more relaxed, cracking jokes with Lori, whose eyes have remained glued to the 7-Eleven the entire time. I watch along with her, but nothing unusual happens. Cars randomly pull in and out of the 7-Eleven's parking lot. Suddenly, a Ford Explorer pulls off the road, parks, and a guy in a baseball cap steps out. He leaves the engine running as he disappears inside the store.

"Now that's a stupid thing to do," Lori says.

The back door flies open, and before I even know what is happening, Cracker dashes out of the car and runs across the street. Ronnie quickly closes the door behind her, and in less than ten seconds, I watch Cracker jump inside the Ford Explorer, reverse out of the parking lot, and drive off down the road.

Lori smiles. "Now that's what we call…"

"Convenience store shopping!" Natice and Ronnie answer in song.

Natice points out the window. "Look! Look!"

A moment later, the guy exits the store with a confused look on his face. He examines the parking space where his Ford Explorer was moments before. He looks around at the other spots, until it dawns on him his Ford Explorer has been stolen.

"Tha's right, dumb ass! It's gone!" Ronnie yells.

The guy looks up and down the street, and not seeing any sign of his Ford Explorer, he reaches into his back pocket. His body lurches forward, and his shoe slams down on the pavement. I'm pretty certain "fuck" is the word flying out of his open mouth.

"Oh shit. He left his phone in the car!" Ronnie says. The girls crack up. I can't help laughing too.

The man finally runs back inside the store and says something to the store clerk, who looks out the window toward the parking lot. "Come on. Let's go." Lori's eyes are filled with tears from laughing. "Show's over."

I pull onto the highway and drive back toward Cantor. "See all the skillful things you're learning in Jersey," Lori says to me.

"Yeah. She's gonna go back home a criminal," Natice says guiltily.

"Shit! Hanging with us, she will," Ronnie says.

I smile and switch lanes. My hands rest easily on the wheel. And the truth is, it was sort of fun.

We meet back up with Cracker behind one of the abandoned warehouses not too far from where she lives. She's already there with the Ford Explorer, along with a buddy of Vince's I recognize from the pizzeria.

"Stay here. I'll be right back." Lori hops out of the car.

"I'm hungry," Ronnie complains.

"You just ate!" Natice says.

"So? I'm hungry again!"

I watch as another guy I don't recognize removes the license plates from the Ford Explorer and replaces them with a set of Pennsylvania plates. Vince's buddy hands Lori a thick envelope.

"Let's go celebrate!" Lori jumps into the passenger seat.

On the way to Lori's house, we make a quick stop at a liquor store. Natice and I stay in the car while the others run inside the store to buy beer. It's the same one where I witnessed Lori and Cracker kick that man half to death. The image of the man's bloody face, eyes begging me to help, has me shifting restlessly in my seat. I grab hold of the seat and turn around to face Natice. "Isn't Lori afraid that clerk might call the cops?"

"Girl, he didn't call the cops the first time 'cause he has a lil' side business selling drugs for Vince."

"What does he sell?"

"Some coke. But ask him for a fifth of Jack, and you get a quarter bag of weed."

"Really?"

"Hell yeah, girl."

"So does everyone get their drugs from Vince?"

"Pretty much. Why you think the cops are always comin' in and asking Pop about him?"

"How is it that Vince doesn't get arrested?"

"I guess he's jus' like you—lucky."

Twenty minutes later, we're in Lori's kitchen, getting drunk. "Don't be muggin' all the smoke. Pass that shit around!" Lori smacks Cracker in the back of the head. Cracker's been holding a joint hostage since we arrived. She takes one last drag before giving it up.

"Cheerleader, come here," Lori says.

I walk over, and she counts five hundred dollars into the palm of my hand. "There you go. Now get your fuckin' air conditioner fixed!"

"Thanks, Mom." I tuck the cash in my pocket. I noticed earlier she gave the others eight hundred dollars each, but I don't care. I'm just happy she's trusting me.

"Ally, clear off the table!" Natice carries in an iPod sound system, clutching a set of keys in her hand.

I clear off the bottles, and Natice places the iPod player down. She chucks the keys onto a nearby counter. "Cracker, hook me up!" Natice yells.

Cracker tosses Natice an iPod, and Natice pops it into the dock. "That's right, it's my birthday!"

"It ain't your birthday," Ronnie says.

"It is if I want it to be." Natice selects an album and hits play.

It isn't long before the four of them are drunkenly dancing in the middle of the kitchen. Ronnie bangs into the table, sending a forty-ounce bottle crashing to the floor. Lori makes a comment about how big Ronnie's ass is and slaps it.

I stand off to the side, trying to act like I'm having a good time as I guzzle beer. Inside, I'm vibrating with anxiety because I can't stop thinking about the set of keys Natice placed on the counter. I know one of those keys unlocks Lori's bedroom door, and I'm as desperate as a drug addict to get inside that room. The police weren't able to come up with anything, but if Lori isn't carrying her gun, it might be in her bedroom. Or on a long shot, maybe Lori keeps a journal or diary. I don't exactly see Lori writing in a diary, but who knows?

So while Natice, Cracker, and Lori take turns slapping Ronnie's ass, I move to the counter, place my beer bottle down, and discreetly pick up the set of keys. I slip them into my back pocket and turn to leave.

Natice sees me exiting. "Where you going?"

"Gotta pee!" I yell back as I leave the room.

I reach the top of the stairs and quickly pull the keys from my pocket. They drop onto the floor, and I feel like I'm in a bad TV movie as I scoop them up and try several before finding the key that unlocks Lori's bedroom door. I hurry inside and slam the door behind me. I can hear the girls and the music downstairs. I quickly scan Lori's bedroom. There aren't too many places to hide a gun or a diary. There's a bed, a closet, and a chest of drawers. The walls are bare, and the room hardly looks lived in. It isn't as nice or as clean as Mark's bedroom. But there are a few signs of sentimentality. Lori has a handful of framed photographs of her and Vince and some with Natice, Ronnie, and Cracker that are displayed on top of a chest of drawers. They all look much younger. On Lori's bed, I notice a worn teddy bear.

I drop to my knees and check under the bed. The only things I discover are sneakers, cartons of cigarettes, and loads of dust. I stand back up and move to the chest of drawers, quickly rummaging through the contents. I come across the red-and-white-striped tank top I first saw Lori wearing. More clothes. Another picture of Vince. Socks. Bras. A few pieces of cheap jewelry.

I move to the closet and search through a pile of clothes, making certain to check the pockets of every sweatshirt and jacket in case something is hidden inside. I hear someone scream, and I jump, my nerves razor thin. It's followed by a burst of laughter, and I continue my hunt for evidence.

On the bottom of the closet is a box. I open it and inside are Blu-ray discs from Target. I stand up, frustrated. *What the hell am I doing?* Detective Thoms didn't find anything. What makes me think I will? Especially eight months later.

I decide to get out of Lori's bedroom before I get caught. I hurry into the hallway, close the door behind me, and as I slip the keys into my back pocket, Cracker appears at the top of the stairs. I pause, worrying she saw me, then I just walk toward her, trying to appear normal, and hoping she'll ignore me. But of course, Cracker doesn't. She stops right in the middle of the hallway, blocking me from going any further.

"Where'd you go?"

"What are you, the hall monitor?"

"Yeah, I am. What the hell you doin' up here?"

"I had to piss. Do you mind?"

Cracker's eyes shift to Lori's closed bedroom door. "It took you long enough, don't you think?"

"I didn't time myself. But I took a shit too, if you really wanna know," I say, interrupting her stare.

Cracker takes her eyes off the door and places them closely on me. "I bet you did."

"Yeah. Well, sorry I didn't call you to wipe my ass. Maybe next time," I say sarcastically. I can tell by the way Cracker's looking at me she knows something isn't right. But she doesn't know what it is. "Now, can you move? I'd like to go downstairs."

She barely steps aside.

"Thanks. You're a real sport, Cracker." I walk past, praying that Cracker doesn't notice the keys in my back pocket.

"Hey, Cheerleader?"

Heart pounding, I turn and face Cracker, trying to think of some messed-up reason I have Lori's keys. Either that, or I'm gonna run.

"Hope you put the seat down." Cracker smirks then disappears into the bathroom.

I go straight to the kitchen and grab another beer out of the fridge. I take a quick sip, hoping to calm my nerves as I watch Natice and Lori laugh hysterically while Ronnie makes the fat rolls on her stomach move in rhythm to the song that is playing. Natice has tears in her eyes, she is laughing so hard. She drunkenly clings onto me.

"Yo, what's up?" Natice says.

I clink my bottle against hers. "Ya know, jus' being sexy," I say with a smile.

They beg Ronnie to do it again. And when she does, I discreetly place the keys on the counter.

CHAPTER 32

I LISTEN TO MY MOTHER'S VOICE on the answering machine. She sounds happy. "Hello, you've reached the Campbell residence, and nobody is home right now. So please leave a message, and we'll return your call!" A beep follows. I wait to see if my father will pick up, and when he doesn't, I leave a message. "Hey, it's Alex. We're heading to the beach now, so I'll give you a call later or tomorrow. Bye, love ya." I hang up, wondering where my parents are. They never screened calls before Jenny's death. Now, they screen all the time.

I chuck the phone down on the dresser next to me, and my Cantor phone rings. The incoming call reads: *Ronnie*. I squint at the number. "Hunh." I exchanged numbers with Ronnie last night, but I didn't expect her to call me so soon.

"Hey. What's up?" I say, excited.

It isn't Ronnie. Cracker is on the other end. "Look out your window."

I push aside the drapes and see Cracker sitting inside Ronnie's car. "Come outside." She clicks off the phone.

I step into afternoon heat and close the door behind me.

Cracker is already walking toward me, holding a newspaper in her hand.

I start to panic. *Why are she and Ronnie visiting me at the motel?* But even more alarming—how does Cracker know what room I'm in? I never told any of the girls, not even Natice. Cracker probably made a visit to the manager's office. This makes me even more worried, but I just try to appear as if nothing is wrong.

"Hey, what's going on?"

"Ever make headlines before?" Cracker asks.

My stomach drops. *This is it. She knows exactly who I am.*

She opens the newspaper: *ATM Robbery. Third in Year.*

"They call you a blond-haired female youth. They don't exactly have all the details right, but it's close," Cracker says, pleased with herself.

I scan the article. *...late Saturday night. Two female youths entered the backseat of the victim's car... produced guns... ordered couple to the ATM to withdraw money... this is the third ATM robbery in the past twelve months.*

Cracker hands the newspaper to me. "You can keep it. Give it to your grandmother for her family album. I have my own copy saved." She smirks.

"Thanks. I'm sure she'll be proud of it."

"So where is she?"

"She went grocery shopping."

"I thought she's sick?"

"She is, but she can still walk. She's not dead."

"Not yet." Cracker smiles with her eyes.

"What do you want, Cracker?"

"I want to meet your grandmother."

"She's not here. I just told you."

"Fine, I'll stick around and wait. You don't mind?"

"I have shit to do," I raise my voice.

"She walked to the store?" Cracker asks.

"Yeah."

"In this heat?"

"Apparently."

"Mind if I use the bathroom while we wait?"

It becomes very clear Cracker is testing me. Perhaps the manager told her I'm living alone and that he's never seen my so-called "grandmother."

"The place is a mess. Now's not a good time." I hope Cracker will give up and leave. But of course, she doesn't.

"I don't give a shit!" Cracker shoves past me. She stops right in front of my room and bangs on the door. "C'mon, Cheerleader. Open the door!"

I feel like I'm trapped on a rollercoaster with no way of getting off. I'm not sure what to do other than keep Cracker out of my motel room no matter what.

I hear a familiar squeaking, and there she is, the old woman who lives a few doors down from me. She comes around the corner, where the sidewalk meets the entrance of the motel, pushing her ShopRite shopping cart.

She has just moved onto the walkway of the motel and is heading toward her room.

"I'll let you use the bathroom. Just don't curse in front of my grandmother," I say to Cracker as I walk toward the old woman and block her from moving forward. "How are you?" I mutter softly in Spanish.

"*Bien. Calor,*" the old woman responds with a tired smile.

A moment later, Cracker arrives at our side.

"Nanna, this my friend Cynthia."

The old woman nods.

"Hi, nice to meet you," Cracker says.

"Cynthia's one of the girls I've been playing basketball with. She's really good."

The old woman smiles, not understanding a word of English.

"So what are you doing now?" I turn to Cracker.

Ronnie honks the horn. "Cracker, c'mon! I'm hungry!"

Cracker looks back at Ronnie and sighs. "What else? We're gonna eat."

I wave to Ronnie. "That's my friend Ronnie." The old woman waves too, and I can't help smiling.

"Well, I better go," Cracker says. "Nice meeting you," she says to the old woman. "See ya later, Ally."

"Yeah, see ya later." I watch Cracker get back in the car and wait until the Jesus-mobile tears out of the motel's parking lot and is fully out of sight before I step out of the old woman's path.

"Sorry. That's a friend of mine. She's a little crazy," I say in Spanish. The old woman nods as if agreeing then pushes her cart past me and heads toward her room.

I open the newspaper and reread the headline: *ATM Robbery. Third in Year.* It's official. I'm a criminal.

I take a deep breath and make sure Cracker and Ronnie aren't coming back here, then I hurry inside my room. I slam the door behind me and chuck the newspaper on the bed. I circle the room, walking back and forth across the brown carpet. Cracker's visit has every nerve ending feeling like pricks of needles. But I also have another problem to deal with: I need to have a conversation with my father. I call him at work.

"Hey, Dad."

"Hey, honey. Having fun?"

"Yup."

"And how are Natalie and her parents?"

"They're good."

"Great. So what's up, kiddo? You coming home soon?"

"Well, I was actually thinking of staying longer."

"Really? How much longer?"

"I don't know. Maybe the rest of the summer?" I say tentatively. "I'm just having a really good time here, and I don't want to leave. Would you care if I did?"

My father is quiet for a moment. "The rest of the summer? Alex, are you sure that's okay with Natalie's parents?"

"Yeah, totally. She already asked them."

"I don't know, honey. I'd like to speak with Natalie's mother first."

I wasn't expecting that response and grow flustered, unsure what to even say. "Sure, but uh, I don't think she's here. I think she went shopping."

"Okay, when she gets back, ask her to call me. And if it's okay with Natalie's mother, you can stay. It's fine with me."

"All right. Thanks, Dad." I hang up the phone. "Fuck!"

CHAPTER 33

LATER THAT DAY, I GO across the street to the Burger King and ask a woman if she'll pretend to be my friend's mother for a school project. The woman looks at me as if I'm crazy and walks off. It takes me another two tries before I eventually find a woman in the Laundromat who agrees to do it for twenty dollars. I stand next to her, nerve-racked, as she carries on a conversation with my father using my Middletown iPhone. But she plays the part beautifully.

"Oh, it's been no trouble at all. Truly. It's been a delight having…"

"Alex," I remind her.

"Alex stay with us." She smiles. "Uh-huh. No, that's not necessary. You really don't have to. Yes, yes. Well, my husband and I are happy to offer our home. We're glad the girls get along so well. Okay. You too. Take care. Here's Alex." The woman hands the phone to me.

"Hey, Dad. So is it cool if I stay?"

My father unknowingly agrees to extend my stay in Cantor.

"Great! I will. Love you too. Bye." I hang up the phone and turn to the woman. "Thank you!" I hand her twenty dollars.

"No problem, sweetie. You need me again, you know where to find me."

The next day at work, I tell Natice about Cracker's visit. "What if Cracker narcs me out to the cops?" I pretend to be worried about the newspaper article when I'm really more concerned with her showing up at my motel.

Natice laughs. "Trust me, she ain't gonna 9-1-1 the cops."

"How do you know?"

"Because she was the one who had the fucking gun." Natice lowers her voice. "Look, Cracker's just trying to scare you with the po po and all that shit."

"Well, it worked."

"Girl, really? You put a loaded gun to your head, and now you're worried 'bout going to jail?" She raises both eyebrows. "This is why I didn't want to get you involved."

"You're right," I say, worried Natice will have second thoughts about including me. "I just don't want Cracker showing up again and scaring my grandmother. You know how she is. And my grandmother thinks I hang out with nice girls."

"Well, we know that ain't true," Natice says with a smile. She looks past my shoulder. "You got company, girlfriend."

I turn around, and Mark Silva walks through the door.

"What up?" He grins at me.

I take a break and go sit with Mark in the back room. He stares down at his sister's initials, L.S., carved into the table then looks up at me. "I have a confession to make."

"Yeah?"

"I lied."

"So soon in our relationship?"

He smiles. "Yo, I'm serious. You asked me if there was anyone. And I lied. I had a girlfriend, which is why I didn't call you."

"So when'd you break up?"

"Yesterday."

"Yesterday?" I shoot him a look.

He laughs. "Yo, it was a long time coming."

"So I'm a rebound?"

"You're too pretty to be anyone's rebound." He sounds genuine.

"So why do they call you Romeo?"

"Yo, you heard that?" His face turns red, and he takes a step back, shoving his hands deep in his pockets. "It's just a stupid nickname. That's all."

"Uh-huh."

"Why they call you Cheerleader?"

"Cracker made it up. It's not a compliment."

Mark nods, aware if Cracker nicknames you anything, it's not likely to be a compliment. "Ah, she ain't all bad."

153

"Yeah, right."

"She's not. She got a heart. It's small. Tiny. And hard to find. But it's in there if you look hard enough."

"I'll have to take your word for it. The last thing I want to do is look for Cracker's heart. I'll pass. Thanks."

Mark laughs then looks at me seriously. "So when you kickin' back to Seattle?"

"Not anytime soon. Why?"

"Don't wanna get attached if you're gonna be takin' off on me."

"Attached, huh? I doubt that, Romeo."

He smiles, revealing his dimple. "Yo, it's true. I'm a Cancer. Sensitive. Look it up. You're probably a Taurus."

I smile. "I am."

"Shit. Figures."

"Why? What's a Taurus like?"

He looks at me, matter of fact. "Stubborn."

We share a laugh, and it feels safe to be around Mark. He is nothing like Lori. After fifteen minutes of talking, Mark walks me back to the front of the pizzeria. As we reach the counter, Mark stops. "Almost forgot." He pulls a CD from his shorts pocket and hands it to me. "It's the band I was listening to that day in my bedroom. Goldfish. I burned it for you." He watches for my reaction.

I smile. He remembered I liked it. "Sweet, thanks."

"Lemme know what you think."

"I will."

"I'm gonna call you for real. Show you some of Jersey."

"Whatevs, Jersey boy. Don't take too long. I won't be in Cantor forever."

He smiles. "Don't worry. I won't." He turns to Natice. "See ya, Natty." He raises a hand and disappears out the door.

Natice walks up to me and takes the CD from my hand. She examines it and smiles. "Romeo must be into you. He only burns for the ones he likes."

"Yup. He's hot for my heat," I say, motioning to a part of my anatomy. Natice shoves me with a laugh.

An hour later, I'm thinking about Mark and cleaning the bathroom when Natice appears in the doorway. "You feel like making some extra money tonight?"

CHAPTER 34

"SKANK, BITCH, MOTHERFUCKER, HO, CATCH a crackhead by her fro..." Lori says, her finger alternating between a Camry and a 4Runner. We're sitting inside the Oldsmobile in a parking garage in Woodbury that's mainly used by people who live in New Jersey and commute into Philadelphia by train. Thanks to a friend of Vince's, Lori knows there aren't any cameras in the building, and the only security is an obese guard who randomly does walk-throughs but who mostly sits in a small office watching TV and eating. It's almost three in the morning when Lori's finger lands on the 4Runner. "Shit, let's take the Camry too."

Cracker and Ronnie laugh as they run out of the car, each carrying a hammer and a Slim Jim, the long, thin metal bar that mechanics use to pop open locked car doors. In their back pockets are wire cutters. Natice chases after them, clutching a handful of pebbles. She's the lookout. If she sees anyone, she'll throw a pebble onto the windshield of the car to let Cracker and Ronnie know. I sit in the car with Lori, waiting for them to hot-wire the vehicles. Once they finish, Natice will hop back in the Oldsmobile, and we'll all drive off.

I watch nervously as Cracker slides the Slim Jim between the windowpane and the door of the 4Runner. It doesn't take her long before she pops open the lock and hurries behind the wheel. Ronnie, though, hasn't slipped the tool into the door of the Camry.

Natice stands hidden behind a cement column, keeping an eye on both vehicles.

"What the hell is she doing?" Lori says as Ronnie runs back to us.

"I got a bad feeling!" Ronnie jumps into the backseat.

"What the fuck do you mean, you got a bad feeling?" Lori turns back and looks at her.

"I got a bad feeling. I ain't doing it."

"Are you fucking kidding me?" Lori's face turns red.

"You know if I get a bad feeling, I don't do it." Ronnie says.

I'm curious if Ronnie got a bad feeling the night my sister was shot and killed.

"Gimme the damn Slim Jim. I'll do it!" Lori grabs it out of Ronnie's hand and is about to step out of the car when the fat white security guard appears from behind a door.

"Lori!" I grab her shoulder.

Lori ducks back inside. "Fuck. Be cool."

The three of us remain perfectly still as we watch the security guard yawn, stretch, and look around as though he's bored.

Natice has noticed him as well and throws a pebble onto the windshield of the 4Runner.

Cracker glances up and sees the guard but doesn't get out of the car. She's still trying to hotwire it.

Natice runs back to the Oldsmobile and hops inside. "Fuck! Fatty never walks out!"

The guard stretches for a few more seconds, and just as he's about to walk away, a ringing cell phone startles him. He looks up and sees Cracker inside the 4Runner. The ringing silences, but from the look on the guard's face, one thing is certain—Cracker does not belong in that vehicle.

"Get out of the car, Cracker!" Lori says, panicked.

But Cracker keeps trying to get the engine started.

The guard walks straight toward the 4Runner, bringing a walkie-talkie to his lips.

"I told you I had a bad feeling!" Ronnie yells.

I hit the gas and head toward the exit. The guard hears my car, looks up, and runs to the middle of the aisle, planting his body right in front of the exit. He talks rapidly into the walkie-talkie as he looks down at my license plate.

I want to scream at the guard, *"You're going to get yourself killed for nothing!"* Before we left Cantor, Ronnie used electrical tape to make the letter O on my plate look like a B and the number one look like a seven.

I floor the accelerator and hit the horn, but the guard just stands there, feet planted.

"Go around him!" Natice shouts.

"How?" I yell.

There is nowhere to go around. I keep my hand pressed against the horn, blasting it and praying he will move. At the very last second, the guard dives out of the way. I crash through the exit, sending the wooden arm flying. I hit the road with a screech and then burn to a quick halt.

"Get in!" Lori yells to Cracker, who escaped out a side door and onto the street.

Cracker jumps inside the car. "Where was the fuckin' cover?" she asks Natice.

"I gave you cover! Why the hell'd you bring your phone?" Natice yells back.

I speed down a two-way street with no idea where I'm going. I just know I need to get off this road, fast, before I get caught. Adrenaline rises, and I feel like I'm going to have a heart attack.

"Slow down!" Lori yells.

I let off the gas.

Up ahead, heading straight toward us, I see flashing lights closing fast. I keep to the speed limit as a police car whizzes past.

Everything seems cool until a second later, I see the cop pull a U-turn, and the flashing lights appear in my rearview mirror.

"Fuck!" Lori shouts.

Tension quickly fills the car. I peel off to the right and down a side street. The cop car gives chase, and I floor the pedal.

"Lose 'em!" Lori screams.

The speedometer climbs from forty to fifty, when I see headlights coming at us. I am going the wrong way down a one-way street.

"Fuck!" I slam on the horn, hoping the car will somehow get out of my way.

Behind us, the cop car reappears. Its flashing lights become brighter and bigger. The siren blares. The cop is hot on our ass. Everyone is yelling, telling me what to do. A head-on tragedy is seconds away. I swerve to the right and barrel into an alley. Garbage cans go flying, and the car scrapes the side of the building. I punch the gas and turn onto another side street. I drive like a maniac, blindly turning down one street after the next.

Finally, we reach a highway. I blow through a yellow light, thinking any moment flashing lights will appear in my rearview mirror. But when I look back, there is no cop car. No lights. No siren.

Another traffic light up ahead changes from yellow to red. But this time, I hit the brake. I haven't even noticed, until then, that I am dripping with sweat. Natice keeps looking back for the cops, and each second feels like an hour. We wait anxiously for the light to change to green. When it does, I lift my foot of off the brake and squeeze the gas pedal. The car stalls and dies.

I turn the key in the ignition. Nothing. "Shit!"

The rest of them start to panic.

"What the fuck? Get it going!" Cracker yells.

"C'mon, Cheerleader!" Lori demands.

I turn the key again. Nothing.

Another pair of headlights approaches from behind. Nobody says a word, and I silently pray in the dark, *Please God, if you're ever going to answer my prayers, answer them now.* I pump the gas—one, two, three times. I turn the key, and *varoom*!

"Go! Go!" Lori shouts.

I hit the gas, and the car explodes forward. The pair of headlights grows dim in my rearview mirror. It was just another car.

"Turn there! There!" Lori yells, pointing to the turnpike entrance.

I approach the tollbooth and with a shaking hand, take a ticket from the automated machine and head toward Cantor. Any second now, I think a cop car is going to appear. I drive paranoid for at least a mile. Or two. Finally, it becomes clear that I've outrun the cops. We've gotten away.

"Fuck!" I yell.

"Good job, Cheerleader!" Natice says, smiling.

I pound the dashboard and scream. It's a weird mixture of fear and exhilaration. "Haaaaaaa! Ha!" I yell in victory. Then all together—Lori, Natice, Ronnie, and even Cracker join me—we fill the car with howls of excitement.

That night, I do my first line of cocaine. "1, 2 Step" plays on the hi-fi system in Lori's kitchen.

"Cheerleader, come here." Lori waves me over. She holds out a key with a bump of white powder on it.

Once again, because it is Lori Silva offering me drugs, I don't refuse. I lean my nostril over the key and snort hard. I almost choke as I feel it drip down my nostril and into my throat.

Lori grins. "That's some good shit."

The drug takes effect almost immediately. A sudden burst of euphoria and energy, along with my high from outrunning the cops, has me feeling invincible. I'm no longer worried or afraid. I'm beautiful and strong and confident and complete. My sadness and pain are gone. The girls start dancing around me, and this time, I am no longer a bystander. This time, I join in and dance.

Natice sings along with the song.

"Sing it, Natty! Sing it, girl!" Ronnie chimes, grinding up against my side.

We may not have stolen a car tonight, but thanks to me, Lori, Cracker, Ronnie, and Natice escaped the police. It's strange to be celebrating and dancing with the girls I'm trying to send to prison, but I feel something I haven't felt in a very long time. I feel alive in the world.

CHAPTER 35

I T AMAZES ME HOW MANY people leave the keys in the ignition of their cars while they go inside a store to buy milk, cigarettes, soda, candy, whatever. It takes me less than ten seconds to run across the street, jump behind the wheel of a Pathfinder, and drive away. Natice beat me across the street and is riding shotgun. She's definitely fast, much faster than I am.

The owner of the Pathfinder has SiriusXM Radio set to classic rock, and Elton John's "Rocket Man" blasts from the speakers as I merge onto a highway. I know by now that Lori and the girls only target towns they know well, towns with 7-Elevens, WaWas, and Quick Checks and are in close proximity to highways that lead directly to the turnpike.

"Goodbye, EZPass." Natice plucks the electronic device off the windshield and tosses it out the window.

By the time we reach the turnpike, "Rocket Man" is at its crescendo. I grab an entrance ticket and head north toward Cantor. Natice opens the sunroof and raises the volume. A rush of wind messes up our hair.

Natice looks over at me and smiles. "How you doin', Cheerleader?"

"Livin' the dream." I smile back at her. I'm also high, thanks to the bump of coke we did before running out of the Olds.

"What are you thinking about?"

I think a rush of excitement—I think a warm summer night—I think a full moon—I think wind on my face—I think that poor bastard whose car I just stole—but mostly, I think, *I haven't felt this good in a long time.*

A week later, I rob my first house with the girls. The house is in a suburban Pennsylvania neighborhood. A girl Ronnie is friends with on Facebook posted pictures of her and her family in South Carolina. *Loving Hilton Head!* the girl wrote on her wall.

I know somehow Detective Thoms is monitoring their pages, except for Natice, who, as I suspected, isn't on Facebook. In the case file, there were notes that Cracker's Facebook page had all four of them checked into Lori's house watching *Game of Thrones* the night of my sister's shooting, which I know is bullshit. The night I outran the cops, Lori had gone onto Facebook earlier and posted some comment about us all playing poker at Vince's. And right now, Cracker has us checked into "Tray's Crib." I wonder if she included me.

"Man, this is one butt-ugly family." Ronnie looks at a framed photo as if she's trying to decipher a math problem.

The girl is someone Ronnie went to grammar school with and who moved out of Cantor several years ago. The girl found Ronnie on Facebook and sent her a friend request. It was just by chance that Ronnie saw her posting. Lori suggested we rob the house while they were away. And within minutes, we steal jewelry, an iPad, a Louis Vuitton handbag, and at least six hundred dollars hidden in a closet.

"Oh shit!" Ronnie laughs as she holds up a huge penis made of purple rubber.

We're in the parents' bedroom, and Ronnie has just discovered it in a bottom drawer filled with pajamas and sex toys. "What the fuck!" She laughs hysterically.

"Oh, these people are freaky!" Natice pulls a black dildo out of the same drawer. "Take that!" Natice slaps the black dildo against Ronnie's purple one. The two start dueling.

"You know where they've been, don't you?" Lori eyes the dildos with disgust.

Ronnie thinks about it and chucks it. "Eww!"

I laugh.

"Ally, catch!" Natice tosses the black one at me.

I duck, and it hits Cracker.

"Hey!"

We play around in the parents' bedroom for a while before returning downstairs to the kitchen. Ronnie searches through the cabinets and finds a bag of Doritos that she takes for the road. Natice and I help ourselves to a couple of fruit-flavored ice pops from the freezer, and we casually stroll out the back door of the house.

A day later, we rob another home in the same neighborhood. This time, the girls don't seem to mind as I break out my iPhone and capture our moments on camera.

"No Instagramming!" Lori tells us.

"No shit. I have an aversion to handcuffs and broads in orange jumpsuits," I reply.

"Hey, Cheerleader! In here!"

I push open a door, and Ronnie is sitting on a toilet bowl, taking a crap while posing with a copy of *Good Housekeeping*. After that, I take a photo of Lori pocketing a gold bracelet from a bedroom, another one of Natice and me lounging on the family's living room couch, then a group picture of us sitting at the kitchen table eating a frozen pizza we heated up.

Later, when I'm alone in my motel room, I go through the photos. I'm definitely getting a charge out of doing all this and may even be growing addicted to committing these crimes, but then it hits me. I suddenly feel bad for the people we are robbing. My excitement evaporates into guilt, and I have to remind myself there is a purpose to all this. An endgame.

I land on a photo of Cracker smiling while giving me the middle finger as she raids a closet. It's tempting to run to the nearest CVS, print these photos, and turn them over to Detective Thoms. The urge to do so is like being handed a piece of chocolate cake while you're on a diet and craving sugar. But I've worked too hard to take a bite. If I show these photos to the police, along with everything else, I'd end up seeing Lori and Cracker spend who knows what amount of time behind bars—six, seven, eight months? Myself right along with them. And for what? For us to get out and return to our crappy lives with nothing changed? I couldn't live with myself, knowing I was this close to nailing them for my sister's murder, and I let it go for a crumb. No, I'm not dropping this ball until I have a perfect three-point shot lined up. I stare at Cracker's face. *You won't be smiling when your ass is rotting away in prison.*

CHAPTER 36

"HOW MUCH IS IT GONNA cost me?" I ask Mark Silva. "Five hundred. Normally, it's seven. But I got him down for you."

"Thanks." I hand over the keys to the Oldsmobile.

A short while later, Mark is treating me to lunch at his favorite family-owned Cuban restaurant while the mechanic at the gas station replaces my broken air-conditioner.

Mark introduces me to what he calls "the original kick-ass Cubano sandwich." It's a submarine-style layering of ham, roast pork, cheese, pickles, mustard, and butter placed between seven inches of sliced Cuban bread, which tastes the same to me as Italian bread. It's pressed with a waffle grill, served warm, and it's amazing.

"I like your watch." Mark wipes his face clean of mustard. He reaches across the table, places his hand on mine, and turns the face of my watch toward him. "It's dope. Where'd you get it?"

I pause and clear my throat. "Thanks. It was a Christmas present."

"Sweet present." He leans back into his chair and stares at me.

I take a bite of my sandwich and wash it down with soda.

"Hey, you listen to the CD?"

"Yeah, I love it," I say, completely lying. I've been too busy committing crimes with his sister to listen to it, which makes me wonder where Mark has been on the nights I've been at his house and if he even knows what his sister is up to. "So I was at your house the other night, hanging out with your sister."

"Oh yeah?" He takes a sip of his soda. "So what'd you guys do?" Then before I can answer, he gives his question a second thought. "You know what? Don't tell me."

"Why's that?"

"Because if you were with my sister, you couldn't possibly be up to anything good."

"Oh really? What do you think we were doing?"

"Shit. I don't know, and I don't want to know." He fusses with his napkin.

"Well, it wasn't anything exciting. We drove around for an hour and then ended up back at your house. It was pretty boring, actually."

Mark nods, and it's hard to tell if he believes me. "Cool." He offers nothing on his whereabouts.

"So you and Lori don't get along, do you?"

He shrugs. "Not really."

"How come?"

"I don't know. We just don't."

"She's not exactly a delicate flower."

"That's for damn sure. She used to beat the shit out of me growing up. But ya know, she ain't all bad. Every once in a while, she'd do something nice, like buy me a pack of baseball cards or make me something to eat when I was hungry. Mom wasn't around much."

"What about your dad?"

"Nope. I'm like an orphan." He pushes the napkin away and taps the table with his fingers.

"No relatives? Grandparents? Uncles?"

He laughs. "I don't know. I think I have an uncle."

I can't imagine growing up without my grandparents. I love them. Right after Jenny's death, though, I became so distant I stopped speaking to them. They cried every time we spoke. I couldn't take their calls anymore. Thinking about them hurts my heart. I make a mental note to call my grandmother when I get back to the motel.

"So what about you, Cheerleader?"

"Cheerleader?" I sit up straight, giving him a look. "Don't go calling me that."

"Why not?"

"Because I like hearing you say my name."

He leans across the table, and his dark-brown eyes and sexy dimpled smile hypnotize me. "A'right, Ally. I won't."

When the check arrives, Mark pays with cash, and we head back to the gas station in his Mustang.

"Your car is spotless." It truly is. There's not even a speck of dirt or loose change on the floor.

"Thanks," he says proudly then looks over at me. "Yo, what's your favorite ice cream?"

"Ben and Jerry's chocolate fudge brownie, why?"

"No reason," he says with a secretive look.

"You gonna surprise me with ice cream?"

"Maybe."

By the time we arrive back at the gas station, my car is ready. The mechanic hands me the keys, and I slide behind the wheel of an ice-cold car.

Mark stands by my open window. "How's it feel?"

"So much better."

"Cool. Well, I'll hit you up later. I gotta work my other job all week."

"What other job?"

"I work the night shift at a warehouse in Philadelphia. Grunt work. I clean the place."

"You're always working, huh?" Now I know where he has been on the nights I've been at his house.

"Like a dog." He backpedals away. "Stay outta trouble, Ally." He wags a finger at me then struts off.

I'm a few blocks from the motel when I see the old woman pushing her grocery cart along the hot sidewalk. It's filled with groceries, and I wonder how she manages in this heat. After parking the Oldsmobile in front of my room, I double back to lend her a hand.

"Can I help you with this?" I ask in Spanish.

The old woman nods with relief, and I take over pushing her cart.

"I'm Ally," I say, choosing not to use my real name.

"Carmela," she says with a thick accent.

When we reach her room, I unlock the door and push the cart inside. Her room is a lot different from mine. It has a tiny living room and a kitchenette. I roll the cart past a couch and stop at a small round table and help unload the groceries. Carmela's hands are so badly ravaged by arthritis they're balled up into fists, but she manages to stock her shelves. We speak Spanish the entire time, and she tells me about her daughter, son, and seven grandchildren. She tells me they visit her, but I've never seen them.

Before I leave, I offer to take her to the grocery store anytime she likes. "Please, anytime. Just knock on my door."

"You're so sweet. Thank you."

She gives me a hug, and I promise myself I'll start visiting Carmela before I go into work at the pizzeria, even if it's only to say hello.

As I walk to my room, I notice I have another missed call from Lea. Since arriving in Cantor, Lea has left me four or five voice mail messages— some, I haven't even listened to. So I decide to finally call her back.

"Where the hell have you been?" Lea greets me.

"I'm in Ocean City."

"Yeah, I heard. What the fuck?"

"How'd you hear?"

"Your dad told someone who told my dad."

Then she launches straight into talking about herself, which today, I'm grateful for. I'm not in the mood to make up lies.

"You were right, by the way."

"About what?"

"About Jay's friend only liking me for a night."

"What happened?"

"He's an asshole! We hooked up and totally had sex. He was like, 'I really like you. I'll call you.' And he never did. I called and texted him, and he never answered any of 'em."

"How many times did you call him?" I'm afraid to know the answer.

"I don't know. Twice, I guess. But then I texted him like six times. I'm like, 'Can you at least respond?'"

"And did he?"

"No. I ran into him last week at Amber's, and he totally blew me off and hooked up with some other girl right in front of me."

I feel bad for Lea because I know she's hurt. "He's a jerk, Lea. Next time, wait." I don't dare ask if she used protection. I hope she did.

"Hey, so any chance I can come visit you in Ocean City?" Lea asks.

I'm not sure what to say to that question, other than the truth. "I don't think it's a good idea. I may not be staying much longer."

166

"Fine. Well, hurry up and come back. You sound good, by the way."

I'm tempted to tell Lea the truth, but I know if I do, she'll freak out and beg me to come home, or she'll threaten to call my dad. And on the slight chance I could convince Lea not to do that, she'd just worry about me the entire time, and I don't need that on my mind. I'm feeling enough anxiety as it is. Besides, knowing Lea, even if she promised not to tell anyone, she would never be able to keep this to herself. It would be all over Middletown. So I hang up the phone, keeping my secret a secret.

CHAPTER 37

"WHAT DO YOU THINK?" RONNIE asks me.

I'm sitting in a chair in her beauty school class, facing a mirror. As part of Ronnie's final exam for graduation, she cut and colored my hair for free. She initially asked Cracker, who refused. So here I am, happy to have been asked.

"You got skills, Rodriguez!"

Ronnie has mad talent. Even with my dark eyebrows, she makes me look like a natural blonde. Her teacher inspects my hair, running her fingers through it. "Good job, Ronnie." She makes a note in a book before moving on to the next student.

I snap a picture of my hair, tag Ronnie in the photo, and post it on Instagram. *#hair #onfleek #workingit #friends.*

I slip Ronnie a twenty when the teacher isn't looking and head out the door with plans to see her and the others later.

***

"This shit feels real." Cracker touches a brunette wig fastened to a Styrofoam head. It's around six o'clock, and we're all together at the pizzeria. Ronnie is showing Cracker and Lori the wig she purchased for practicing cutting hair.

"It *is* real—it's a hundred dollars real. So stop touching it," Ronnie says.

Cracker promptly removes her hand. "Eww. This is someone's real hair? That's nasty!"

Natice examines the wig and snatches the Styrofoam head off the table. "Cracker, go long!"

"Hey!" Ronnie throws up her hands to block the pass.

But she's too late. Cracker catches the Styrofoam head. The wig remains firmly attached, its dark hair bouncing up and down as Cracker and Natice toss the Styrofoam head back and forth over Ronnie's head, playing a game of Monkey in the Middle.

"C'mon, y'all! Give it back! I ain't playing. That shit's expensive!" Ronnie chases after it as Cracker chucks the head to Lori, who tosses it to me. "Yo, Ally. C'mon!" Ronnie waves her hands in the air, trying to block my pass.

I throw it to Natice.

"C'mon, yo! Give it back!"

Finally, the Styrofoam head drops out of Natice's hands, and the wig falls off. Ronnie dives on top of it, trapping it underneath her body. We bust up laughing.

"Dammit, you guys!" Ronnie stands with the mangled wig in her hands. She untangles the hair and places it back on top of the Styrofoam head. "Chanel, you all right, girl?"

"Chanel?" Cracker scrunches her face as if she just smelled something bad.

"Yeah, I gave her a name," Ronnie replies.

My cell phone rings, and I answer the call, laughing. "Hello?"

"Yo, it's Mark. What you up to?"

"Nothing much. Working."

"You working on Sunday?"

"No, why?"

"How 'bout you come over, and we watch *Rocky*?"

"In your bedroom? What happened to showing me Jersey?"

He laughs. "Yo, I promise to behave myself. Have you ever seen it?"

"I saw half of it once on TV."

"Half of it? You gotta see the whole thing. You gotta."

If it had been any other boy, I never would have agreed to watch a movie in his bedroom, but because it's Mark, I'm more than happy to have time alone with him. "Fine, but you gotta promise to keep your sensitive hands off my heat."

He laughs. "Yo, I promise."

We pick a time, and I click off the phone. I head to the front counter, biting my lip and walking on the tips of my toes.

"Ally has a date! Ally has a date!" Natice teases. Her expression changes.

I follow her stare out the window as a Ford Taurus pulls up in front of the pizzeria, and Detective Thoms steps out from behind the wheel. Another man—younger, Latino—gets out on the passenger side.

Natice hurries around the counter. "Lori! Thoms is here!" she yells to the back.

"Who's that?" I ask.

"Just some asshole cop." Natice nervously watches the door as Thoms and his partner approach.

She's not the only one who's nervous. I only have seconds to get out from behind that counter before I'm seen. "Be right back. I have to take a leak."

I'm not a second too soon as the door opens, and Detective Thoms's familiar voice is behind me. "Hello, Natice."

I hurry into the back room and, not seeing Cracker, I bump into her. "Watch it!" she yells.

"Sorry." I quickly step around her and escape into the bathroom.

Cracker stares after me, annoyed. She moves next to Lori. "Why you think he's here?"

"Who the fuck knows?" I hear Lori say from behind the door.

I crack open the bathroom door and peer out just as Detective Thoms walks past. He is dressed exactly the same as the last time I saw him, right down to his dark-blue button-down shirt.

"Hi, girls."

"What up, Detective T?" Ronnie says.

"You look like you lost a little weight, Ronnie," Detective Thoms tells her.

Ronnie proudly holds her stomach. "I've been runnin' and shit. You know."

Thoms smiles and turns to Cracker. "Cynthia, how are you?"

"Oh, I'm fantastic," Cracker says in a sarcastic voice.

Lori smirks but remains quiet.

"Hey, Detective Thoms, how come you never brought this fine piece of Latino meat in here with you before?" Ronnie says, referring to his partner, who is much better dressed in a suit and tie.

Thoms's partner smiles without saying a word.

"Girls, this is Detective Moreno. I'm sure you'll be seeing a lot more of him."

"I hope so because he's fine," Ronnie says in Spanish.

"I'd beat it." Lori laughs.

"Keeping out of trouble, Lori?" Thoms asks.

"If I were in trouble, you'd know it. Wouldn't you?"

"No new car, yet, huh?"

"Nah. Insurance didn't pay much."

"Oh, by the way, Detective Moreno ran into your mother not too long ago," Thoms says. "When was that, Moreno?"

"Six, maybe seven weeks ago," Moreno says matter-of-factly.

"She had a little trouble coming up with the bail money," Thoms remarks. "She may not be home for a while."

"Tha's a shame. I guess I won't be throwing her a welcome-home party. I'll jus' have the house all to myself," Lori says.

"I guess you will." Thoms faces Moreno. "Did you know I went to school with Lori's mom?"

"I didn't know that," Moreno responds.

"Yeah, she had Lori when she was, what... fifteen? Sixteen?" Thoms turns to Lori for a reaction. But there is none. "I remember her mother would come to school wearing these skirts that barely covered her ass. She started tricking pretty early. Made good money too. Anyway, no one ever knew who Lori's father was. Shit, I was even worried for a while." He laughs, but again, Lori doesn't bite. "How's your brother?"

"He's great. Probably at home watching TV." Lori smiles sarcastically.

Thoms returns the smile. Then he gets close into Lori's face, and his tone changes. "Don't worry, Lori. Something will turn up. And when it does—just like your mother—I'll nail your fucking ass."

"Sounds like fun," Lori says.

"Stay out of trouble, girls," Thoms says to the others. He leaves with his younger partner trailing after him.

I wait another minute or two before I come out of the bathroom. Natice has just walked back from the front. She approaches Lori, who for the first time ever, looks upset. We all know Thoms hit a deep wound. Natice told me early on that Lori had once stabbed a kid in her class with a fork because he called her mother a prostitute. She was only twelve.

"Forget him, Lori. He's an asshole," Natice says.

"I swear to God, one of these days I'm gonna fucking kill him. I'll shoot him myself," Lori says.

"We should do it! Let's find out where he lives!" Cracker says.

"Yo, I want nothing to do with that." Ronnie walks away.

"Don't be stupid, Cracker," Natice says.

"Why's that stupid?"

"You're gonna shoot a fuckin' cop, now?" Natice says.

"I don't give a shit!" Cracker responds.

"I tell you what. If I ever get the chance, I will," Lori says.

No one says a word after that.

I walk toward the front and see Detective Thoms and Moreno still in the parking lot, arguing. Thoms points to the pizzeria, yells something to Moreno, and disappears behind the wheel. Moreno takes a few seconds to cool off before getting inside the car. His door is barely closed when Thoms speeds off.

I walk away from the window and look back at the girls. Cracker and Ronnie have moved on to the basketball toss game. Natice is in the bathroom, and Lori sits at her back table alone. She looks up and catches me staring at her.

I feel something for Lori that surprises me—compassion.

CHAPTER 38

"You're gonna shoot a fuckin' cop now?" I can't get Natice's words out of my head. I suspect that she meant Cracker has shot someone before and that *now* she wants to shoot a cop. My guess is the *before* is my sister or the store clerk, and my goal today is to find that out as I watch *Rocky* with Mark.

We're lying on his bed, eating Ben & Jerry's ice cream straight from the containers. Mark has his favorite—cookie dough—and for me, of course, he remembered my favorite: chocolate fudge brownie. On screen, Rocky is ice-skating with Adrian while Mark tells me how *Rocky* got made. He says that Stallone was a struggling actor and had maybe two hundred dollars to his name when he wrote *Rocky*.

"A movie studio wanted to buy it for a hundred thousand dollars, but Stallone wouldn't sell the script. The only way he would let the studio buy it was if he got to play Rocky. They said yes, and *Rocky* and Sylvester Stallone were born. Stallone didn't quit on his dream."

"What's your dream?"

"I'm gonna produce music. For a year, I've been hounding companies in New York and Philly, tryin' to get a job. I've been stalking 'em."

"Sweet." I say, genuinely impressed. I toast his spoon with mine, and it makes a small clinking sound.

"Yeah. Most sent we're-not-hiring bullshit emails, but then outta nowhere, I got a call from this label in Philly that said I could do an internship."

"Look at you. That's badass."

"Yeah, they almost didn't give it to me 'cause I'm not in college. But I kept hounding 'em. 'Please, I'll do anything. I'll sweep the floors!' Yo, it paid off. I start in September." His face lights up. "I can't wait! I'll be working forty hours a week for free. But I don't care. I'd pay them to let me work there!"

"I expect free music."

"Yo, absolutely."

Inside, however, I know by the time Mark starts that job, he and I will no longer be friends. For all I know, he may go to prison along with Lori if it turns out he withheld information about her involvement in Jenny's murder.

"What's wrong?" He catches the sadness in my eyes.

"Nothing." I think about how different Mark is from his sister. I'm grateful Lori is at Vince's for the night. I wouldn't have felt comfortable in the house if she were home, even with our newfound phony friendship.

"Come here."

"No," I say, well aware of what he wants from me.

"Fine, I'll come to you." Mark moves in for a kiss, but I turn my head to the side. He makes a second attempt, and I roll over on top of him, pinning his arms to the bed.

"Yo, I'm gonna call you Rocky."

"Whatever, Adrian." I look down at him.

"That's right. I'm a lover, not a fighter." He laughs.

"So tell me something about you that I don't know, other than you're sensitive."

Mark smiles. "I watch soap operas."

"Soap operas?"

"Yup."

"Which one?"

"*Days of Our Lives*."

"I don't believe you."

"Yo, it's pretty good, Ally. You should check it out."

"Okay. What's the worst thing you've ever done? The worst lie you've ever told?"

Mark gives this question plenty of thought. "I could tell ya, but I gotta get somethin' in return."

"Name it."

"One kiss."

"Just one?"

"You'll want more."

"Oh really?"

I lean down, and our lips meet. Mark's are soft and gentle, unlike kissing Jay, whose make-out sessions always left my mouth feeling scratched and raw. We kiss for a while before Mark smiles up at me.

"I like you," he says.

"Me too." It's not exactly a lie.

"C'mon, Rocky." Mark pulls me back down beside him. He slips his arm around me, and we go back to the movie.

Unfortunately, Mark never answers my question, and I fall asleep right after Rocky climbs the steps in Philadelphia.

I wake up to something cold and hard pressing against my forehead. I open my eyes to see Cracker standing above me, holding a gun to my forehead. She pushes the barrel deeper into my skin. I feel the blood drain from my face, and I think of my parents now with two dead daughters. I've wanted to die so many times before, but not at the hands of Cracker. *Will my body be found? Will my parents wonder what I was doing when they discover I never went to camp? What will they think?* I want to tell my father how much I love him. I want my mother to know I forgive her for the awful things she said to me in Jenny's bedroom, something she never apologized for. "Please don't..." is all I can think to say to Cracker. But the words don't come out. I think for sure I am dead.

Then Cracker smirks, and it becomes obvious that this sick bitch was fucking with me. She lowers the gun. "Lori wants to see you outside."

It takes me a moment before I'm able to breathe and crawl out from under Mark's arm. I sit up with the shakiness of a car crash survivor, heart thumping, short of breath. "What for?" I finally say.

"Come find out. And don't wake your boyfriend."

I look down at Mark as he sleeps, and my gut nudges me to wake him, but I leave him alone and rise unsteadily to my feet. I slip into my shoes, grasping onto the chair for balance.

"Go. Move." Cracker motions me with the gun to walk ahead of her.

"Do you mind putting that away?"

"Just fucking walk." Cracker lowers her arm.

Mark stirs but remains asleep as I leave his bedroom. Cracker follows closely behind me, gun in hand. I steady myself against the wall, placing one foot in front of the other on the carpet. The house is eerily quiet. I can barely see what's in front of me as I walk down the stairs, through the dark living room, and into the kitchen, where the back door has been left open.

"So what is it?" I ask.

"You'll see," Cracker says.

I step outside, and waiting for me are Lori, Natice, and Ronnie. Nobody says a word.

"What's up?"

Lori walks over to me and puts her arm around my shoulder like a good friend. "C'mon, Ally. Let's go for a walk."

A flashlight clicks on, and Natice steps ahead of us, leading the way toward the abandoned schoolyard. Ronnie moves to the opposite side of me, and Cracker continues to follow from behind. I am blocked in by all four of them.

"We got a problem," Lori says. "The problem is you ain't one of us."

It only takes me a second to realize Lori knows exactly who I am and that I made a big mistake by not waking Mark. But if I had woken Mark, would he have done anything?

I follow Natice's every step, wondering what she is thinking, and as I'm about to make a run for it, Lori stops me.

"So whaddya say, Ally? You wanna get your ass jumped in?"

I hold her stare, and I see the faintest smile emerge. Then I look at Natice and Ronnie; they're smiling too.

"What's that?" I ask.

"Something we're bringing back, just for you," Cracker says, excited for whatever is to come.

"C'mon, Cheerleader! Say yes!" Ronnie yells.

"Black diamonds are forever, baby!" Natice holds up her fist and shows off her tattoo.

I don't have to think twice. "I'm in."

What follows is a beating far worse than what I witnessed in that liquor store. Lori punches me in the face. Cracker hits me in my gut. I bend over and struggle to breathe, feeling the pain of both blows. A series of punches follows from all four. I'm hit in my face, head, and body. Everywhere. I take a step forward, trip, and hit the ground. From there, I'm kicked mercilessly, shoes and sneakers from all angles. I huddle in a small ball, trying to keep my face from being kicked in. My arms are struck. The back of my head is kicked. I wish for the beating to end. I almost black out. Then I hear Lori's voice.

"Get up! Get up, Cheerleader!"

Natice and Ronnie help me to my feet. I feel drunk. I can hardly see. I cough and spit out blood, and it drools off my lips. I leave it hanging there as I am punched in the stomach by Ronnie. Then for another ten seconds, I am hit and kicked. It seems like an eternity. Finally, someone takes hold of my head. I look up to see Lori's face. The last thing I remember is her knee. Everything goes black after that.

CHAPTER 39

I CRACK OPEN MY LIPS, AND it feels as if a knife has sliced them apart. My face hurts, and my head feels as if it will explode at any second. My left eye is swollen so badly I can barely see out of it. I look down at my throbbing right hand and see that my pinky finger is grotesquely swollen. I sit up and take notice of my surroundings. Sharing the bed with me are tons of stuffed animals. On the floor below me are piles of clothes, and pushed up against a wall is a desk cluttered with books. For a moment, I think I'm in Jenny's room. But I am not. I'm in Natice's bedroom.

I push myself to the edge of the bed and moan as I rise to my feet. I'm standing on a bright-purple carpet. I take a step and catch my reflection in a mirror. I almost cry. I look like Rocky Balboa.

"What the hell are you doing?" Natice rushes in from the doorway and yanks me away from the mirror. "Girl, do not look in that mirror." She gently sits me back down on the bed. "How's your head?"

"Is it still there? It fuckin' kills."

"Here, take this." She hands me a glass of water and a small white pill.

"What is it?"

"Vicodin."

The same drug my mother takes, although she takes three or four at a time. I pop it into my mouth and chase it down with a gulp of water.

"I think you should stay here for a while. You don't want your grandmother seeing you like this." Natice examines my left eye.

"Don't worry. I'll just tell her I got in a car accident."

"That's not a bad idea." Natice looks impressed.

"I was kidding."

A minute later, I make a call to my Middletown cell phone and pretend to talk to my grandmother. I ask if I can spend the rest of the week at a friend's house. Of course, my pretend grandmother says yes. After the call, Natice applies a splint to my finger, forming it with two old Popsicle sticks and tape.

"There. Not bad," Natice says.

"Beautiful." It looks ridiculous.

We both laugh.

"Oww. My face hurts."

An hour later, the Vicodin has kicked in, and I realize why my mother takes it. I feel numb inside, like a zombie with zero feelings. "So when did you guys decide to do this?"

"About two weeks ago. Cracker was against it until she realized she'd get to punch you in the face."

"Of course."

"We were just waiting until my stepfather wouldn't be home."

"So where is he?"

"Right 'bout now, he's probably in Georgia. He's a truck driver. Delivers beer all over the damn country."

"I hope he left some behind."

"Shit. I a'ready put half a case in the fridge. Thank God, he's hardly home."

"Why's that?"

Natice shrugs. "He's kind of an asshole."

"Any grandparents? Or just him?"

"Just him. My mom grew up in foster care. But she did a'right for herself. She got out of the system, put herself through college, became a nurse."

"What about your dad?"

"Never met him. All I know is that he worked at the same hospital my mom did. Prick was already married with kids."

"Shit."

"Yeah, he wanted her to abort me. But she didn't, and here I am." Natice smiles.

"Is that your mom?" I ask, noticing a framed photograph of a beautiful black woman on a nearby shelf.

"Yup."

"Wow. She's stunning."

"Yeah, she was." Natice stares at the photograph for a moment, then she stands up, pulls another photo off the shelf, and sits back down next to me. "Look at this." The photo includes Ronnie, Lori, Cracker, and Natice when they were all much younger.

"Look at my hair. Platinum blond. I have no friends, Ally. 'Cause if I did, they never would'a let me walk around with this head."

She holds the picture for me to see. Her hair looks worse than any bad hair day I have ever had. We both laugh.

"Owww, don't make me laugh." I grab my jaw.

I call in sick to the pizzeria, using the excuse I got into a bad car accident, and for the next three days, Natice and I order in food and watch movies nonstop in her bedroom. Old shit from the early 2000s: *Final Destination, Elf, Scary Movie, Love and Basketball,* and *300.* We binge watch *Scandal* and a bunch of new shows on Netflix.

We are lying on her bed when Natice crawls up underneath my arm and kisses my cheek. She smiles at me. "I'm glad you're here."

"Stop wanting me, Natice."

She laughs and elbows me.

"Owwwwww…" I smile, holding my tender side.

Natice is easy to like, and her affection, much like Mark's, feels good. It's something, before Jenny's death, I could never get enough of. A kiss or a hug or to be told, "I love you." I was like a bottomless pit for affection and love. Since Jenny's death, I've been unable to accept it. *Until maybe now.*

When we aren't watching movies, or when I'm not fast asleep thanks to the Vicodin, Natice entertains me with stories of her and the girls, none of which ever includes the convenience store robbery. One day, feeling brave, I flat out ask the one question that will put an end to my stay in Cantor.

"Has Cracker or Lori ever killed anyone?" I try to sound casual about it.

"Why you asking me that, Ally?" Natice says harshly. "If they did, you think I'd tell you?"

My mouth hangs open, and I stutter for a second. Then I shrug as if it's no big deal. "They carry around guns. Sooner or later they go off, right?" I purposely look as far away from her dresser as possible, hoping Natice follows my stare and doesn't notice my iPhone recording our conversation.

"It's none of your damn business." Natice kicks at the bedspread to flatten out a wrinkle.

It's the only uncomfortable moment between us. But I realize that Natice is not only protecting Lori and Cracker, she's also protecting me. She quickly changes the subject, and I'm at least grateful Natice doesn't hold grudges or stay angry long. She asks me about Mark and then about my family, wanting to know if I come from a normal home.

"What's normal?" I say.

"Shit. I don't know. But if there is a normal, I'd love to know what it feels like."

"Me too. But I get along great with my dad. My mother… I don't know, sometimes I wonder if she even likes me." I feel like shit because I know she doesn't like me. Right before Jenny's death, I overheard my mother tell a friend of hers that she couldn't stand the sight of me and that I was a bitch. They didn't know I was in the house when they were talking in the kitchen. I've always felt as though my mother hated me. No connection. Nothing. My mother hates me, and that's the truth.

"I'm sure your mom likes ya." Natice gives me a hug. "And if she doesn't, I do." She kisses the top of my head, and I almost cry.

"Thanks, Natty. I mean that." I dread having to go back to my empty motel room. Then, sensing Natice is more vulnerable or willing to open up, I ask, "How did you get over your mom dying?"

"I don't know. I think at first, I dealt with it by getting in all sorts of trouble. Then I guess I jus' accepted she was gone. I still talk to her. People probably think I'm crazy, but I don't give a shit. Though some days it's weird. There'll be a day I forget I had a mom. And that scares me. But I jus'… I don't know… what choice do I have, ya know?"

I nod, feeling sorry for both Natice and myself. But unlike Natice, I know for certain there will never be a day that I forget Jenny.

A few times, I wake up to find Natice studying while listening to music on her headphones. And when Natice isn't in the room and is off taking a shower or doing something downstairs, I take the opportunity to search her bedroom. If I can't get a confession out of her, my hope is that she keeps a diary or journal, and within its pages is something incriminating about Jenny's shooting. It wouldn't be odd or out of the ordinary for Natice to keep a journal. But so far, I haven't found anything.

What does happen, though, is that Natice and I grow closer as friends.

"You talked in your sleep last night," Natice says as I wake up beside her.

"I did. What I say?" I ask, nervous to hear the answer.

"I don't know. I couldn't understand you. Something 'bout going to the beach."

"I must've been dreaming."

"You think?" She shoots me a look then rises from the bed. "I'm gonna take a shower, and then I'll make breakfast. You want pancakes or eggs?"

"Pancakes."

"Cool. I make a mean chocolate chip." Natice smiles and leaves the room.

I wait until I hear the bathroom door close and the water running before I slip out of bed and pad over to Natice's desk. Lying on top is a research paper titled, *The Impact of Government Spending On Economic Growth.* I pull open the desk drawer and shuffle through the junk. I find random items but nothing of importance. Then I hear a creak at the door.

Standing in the doorway is a man whose large body fills the frame. His eyes are dark, bloodshot, and tired. Startled, I realize this must be Natice's stepfather.

"Hi. I'm a friend of Natice's." I take a step away from her desk.

He stares at me coldly. It's unnerving. Finally, without a word, he walks off.

By the time Natice is done with her shower and back in the room, she knows her stepfather is home. "Fuck, he wasn't supposed to get home until the end of the week." She changes into clothes.

"It's okay. I should go anyway. My grandmother called when you were in the shower. I need to get back to help her out."

"You can't stay?"

"I'd love to, but I have to go." And I would stay. I'd never leave her house if her stepfather weren't home. I'm uncomfortable being in the house with him, especially with the way he was looking at me. "Thanks for bandaging me up."

"No problem, Ally."

As I walk out the door, I get an overwhelming sense that Natice is also afraid to be home alone with her stepfather.

CHAPTER 40

"HURTS LIKE HELL, DOESN'T IT?" Lori digs a small, razor-like instrument into my skin. I am sitting in her kitchen, surrounded by the girls.

"Not as much as my ass-kicking," I say.

She digs the needle in deeper.

A minute later, Mark enters the kitchen without seeing me and goes straight for the refrigerator.

Natice slaps his ass. "What up, Romeo?"

He searches for something inside. "Don't you all have a home?"

Ronnie steps next to him. "Nope. We're moving in. Cracker's gonna share your bed with you."

"I think that spot's already taken," Natice says.

Mark turns and finally sees me. He watches his sister tattoo my skin, and I know he is disappointed. I think back to the last text I got from him: *Is it true?* I knew without asking he wanted to know if I got jumped in.

I wrote back: *Yes*.

I hadn't heard from Mark since, but it doesn't surprise me. He obviously meant what he said the night we watched *Rocky* together, when he told me he could never date a girl who was part of Lori's gang. "It's a rule of mine," he'd said. I broke his rule, and it's either his pride that has kept him from calling me—or maybe it's how he protects himself.

"Come on, Romeo. Have a drink with us," Natice says.

"No, thanks." Mark slams the refrigerator door closed and walks out of the kitchen without a word to me.

"What'd you do to him, Ally?" Natice asks.

"Nothing," I say, but I'm just as disappointed as Mark. I was hoping to use him against his sister. And I did like him. It feels weird to be ignored. But I don't fault Mark. I made a choice, and there was no way I wasn't going to join Lori's gang, with or without his dating me.

Lori finishes. "What do you think?"

I stare down at my right hand. On it is a small black diamond tattoo. It's reddened around the sides.

I smile and instantly forget about Mark. "I like it."

Ronnie dances in front of me. "Go, Cheerleader! Go, Cheerleader! Go, Cheerleader!"

I stand, and each one of them hugs me. Lori, then Ronnie, and Cracker, who barely touches me.

Natice slaps a wet kiss on my cheek.

"Ahhhhh." I laugh.

Lori hands everyone a beer, and we drink. "Welcome to the family!"

If anyone had told me that one day I would become a member of this gang or that I would become friends with my sister's killers, I would've thought they were crazier than I am. But it happened. I've become friends with these girls.

"A'right, Cheerleader!" Ronnie yells, making the rolls on her stomach move in rhythm to her repeating, "Go, Cheerleader. Go, Cheerleader!"

We bust up.

I genuinely like Ronnie. I think if she had gone to my high school, we would've been friends. She's funny and childlike and innocent and silly. And I love her giant laugh. In some ways, she reminds me of Jenny. She's always happy. A bit unpredictable, which makes me nervous, but overall, I dig her.

"You need to go on a diet!" Cracker tells her.

"Shut up, Cracker!" Ronnie pushes her away.

Cracker laughs.

I still fantasize about Cracker losing that game of Russian roulette. In the time I've spent with her, she is only ever happy when she's being spiteful. It brings her extreme pleasure to see someone else hurt or miserable like herself. The thing that is most difficult about being around Cracker and Lori is acting as though I like them when I hate their guts. I suppose with Lori, her sadistic nature is a product of her childhood. As I watch her enjoy herself, I can't help thinking about what Natice shared with me when

I stayed at her house. Some of the stories were difficult to hear—Lori's mother prostituting Lori for drugs when she was barely twelve, or her being repeatedly raped by one of the mother's boyfriends until Lori finally stabbed him with a knife when he was passed out drunk. It makes sense that Mark is much different from Lori. He wasn't subjected to most of what she endured as a child. But regardless of Lori's awful childhood, it doesn't make me any less determined to see her punished for my sister's murder.

"Black Diamonds are forever!" Lori raises her forty-ounce bottle of beer.

I force a smile and tap my bottle against hers. "Legit."

"That's right!" Natice joins.

A few hours later, we leave Lori's house, fully wasted. Natice happily clings to me.

"Ally, what up!" She grins at me before hopping into the backseat of the Olds with Ronnie and Cracker. I wish Natice would ride shotgun, but of course, that seat's always reserved for Lori. It's reassuring that Natice at least refuses to carry a gun. Both she and Ronnie have repeatedly made comments to Lori and Cracker to keep their guns at home, which makes me wonder where exactly they hide them.

"Cheerleader, how you feeling?" Lori asks.

"I'm feelin' sexy," I say, causing Lori to smile.

"Yo, Fathead, raise that shit!" Natice says to me from the backseat, laughing.

"Someone's in a good mood." Lori turns around.

"Damn straight!" Natice answers.

I think my joining the gang has made Natice happier—that or the cocaine she snorted at Lori's.

I raise the volume and aimlessly drive us around Cantor as the Pussycat Dolls' "Don't Cha" blasts from the speakers.

"I haven't heard this song in years! Damn, it brings me back!" Natice says as she and Ronnie sing along.

Ronnie shakes her boobs when the song comes to an end. We all crack up. Ronnie's either shaking her boobs, ass, or stomach. She has a special gift of making her body parts move in ways that no one else can imitate.

"I tell you all about that boy in my history class?" Natice says.

"You ain't hooked up with him yet?" Lori asks.

"Shit, girl. That boy is shy. And he goes to church every Sunday. But I don't care. I'm gonna find out where he goes, and I'm gonna be sittin' in the front pew, honey!"

"Amen to that!" Ronnie adds.

"Yo, Natty, what I gotta do to get into community?" Cracker stuffs a handful of Cracker Jacks into her mouth. "I was thinkin' of maybe gettin' a degree like you. Learn how to run my own business or something."

"Community would never take you, Cracker," Lori says.

"How do you know?" Cracker shoots back.

"Because you didn't even graduate! Shit, you need to get your GED. Then you gotta take the SAT."

"What's an SAT?" Cracker asks.

"A test you can't pass, dummy!" Ronnie says.

"You don't need it for community. You just have to apply," I say.

Cracker thinks about it. "Yeah. All right. So Natty, what you get on that test?"

"My girl got over an eighteen hundred on her SAT!" Lori high-fives Natice.

"You cheat?" Ronnie asks.

"No! I got skills," Natice says.

"How could someone get an eighteen hundred on a test?" Cracker asks, confused.

"It ain't like a normal test, Cracker. It's different parts of one big test. Math. Reading. Writing. And they all add up to twenty-four hundred," Ronnie explains.

"How the hell can a test add up to two thousand and four hundred? That don't make sense. Why don't it just add up to a hundred?" Cracker literally scratches her head.

"Forget it, Cracker. Just go into the army or something," Lori says.

"Yeah. Go be all you can be!" Natice jokes.

We laugh, and Cracker's face burns red with embarrassment. She flips us the middle finger. "Why don't you all sit on this and be all you can fuckin' be?"

I'm still laughing when Lori yells, "Ally, pull in here!"

I look up and see that she is pointing to the store where Jenny was shot and killed. My smile vanishes, and I feel sick to my stomach. I hadn't even noticed my surroundings until that moment. I see Cantor High School East on the right.

I turn off the road and park in front of the store.

"Man, I hate this place," Ronnie says as the car goes silent.

I stare at the glass door wishing I were dead. It triggers a wave of intense sadness that I have to fight back to keep from crying. Everything looks exactly the same as it did on the night Jenny died. In all the time I have been in Cantor, I haven't once driven past this store. I couldn't bring myself to do it. I was too afraid. And now, here I am with the girls responsible for her death.

"Natty, you want anything?" Lori asks.

"Nah."

Lori and Cracker get out.

"Cracker, get me some Slim Jims!" Ronnie yells.

"Get 'em yourself, fat-ass. I ain't your bitch."

"You suck, Cracker. You know that?" Ronnie hops out of the car. She grabs Cracker from behind, and the two playfully fight as they enter the store having a great time.

My eyes grow wet, and the time passes slowly and painfully. I hear a familiar sound. I look in the rearview mirror and see Natice wiping white powder from her nose.

"Want some?" she holds up a small vial.

I shake my head no. "Why does Ronnie hate this place?"

Natice shrugs. "There was a robbery earlier in the year. A girl died. The store just sucks."

"What happened?"

"She was shot."

"Somebody you knew?"

"No." Natice glances out the window, sad.

Suddenly, Lori, Cracker, and Ronnie emerge from the store. Seconds later, they're back in the car.

"Let's hit Pop's!" Lori slides a cigarette in her mouth and sets it ablaze.

I force back the tears and speed out of the parking lot. My hatred of Lori grows to epidemic proportions. I want her dead. I want to rip that lighter out of her hand and set her on fire. I want to watch her scream. I want her to feel unbearable pain. I no longer want to be in the car with any of them, including Natice. If I had a gun in my hand right now, I'd use it.

We cruise past Tray's house on the way to the pizzeria, and I am still spinning with fury and grief, barely keeping it together, when Ronnie yells, "Oh snap! This fat-ass bitch is crazy!"

I look out the window and see Tonya, the purple-bandana-wearing girl from the Locust Park gang, straddling Vince's legs as he leans up against his Mercedes. Surrounding Tonya and Vince are the other girls from Tonya's gang.

"Oh fuck," Natice says.

"That lyin' mothafucker! Ally, stop the fuckin' car!" Lori demands.

I hit the brakes, and before the car even comes to a complete stop, Lori, Cracker, Ronnie, and Natice jump out.

Vince sees Lori heading his way and promptly pushes Tonya away from his crotch.

"Yo, Tonya!" Ronnie shouts.

Tonya turns, and Ronnie throws the forty-ounce bottle she is holding right in Tonya's face. It lands with a gnarly thud, sending Tonya to eat the asphalt. Two of Tonya's girls double-team Ronnie, who manages to get one good punch in before she is pummeled to the ground by their fists. Cracker and Natice run to help, pulling the girls off Ronnie and landing a stream of punches. Cracker gets clawed in the face by one girl and then turns into a beast, punching the girl in her head, throat, neck, anywhere her fists will land. Lori grabs another Locust Park girl from behind and slams her to the ground. A switchblade falls from the girl's hand, and Lori kicks her in the face.

Vince, Tray, and two other buddies holler and crack jokes, while one of Tonya's girls and another guy help Tonya to sit up. Blood runs down her face, and she looks stunned and disoriented. In her hand, she clutches her purple bandana.

Why did Jenny have to die? And why did one of these girls have to kill her? Anger boils inside me. Tears roll down my face. Unable to take another second of the pain, I throw open the car door and step onto the street. I stalk one of Tonya's girls from behind, and with my forearm leading the way, I level her. I put my knee against her chest and pin her to the ground as my fist hammers away on her face in a homicidal rage. I punch her again and again and again.

"Ally! Ally!" Natice yanks me off the girl, whose face, along with my fist, is now covered in blood. "Let's go!"

I stand over the girl's body, breathing heavily, wondering if she is even alive, until I see her take in a breath and choke on blood.

"Now!" Natice shoves me into the backseat of the Olds, which appears next to us. Ronnie is behind the wheel and speeds away as soon as Natice slams the door.

"Look what the bitch did to me!" Cracker examines her scratched-up face in the side-view mirror.

"Ronnie!" Natice yells. "What the hell?"

"Hey, I can't help it. I got good aim."

"From two fuckin' feet away? How could you miss?" Cracker says.

Then all at once, Ronnie, Lori, and Cracker bust up laughing.

"Shit, y'all crazy!" Natice says, smiling. She looks over at me. "Damn girl, I thought you were gonna kill her." Her smile vanishes.

I arrive in my motel room and go straight to the bathroom. I click on the light and wash the girl's dried blood off my throbbing and swollen hand. I'm trembling so badly I can't stop. Little bursts of air pass my quivering lips. A choked sound emerges from my throat. If it weren't for Natice, would I have beaten that girl to death? I look up in the mirror. *Who am I becoming?*

CHAPTER 41

RONNIE IS BRAIDING CRACKER'S HAIR when I arrive at the basketball courts in the park. It's been two days since I've seen the girls, and I haven't done much with myself other than sleep and ice my hand. The day after the fight, however, I did spend the entire morning calling all the hospitals in Cantor to see if any seventeen- or eighteen-year-old girls had been admitted to the emergency room as a result of a gang fight. Unfortunately, the hospitals were unable to give out any information, although one woman said, "Several young females have visited our emergency room this week."

"Where the hell you been, hooker?" Natice holds a shopping bag.

"Grandmother duty."

"What up, Cheerleader?" Ronnie says.

Lori tries to peek inside the shopping bag, but Natice quickly pulls it away. "Hold up. Not yet!"

They seem to have forgotten the fight with Tonya's girls, but I can still see it vividly—the blood, the fists, the bottle busting open Tonya's face.

"Jesus, show us what's in the bag already," Cracker says.

Natice swings the bag in front of us. "I got a little something for my girls. Figured we need to be lookin' good out here."

"Shit, I already look good." Ronnie sucks in her stomach and stands tall.

"Now, you're gonna look better." Natice pulls a handful of white tank tops out of the bag. They're numbered with a black diamond on the front of each.

"Come on. Don't be shy. One for everyone."

Cracker greedily grabs the Number 1 shirt. "Look at you, being all generous."

"Ally, what number you want?" Natice asks.

"Number 2," I say, selecting Jenny's number.

We clobber the other girls, and I have one of my best games. No one talks about the fight with Tonya and her girls, except for Cracker, who asks Ronnie how the scratch is healing on her face. As it turns out, Cracker is incredibly vain about her looks.

After the game, Lori is off talking with Vince while Cracker, Ronnie, and I sit around drinking water and watching Natice imitate my play. Natice moves her hips quickly from side to side then spins around. "Ally shook the shit outta that girl!"

I laugh at her impression of me. I feel my arm being nudged.

It's Cracker. "Yo, Cheerleader, how many points you have today?"

"I don't know… eighteen?"

Cracker takes the number in, aware that I scored more than she did. "Where'd you learn that move?"

"My dad taught me."

"For real?"

"Yeah. I can teach you if you want."

"A'right. One of these days, I'm gonna beat you on points."

"Well, hurry up, already."

"Shit. Whatever, Cheerleader." Cracker smiles and lets out a happy laugh.

"Cracker!" Lori yells, appearing from behind us.

Cracker turns, and Lori's open hand strikes her hard across the face.

The slap stuns all of us and knocks the bottle of water out of Cracker's hand.

"What the *fuck*!" Cracker holds her face.

"Are you fucking stupid or something? You made a fuckin' scrapbook?" Lori says, trying to keep her voice down.

"Yeah. So what?" Cracker responds.

"So what?" Lori steps into Cracker's face, her pencil-thin eyebrows ready to snap.

"Jesus, Cracker…" Natice says in disbelief.

"What, Natice? You got a problem?"

"I got a fuckin' problem! Who else you show it to?" Lori asks.

"No one. Just Tray's friend," Cracker says.

"Take your stupid ass home now and burn that shit!" Lori orders. "Ally, give her a ride!"

Cracker is silent for most of the ride, except for when I hear her say, "Lori hits me one more time... I swear to God." Meanwhile, I'm a ball of nerves, trying to think of an excuse to get inside her apartment. If Cracker has a scrapbook, I want to see exactly what's in it. It isn't until I park in front of her building that I turn to her and ask, "Mind if I use your bathroom?"

"I don't give a fuck." Cracker slams the door.

I follow Cracker up four flights of filthy stairs and down a long, dingy hallway. Crack vials and dirty syringes litter the ground. The walls are caked in grime, snot, and God knows what else. Cracker doesn't say a word, and once again, I get that sinking feel of being on a rollercoaster. Steadily climbing up to the top, I wonder—will Cracker even show me the scrapbook?

Finally, we reach the end of the hall, and Cracker unlocks the door to her apartment and pushes her way in. I trail from behind and see the two young faces I saw staring out the window when I first stalked Cracker's apartment: a younger brother and sister. They sit on a worn couch watching TV and drinking soda. Behind them is a bedsheet used as a curtain. We cross in front of the TV, and Cracker slams a button, sending the TV into darkness.

"Hey!" her brother yells.

"Shut the fuck up," Cracker tells him.

I step out of her brother's way as he moves off the couch and turns the TV back on. At least Cracker treats her family the same as she treats me. A moment later, we pass a kitchen where her mother stands, smoking a cigarette and cursing up a storm while she hurls dishes into the sink. Cracker ignores her and leads me down a narrow carpeted hallway. She stops at a closed bedroom door, pulls a key from her pocket, and unlocks a padlock clamped and hinged to the frame.

"Bathroom's down there." Cracker points to the end of the hall. She inserts the key and clicks open the padlock.

I keep walking, and the smell of urine grows stronger as I reach the bathroom. I enter and almost puke. The toilet bowl is stained with piss and shit, and looks like it has never been cleaned. My sneakers stick to the floor, and strands of long red hair clog the rusted sink. I cover my nose, wait a few torturous minutes, flush the toilet with my foot, and quickly get out of there.

As I approach Cracker's bedroom, I hear her mother's voice becoming louder. I reach the doorway, uncertain what to do.

Her mother stands in the middle of the room, yelling at Cracker while holding her lit cigarette in one hand and a can of Budweiser in the other. "I ain't your fucking maid! You hear me? You left the kitchen a fuckin' mess!" She turns and notices me standing in the doorway. "Who's this?"

"A fucking friend!" Cracker says, having just pulled the scrapbook from under her bed.

I say nothing and stand there, wishing I were invisible.

"Are you done?" Cracker says to her mother.

Her mother examines Cracker in her basketball clothes and makes a disgusted face. "Is that all you're gonna do? Play basketball all day? My daughter's a fucking dyke."

"Is all you're gonna do is drink? My mother's a fucking drunk," Cracker says.

Her mother descends on Cracker like a vulture and yanks a fistful of Cracker's hair. "Who the fuck you think you're talkin' to, huh?"

The scrapbook drops onto the floor, and Cracker rises with a closed fist, hatefully eyeballing her mother.

"Go ahead. Do it. I'll call the cops and have your ass thrown in jail!"

Cracker stands there for a few more seconds, then she abruptly bends down and collects a handful of loose photographs that have fallen out of the scrapbook.

"I want you out of my house! Today!" Cracker's mother steps on one of the photographs.

"Fine!" Cracker shouts with a breaking voice.

"See if one of your goddamn friends takes you in!" Her mother staggers past me in a haze of booze.

Cracker keeps her head down as she collects the scrapbook. She's crying, and I want to say something, but what can I say? I hate Cracker's mother even more than I hate Cracker.

Cracker looks up and yells, "Fucking cunt!" She sits down on the bed and fixes the scrapbook as if it is a prized possession.

I suddenly feel sorry for Cracker. My mother hasn't always been the kindest to me with her words, but she's never hit me or been this cruel. And even when her words were unkind, I always had my father to overdo the affection. Cracker has nobody. Even her best friend hits her.

"This one's you," Cracker says with a smirk.

She holds open the scrapbook, showing me a newspaper article. It's from the ATM robbery, the one where Cracker shoved the gun in the old woman's face.

"Can I see it?" I sit down next to her.

Cracker hands the book over to me. She is proud of it. I purposely flip the pages backward and come across various articles on crimes. An auto theft at a 7-Eleven store,

a home robbery, another ATM holdup. Some articles are taken from newspapers. Others are printed out from the Internet. Some crimes I participated in. Others, I didn't. I turn another page and another then stop. My stomach sinks. I feel as if I have been punched breathless.

Teenager Dies in Convenience Store Robbery. "Why do you have this one?" I watch Cracker closely.

She stares at the newspaper headline then looks at me. I see a hint of hesitation in her eyes, as if something in her gut is telling her not to answer that question. I know I am right when she takes the book from my hands. "You used the bathroom. Now you can go."

I stand to leave. "Let me know when you want to get together. I'll show you that move."

"Yeah, right," Cracker says suspiciously.

I pretend not to notice her tone or her look. "See ya later." I walk out.

An hour later, I'm sitting on my motel bed looking over the case folder when Natice calls. "What's up?"

"Cracker almost burned down her apartment."

"How?"

"Dumb ass put the scrapbook in the tub, set it on fire, and blew the whole damn shower curtain up along with it."

"Shit..." I was hoping Cracker didn't destroy the scrapbook and that it could somehow be used as evidence linking her to my sister's murder. "What happened?"

"Dumb ass was at least smart enough to turn on the water and put out the fire. But her mom kicked her out. She's staying at Lori's."

CHAPTER 42

I KEEP THINKING ABOUT THE SCRAPBOOK and the article on my sister's death. Seeing it in Cracker's hands only confirms she had something to do with Jenny's murder. Why else keep that article? If all the other articles in the book are from crimes Cracker participated in, surely she participated in that store robbery. This, along with watching her mother verbally and physically abuse Cracker, has made me want to take a trip home to visit my dad. The only problem with returning home before my plan is complete is my Jeep. *How am I going to show up at home without it?*

This is on my mind as I stand behind the counter at the pizzeria, watching the time slowly pass. I start to wonder if my Jeep is still for sale or if it's been sold. I pull out my Cantor iPhone and do a quick Internet search for Tom's Used Car Lot. Not finding my Jeep online, I decide to call. The phone rings several times before I hear Tom's friendly voice.

"Tom's Used Car Lot."

"Hi, do you have any SUVs or Jeeps for sale?"

"I don't have any SUVs, but I do have one soft-top Jeep."

"What color?"

"Blue. It's in great shape. Almost brand new. Why don't you come in and take it for a test drive? I'm pretty sure you'll love it."

"How much is it?"

"Eight thousand nine hundred and ninety-five, but I can work with you."

It's almost four thousand dollars more than what he paid me for it, and I don't have the money to buy it back, even with the Olds as a trade-in. I tell Tom I only have five thousand dollars to spend on a car, and when he tells me he can't go that low, I thank him for his time and hang up. *I could always tell my dad my Jeep was stolen. Or I could steal it back.* I grow excited thinking about this idea. I never gave Tom my spare key. So if I wanted to steal my Jeep, it wouldn't be too difficult.

I am seriously considering doing this when the front door opens, and Mark walks in. Next to him is the blonde I had seen him with.

"I'll meet you in there," Mark tells her. The girl gives me a glance then heads to the back room, leaving Mark and me alone. I haven't seen him since the day I sat in his kitchen while Lori inked my skin. I'm still not used to having the black diamond on my hand. I feel like an imposter. But an imposter as my old self or new, I'm not quite sure.

"How are you?"

"Great. Can I get three slices and two Cokes?" Mark says coldly.

"Sure. No problem."

I toss the slices into the oven and stand at the counter, waiting for the pizza to be ready. Neither Mark nor I say a word. I straighten out the napkin holder, giving myself something to do, while Mark swipes at his gigantic phone, laughing at something he reads on screen, as if I'm not even in the room. Being ghosted right now only reconfirms one thing: there's no way I'm getting Mark to tell me the truth about where Lori was on the night of my sister's murder.

A moment later, I pull the slices out of the oven and return to the counter with the Cokes and pizza on a tray.

"Twelve dollars."

Mark hands me the exact change.

"I guess you're back with your girlfriend?"

"Guess so." Mark walks off with the tray.

"Why do you think we call him Romeo?" Natice appears next to me.

I'm more pissed than upset but not for reasons Natice thinks. "What are you doing later?"

"Nothing. Why?"

"I need a favor."

"What?" Natice leans against the counter and studies me.

"I want you to teach me how to hot-wire a car."

Natice pops off the counter. "Not a problem." She breaks out her phone to make it happen.

It's after two a.m. when Natice and I arrive at a chop shop in an abandoned industrial section of Cantor.

"You can use that one over there." Tray points to a Honda Accord. Surrounding it are other stolen cars in various stages of being dismantled. The parts will be sold for more money than the cars are actually worth. Tray runs the shop for Vince.

"Thanks, cuz," Natice says. "C'mon, Ally."

Natice grabs a hammer and wire cutters off a wall and leads me to the Accord. We climb inside, and she goes right to work. "You jus' break the column. It's plastic." Natice demonstrates with ease as she uses the hammer to pull apart the dash. It cracks loudly and snaps apart.

"Yo, easy on that shit! It's clean," Tray says.

"Shut up, Tray. Go away!" Natice tells him. She reaches under the dash and pulls out a bundle of colored wires. She strips four down to about an inch of metal then pulls aside two reds. "The battery wires are always red. Twist 'em together like this, then tie the ignition wire to 'em." She connects a brown wire to the twisted red wires, and the dash lights and radio come alive, startling me. Natice laughs. "That turns the shit on. Then jus' spark it." Natice barely touches the end of a yellow wire—the starter—to the battery wires, and the car roars to life. She pumps the gas pedal, revving the engine, causing it to grow louder. "You're good to go." Tray looks over at us, shakes his head, then returns to what he is doing.

"Pull the ignition wire off the reds." Natice separates the brown wire, keeping the reds still attached, and the engine dies. "That'll kill it."

"Cool," I tap my feet on the floorboard, excited. "Thanks for the lesson."

"Glad my skills can be of service," Natice says with a smile. "Just make sure you crack the steering wheel hard. Otherwise, you won't be able to turn the damn thing. And stay away from new cars, anything that uses a transponder key to start the engine. Forget it. That shit's advanced. You'll never figure it out."

She grabs the radio knob and searches for a song she likes. I watch Natice and wonder why she risks going to prison by stealing cars, especially since she's in college and has a job.

"Can I ask you something?"

"Sure. What?"

"Why do you do this, steal cars and rob houses?"

"It's the fastest way to make money. And besides, I've been doing it for so long, I don't know how not to do it."

"Yeah, but you're smart. You're in college. You can get financial aid. Aren't you afraid you'll wind up in an orange jumpsuit?"

"If I tell you something, you promise to keep it to yourself? Not tell the others?"

"Sure."

"I applied to a four-year college in California."

"That's awesome. Nice job!"

Natice smiles. "Yeah. I'm waiting to hear back. I jus' feel like I'm abandoning the girls. You know?"

"I hope you get in, Natice. I really do."

"Yeah, me too."

I hold up my hand and give Natice a high-five. I'm happy for her, but if Natice feels guilty about leaving Lori, Cracker, and Ronnie behind, then I doubt I will ever get her to tell me anything that convicts them of my sister's murder.

We're about to step out of the car when the Pussycat Dolls' "Don't Cha" comes on the radio. "Hell yeah, girl!" Natice says and starts singing. "Come on, Ally. Sing with me."

She raises the volume, and Natice and I sing along. When it ends, she looks over at me and smiles. "You have the worst voice!"

"Please. My voice is bad ass," I say, well aware of how truly awful it is.

"Girrrrl, it's jus' bad."

We share a laugh, and Natice pulls the red wires apart, silencing the radio.

I grab the door handle, ready to leave the car, and a noisy silver truck pulls into the garage. A white guy with a shaved head and tattooed arms steps out from behind the wheel. He's greeted by Tray.

"What up, dog?"

"How you doin', man?" the bald guy says.

They bump fists, and I stare at the bald man, knowing I have seen him someplace before.

"Fucking criminal," Natice says.

"What do you mean?" I ask.

"He's a cop."

I know exactly where I've seen him—*Fuck!* He's the plainclothes officer who poked his head inside Detective Thoms's office the last time I was there with my parents.

"What's he doing here?"

"He's fuckin' dirty." Natice stares hatefully at him. "That's how Vince keeps himself from getting busted. He's got a cop on his payroll."

"He looks like a real sweet guy," I say, praying the dirty cop doesn't notice me. "What's his name?"

"Rawlings."

It hits me. That's what Thoms called him. *"Give me ten, Rawlings."*

"He's a total prick. C'mon, let's go." Natice steps out of the car. But I don't dare follow after her—mainly because Rawlings, the dirty cop, is standing right in front of the exit as he carries on a conversation with Tray. There's no way I can get out of the garage without walking past him. I sit there, trying to figure out an escape, when Natice stops to talk to Tray, interrupting his conversation with Rawlings.

Rawlings stands there idly, looking bored, then sparks up a cigarette and turns so that his back is facing me. I figure this is my chance, and I open the door and step out of the car. I hurry toward the exit, hoping this scumbag dirty cop doesn't turn around—but of course that's exactly what he does. He faces me, exhaling a cloud of smoke as our eyes meet. I bring a hand to my face, coughing into it as if I have something stuck in my throat. As I walk past, I feel Rawlings's eyes burning a hole in my back.

"Ally, hold up!" Natice yells after me.

I walk faster, practically running to get to the Olds. I know Rawlings is staring after me—recognizing me.

I hop inside the Olds and lock the door. I start the car and hit the gas, but the engine stalls.

"Fuck!" I turn the key again and again. Finally, the engine roars to life just as the passenger door flies open.

"Damn, girl. You gonna wait for me?"

"What? Yeah..." I say, rattled. I look back up, and Rawlings is walking off with Tray.

"Someone's in a hurry to get home." Natice climbs inside the car.

"You could say that." I hit the gas pedal and get the hell out of there, fast.

CHAPTER 43

I'M SPENT BY THE TIME I return to my motel room, but I don't want to wait another second or day to go home, so I call a cab with my Cantor cell phone, throw a bunch of clothes in a duffel bag, and in less than ten minutes, a cab is waiting outside my door.

"Can you drop me off here?" I ask the cab driver, pointing to a 7-Eleven store less than a mile from Tom's Used Car Lot. I pay with cash and walk the rest of the distance. I've only taken about ten steps when I break into a jog, fearing that between now and the time that I called Tom, he has already sold my Jeep, but as I approach the lot, I come to a complete stop, and my lips curl into a smile at the sight of my beautiful blue Jeep facing the highway with an $8,995 price tag taped to the inside of the windshield.

A sense of relief washes over me, like seeing an A marked on a test when you were expecting to fail. "Thank God." I unlock the driver's-side door with my spare key and fall in love with my Jeep all over again. I climb behind the wheel, start the ignition, hit the gas pedal, hop over the curb, and in less than thirty seconds, I steal back my Jeep without having to hot-wire it.

When I arrive in Middletown, it's a little before seven in the morning—too early to go home, so I drive down to Sandy Hook Beach, twenty minutes past my parents' house and the first stop along the Jersey Shore. I park at the very last section, where Jenny used to love to come, by the Seagull's Nest restaurant, overlooking the ocean. I take off my sneakers and step out onto the sand, passing the restaurant on my left and walking down toward the shoreline. I'm grateful nobody else is here, except for a lone jogger off in the distance. I sit with my feet touching the water and listen to the waves crash. A sense of calm washes over me. But then my feelings of missing Jenny resurface, and I begin to sob.

I leave the beach about an hour later, and my father is pushing a lawn mower across the grass when I pull into the driveway and park in front of the basketball pole. My father shuts the mower and walks toward me, smiling.

"What'd you do to your hair?" he says affectionately.

"I wanted a change."

His smile widens, and he gives me a great big hug. "I missed you, kiddo." He kisses the top of my head.

"I missed you, too." I tighten my grip on him, smelling his cologne. It's like being wrapped in a warm blanket.

"C'mon, I'll make you some breakfast." He gives me another kiss, wraps his arm around me, and leads me into the house.

"Where's Duke? I can't wait to kiss his big, furry head."

"In the backyard. He kept trying to bite the lawn mower. He'll be excited to see you." He pushes open the front door.

It's difficult when I first enter the house, but then I knew it would be. I'm immediately greeted by the family photographs lining the foyer walls. In each one, Jenny looks happy and alive. I want to die, knowing I will never see my sister again, but I keep walking, following my dad into the kitchen.

And there he is—Duke's handsome face panting at me from behind the screen door. He barks, and his tail goes nuts. My heart fills with joy seeing his big dopey face. As soon as I open the door, he's all over me, jumping and barking, tail thrashing.

"I missed you!" I wrestle the big dopey bastard to the ground, and his paw almost catches me in the face. "How's my big, handsome boy? Huh? I missed you sooooo much." I give his face several kisses before snuggling into his soft, furry body. I hold onto him for dear life.

"You want eggs? Bacon? Toast?" my dad asks, happy to have me home.

"Sure." I stay seated on the floor, my hand stroking Duke from head to tail. I glance around the kitchen, barely recognizing the toaster oven or the refrigerator, and is that a new coffee machine, or has it always been there? Everything looks so foreign to me now, especially compared to where I've been.

My father opens the refrigerator, pulls out a bunch of food, and goes to work making me breakfast. "So tell me everything. How's Natalie?"

"She's good."

"Did she bleach her hair too?"

I think about Natice's photograph when she was younger. I smile. "No, just me, Dad."

"And how's your jump shot?"

"Solid. It's tight."

"Tight, huh? Good. So what else did they teach you at camp?"

Armed robbery. Car thefts. Break-ins. "A few things."

My dad finishes at the stove and places a dish of warm eggs and bacon down on the table. I rise from the floor, and Duke follows me to my chair.

My dad ruffles my short blond hair. "Eat up, kiddo. You're looking a little skinny."

It's true. I've lost at least five or seven pounds since I left.

My father sits down beside me with his own plate of food. Duke takes his normal standing position between us, and I toss him a piece of bacon that he snatches from the air, not even waiting for it to be swallowed before he's begging for more. A warm sensation fills my body. It's been so long since I ate breakfast like this, between Dad and Duke. I had almost forgotten how happy it makes me. I only wish Jenny were with us. I look up and notice the basketball schedule has been removed from the refrigerator door.

"So when's Natalie's birthday?" Dad asks, already aware that I plan on returning to Ocean City for her fictitious birthday party.

"Next weekend. It'll be on the beach."

"Good. Well, I'm glad you're having fun." Dad smiles, looking especially handsome. His face is clean-shaven, and his hair is recently cut. "We should buy Natalie's parents a gift for letting you stay there. Make sure you give me their address before you leave. Okay?"

How am I going to give him an address? I shrug nonchalantly and say, "How about a gift certificate? There's a really nice restaurant they always go to. I can pick one up for them. I know they'd like it."

"Sure. Just let me know. You plan on seeing Lea while you're home?"

I hesitate. "I don't know." I suddenly feel bad. I've totally ghosted her.

"Well, you don't have to if you don't want to."

202

"Yeah, I don't think I will," I say, softly. Then I swallow a bite of my eggs and watch my dad closely. "So what's going on with you?"

"I'm okay," he says with confidence. "I started playing poker with some guys at the office."

"Really?" I tilt back in my seat. My father hasn't done anything outside the office since Jenny's death, other than to go to the gym and keep a watchful eye on my mother.

"Yup." He nods proudly.

"How bad are you?"

He laughs. "I only lost a hundred dollars the other night. Probably why they invited me into the game."

Dad and I share a smile, and for a moment, I forget I have a dead sister.

"What happened to your hand?" my father asks, noticing the Band-Aid covering my black diamond tattoo.

"Oh, Natalie's cat scratched me."

I hear footsteps, and a moment later, my mother enters the kitchen. She sees me sitting at the table and looks surprised even though she knew I was coming home.

"Hi, Mom." I rise to hug her.

"What did you do to your hair?" She crinkles her nose and eyebrows. And in a matter of seconds, the whole energy in the room changes.

"I jus' needed a change."

We hug briefly, and I sit back down next to my father. I'm not the only one who's lost weight. My mother looks emaciated.

"So who's this new friend? Tell me about her," my mom says, making an effort at conversation.

"A girl I met at camp. She's really cool."

"Camp," my mother comments bitterly. "You're not even going to college, but you went away to basketball camp."

"It's fine, Mary." My father warns my mother with a look not to start any trouble.

But of course my mother ignores the look. "I called the governor's office. They still won't get involved in your sister's case. They sent me a letter saying it's being thoroughly handled by the local authorities. What they mean to say is thoroughly mishandled."

"Maybe something will turn up."

203

"Like what? What's going to turn up, Alex?"

"I don't know. A confession. The gun. You never know."

My mother looks at me as if I'm stupid. "A confession? Really, Alex?" She shakes her head and continues her tirade. "They're the ones to blame, letting Cantor get the way it is. It has one of the worst crime rates in New Jersey. I—"

"Mary?" my father interrupts.

"What?"

"Can we just enjoy breakfast with our daughter?"

"I stopped enjoying breakfast eight months ago, John." My mother walks out of the room, leaving Dad and me upset.

"I'm sorry, Alex. She's still…" My father can't finish his words. I can tell this is all wearing on him. I wonder if my father only stays with my mother because of me.

"It's okay."

My father forces a smile. "I love you, kiddo."

"Love you too, Dad."

He winks and ruffles my hair. "I like it. It looks good."

"Thanks." I smile back, and we force ourselves to finish eating.

After breakfast, my father returns to mowing the lawn, and I visit Jenny's bedroom. I pick up a framed photograph of the two of us on her dresser. "I miss you, Jenny." I stare at her face.

A moment later, I hear a creak by the door. I turn and see my mother watching me from the hall. She walks silently away.

After taking a much-needed nap, I meet up with Dr. Evans at a nearby Starbucks. He's sitting at a table when I arrive, and just like my father, Dr. Evans greets me with an enthusiastic smile and a warm hug. He's wearing shorts and a white T-shirt.

"You cut your hair?"

"Yeah."

"It looks good. I like it."

"Thanks."

"What is it?" he asks.

"It's so weird seeing you in a T-shirt. I don't know. I'm not used to it."

"My summer attire," he says proudly.

We share a smile, and I'm instantly glad I made time to meet with him.

Same as with my father, there's a sense of warmth being around Dr. Evans. But I don't have to pretend to be happy when I'm not. Or lie about my feelings. I can just be myself—well mostly myself, with a few exceptions.

"So your dad told me you're staying in Ocean City for the summer?"

"Yeah, I met a girl at camp, and we hit it off."

"That's great. So how was camp?"

I tell Dr. Evans camp was brutal. Brutal, in the sense that it was a lot of running and drills. "But I loved the scrimmages, and Natalie and I were always on the same team, so that was cool." I make up stuff about Ocean City the way I had about Seattle. I also share with Dr. Evans that I've become close friends with all of Natalie's friends. "They've been helping me keep busy."

"And what about the nightmares? Have you had any while you've been away?"

I realize I haven't, which surprises me. "No."

"That's great." Dr. Evans glances down at my hand and sees the Band-Aid. "What happened?"

I press down on the Band-Aid, making sure it is firmly stuck in place. "Oh, Natice's cat scratched me." A second later I realize what I said and quickly correct myself. "I mean Natalie's cat."

CHAPTER 44

I STAY IN MIDDLETOWN ANOTHER THREE days with a nagging worry the police are going to show up at my parents' house and arrest me for the stolen Jeep parked in our driveway. But I'm probably safe since that used car lot is so far away. I push the thought from my head and try to relax. My father and I go to see two movies together, play a few games of tennis, and shoot basketballs. We have dinner one night with my mother, and it's difficult. She doesn't talk about Jenny or the governor's office, but she is depressed. I doubt any of the medications she's on are helping. I also notice her drinking has increased, as well as my father's. I don't call Lea or any of my other friends while I'm at home. Lea would just bug me to come out with her and then talk about herself the entire time. Instead, I spend most of my time lying on the couch, watching movies with Duke right beside me.

Oddly enough, I find myself missing Natice. Before I left Cantor, I sent her a text telling her I had to fly home to Seattle for a family emergency, but I haven't spoken to her since she showed me how to hot-wire a car.

I wait until my parents are asleep in their bedroom before I break out my Cantor phone. Duke is at the foot of my bed, eyes closed, sleeping, and I'm already hating myself, knowing I'll be leaving him again.

Yo, what up, sexy? I text.

Almost immediately, Natice texts back. *Where the hell you been? Girl, you don't call?*

Sorry, it's been cray cray, I write back.

So what happened? Natice asks.

My mom. Bit of a mental breakdown. It's half true. I add an emoji with a grinning face and smiling eyes.

Shit. Sorry girl. You okay?

Yeah, I'm fine. She's doing better now.

Cool, Natice writes. *You need anything, lemme know.*

Thx. I will.

Sooooo you coming back?? I sense that Natice is worried I may not.

Yeah def. I'll be back next week.

I receive a smiling-face emoji. It's followed by, *Pop has been on the rag all week!* That one is followed by an angry, red-faced emoji.

How's his breath? I write. I send it with a smiling pile of poo.

Natice stops texting and calls me. She sounds happy to hear my voice and fills me in on some of the drama that has been going on while I've been gone, mainly a few fights between guys and something about toilet paper being stolen from the bathroom. The biggest news, though, is that she finally hooked up with that boy in her class. "Girl, I felt like I was kissing a Saint Bernard. I swear I needed a towel to dry off my face."

We share a few more laughs before we get off the phone. "I'll see you soon."

When it comes time for me to say goodbye to my parents and return to Cantor, a five-hundred-pound bag of guilt weighs on my shoulders for leaving my father. I know how much he's loved having me home and that it's been good for him. But I remind myself why I'm returning to Cantor—to get the evidence to send Jenny's killers to prison.

As I say goodbye to my mother and look into her face, a sense of determination hardens like cement. The next time she sees me, I will have turned up something the police can use. I promise her that without saying a word.

CHAPTER 45

"How much do you think we can get for it?" I ask Natice, who stares at my blue Jeep in amazement.

"Girl, where'd the hell you steal this from?"

I smile. "I went convenience store shopping at a 7-Eleven."

A few hours later, Tray is counting out a roll of hundreds and placing them into the palm of my hand. In total, he gives me three thousand dollars. It's the second time I've received money for my Jeep. At least now, when I tell my parents my Jeep was stolen, it won't be a lie. I feel like shit for ripping off Tom, but I have a game plan, and I'm sticking to it. One day, I'll pay him back. I hand half the money to Natice.

"What are you doing?" Natice pushes away the money.

"Put it toward California."

"I didn't do shit for it. You need it."

"It's a gift. Besides, if the keys weren't in it, I would'a needed your hot-wiring lesson to fall back on."

Natice laughs. "A'right. If you're gonna put it that way... thanks, Ally." She happily takes the money.

"Now let's go shopping."

Hours later, we end up at Lori's house, drinking beer and enjoying the gifts Natice and I purchased with the money from my Jeep. Cracker is playing around with a digital video camera and recording Ronnie, who stuffs potato chips into her mouth.

"Lemme see." Ronnie turns the display on herself. "Damn I am fine." She wedges another chip into her mouth.

"Be honest. You all stole this shit." Lori opens a carton of cigarettes.

"Nope. We bought it," Natice tells her.

"K-Mart was having a sale," I say.

"Yeah. Blue Jeep special!" Natice jokes.

We are surrounded by spent beer bottles as Ronnie entertains us with random childhood stories. The entire time, she holds Chanel, the Styrofoam head from her beauty school class. Cracker is recording with the camera when Ronnie turns Chanel toward the lens.

"Say hi, Chanel! You're on camera, girl!"

"Gimme Chanel." Natice drunkenly applies red lipstick to her Styrofoam lips. "There you go, girl. You lookin' good!"

Everyone laughs.

"Let's play a game!" I say.

"We ain't playing no Russian roulette," Lori says.

"Damn straight," Natice comments.

"Nah. It's called 'I never.'"

"Boring-ass grade-school game," Cracker says, aiming the camera at me.

"Come on. It's fun. You say something you never did, and if you did it, you drink."

"A'right! A'right! I'll go first," Ronnie says. "I never wet my pants in fifth grade and then said I spilled 7Up on myself."

Natice drinks. "You low down. You know that?" No one else drinks, and Ronnie busts up laughing.

"Who says they spilled 7Up on their pants?" Lori smiles and looks happy.

"Shit, why not Diet Coke?" Ronnie jokes.

"I was traumatized, a'right! And there was a boy in the class that I liked. Thank you very much!"

"There's always a fucking boy," Cracker says.

"My turn. I never stole a car," I say.

"Wait, you just stole a Jeep. You can't be saying I never," Natice says.

"Whatever. New rules."

"New rules?" Natice scrunches up her face. "A'right. Whatever, Cheerleader."

Everyone drinks.

"I never stole from my mother," Cracker says.

Everyone drinks except Natice. "You all are rotten," Natice says.

Lori is next. "I got one, and all you bitches better be honest. I never, in seventh grade, puked in someone's bed and then covered that shit up with a sheet and let my ass crawl into it!"

No one drinks.

Finally, Ronnie lifts her beer and takes a sip, then promptly spits it out laughing.

"I knew it! I knew it was your stank ass!" Lori says.

Ronnie continues laughing. "Yo, that peach schnapps fucked me up!"

Natice playfully kicks Ronnie. "You nasty!"

"All right. My turn. My turn," Ronnie says, calming down. "I never stole a Mercedes Benz!"

Everyone drinks, except for me.

"I never got chased by the cops." Cracker smiles into the camera and takes a sip. The rest of us follow.

"I never killed anyone," I say.

It's followed by silence—then Cracker drinks. And so do I.

"Bullshit," Cracker says.

"Why would it be bullshit?" I respond.

"You killed someone?" Cracker aims the camera at me.

I meet her stare. "Yeah."

"So what happened?" Lori asks.

"Yeah, what happened?" Natice sounds surprised I never told her this.

"She played Russian roulette with them," Ronnie jokes.

They all laugh, except for Cracker.

"About eight months ago, I was driving home from a party. I went through a stop sign. Hit a guy. He lasted a week in the hospital. Then he died."

"Shit, that doesn't count," Cracker says.

"How the hell does that not count?" Natice asks.

"Fucking drunk driving?" Cracker shoots back.

"If I hadn't hit him with the car, he wouldn't have died," I say.

"So it was an accident!" Cracker says.

"She still killed a guy," Natice says.

"Don't be stupid, Cracker." Ronnie rolls her eyes.

"What's fucked up is that the guy had been drinking too. When they opened up his car, there were cans of beer all over the place. They never tested me for alcohol. They thought he caused the accident." I do my best to look remorseful.

Lori takes a sip of beer. "Shit. You're lucky. If it was me, they would'a arrested my ass without a test and with the empties in his car."

"Whatever. That still don't fuckin' count," Cracker says.

"So who'd you shoot?" I ask, aware the video camera is still recording. "Some old lady for her purse? A teenager for a stick of gum?"

"Who said I shot anyone?" Cracker asks.

"I see. You strangled them to death."

The girls laugh.

Cracker stares at me, camera in hand. "I noticed none of y'all drank." She looks around at the others.

"Shit, I didn't kill anyone." Ronnie takes a sip of her beer, seemingly out of thirst.

"So who was it?" I ask.

"Someone who got in my way." Cracker promptly shuts off the camera.

The room turns quiet, and something tells me Cracker knows I was trying to get a confession out of her. I see the familiar look of distrust surface in her eyes and fear any second, she is going to share this with the group, but instead she surprises me and says, "I never did an armed ATM robbery... on my own."

Everyone drinks, except for me.

"Who thinks it's time that Cheerleader does?" Cracker says.

I take a sip of my beer. "I do."

The last thing I want to do is attempt another armed robbery, but I also don't want Cracker any more suspicious of me then she already is—or Lori, for that matter. Maybe I pushed it too far with the "I never killed anyone" question. Or maybe I'm just feeling paranoid. But I did show up at Lori's house with a video recorder and then suggest we play that game.

"Look, Ally, if you all are doing this, I can't be a part of it," Natice tells me. "I jus' can't do guns."

"Let's go!" Lori emerges from the upstairs. In her hand, she holds a pair of Latex surgical gloves and her gun.

My anxiety level rises from a six to way past ten. *Last time, I got lucky and nobody got hurt. But what if I'm not lucky tonight?* "Natice, I got an idea." I crack my gum and quickly whisper it to her.

"You ready, Cheerleader?" Lori asks.

"Let's go," I say confidently.

"Natty, you in?"

Natice looks at me then turns to Lori. "I'm in."

"A'right! Natty's in!" Lori claps.

As we head out the door, I'm grateful for one thing: I now know that Lori stashes her gun upstairs, although I wonder exactly where, since the cops were unable to find it, if it is the same gun that was used in the store robbery. My guess: Lori keeps this one hidden somewhere in her mother's bedroom.

CHAPTER 46

WE MAKE A QUICK STOP at Ronnie's house before heading to the Turnpike. Forty minutes later, I am sitting in the backseat of the Olds with a nude nylon stocking covering my face and Lori's gun held in my latex-covered hand. We're someplace in South Jersey, staking out an ATM and waiting for victims.

I pull at the stocking. "Fuck, I can't breathe under here."

The girls laugh, including Natice. The nylon stocking belongs to Ronnie's mother. The woman has no clue her daughter's depleting her supply, and this time, Ronnie stole it from a drawer in her parents' bedroom while they slept, inches away from her.

"We got a winner!" Ronnie yells.

A black BMW pulls up to the ATM with a guy and a girl inside.

Lori shouts, "Go!"

My adrenaline kicks in as I jump out of the car and sprint toward the BMW.

As I get closer to the car, I see the girl and guy starting to fool around. The girl has just lowered her head into the guy's lap when I open the door and land in the backseat. They both jump. The girl screams as she sees the gun aimed at her.

"Please don't kill us!" the girl begs.

"*Shut up!* Shut the fuck up!" I scream.

"Please don't shoot," the guy says calmly, holding up his hands.

"Go to the ATM, and take out as much money as you can! She's gonna stay here with me until you come back."

"Brent, don't! Don't!" the girl cries.

"Shut up! I swear to God, *shut up!*" I aim the gun directly at her.

"Okay. It's cool. I'm going!" The boyfriend zips up his fly.

"Where's your phone?"

"Right there." He points to the console.

"Leave it. Come back with the money. And everything will be cool. Do you understand, Brent?"

"Yeah." He sounds scared and uncertain.

"Brent, no!" the girl screams.

"She'll be fine as long as you bring me the money. Now go!"

Brent looks at his girlfriend then stares at the gun in my hand, rethinking his decision to leave the car. He starts shaking his head no. "I can't do it. I'm not going."

I aim the gun at him. "Brent, you have five seconds to leave this car. Do you understand? I promise you. All I want is your money. I won't hurt her. I swear."

But he doesn't move. He remains in the front seat, and I worry that any second, Cracker will hop in the car with her loaded gun. After weighing the decision a moment longer, Brent decides he can trust me. He turns to his girlfriend.

"It's cool. I'll be right back. Just stay calm. Okay?"

"Hurry!" she says.

He finally gets out of the BMW.

"Don't do anything stupid," I say to the girlfriend, keeping the gun trained on her.

She muffles her cries, and we both watch Brent. He hurries up to the ATM, inserts his card, quickly presses some buttons, and nervously looks back at us. Seconds later the money slides out. Brent yanks the cash out of the slot and runs back to the car.

"Here. It's nine hundred." He hands me a wad of bills.

"Good job. I'm proud of you." I stuff the money in my pocket before snatching his cell phone off the console. The drunk girlfriend, without being asked, throws her phone to the backseat. I grab it and run out of the car.

I haul ass to the Olds, dive into the backseat, and Ronnie speeds away.

"Nine hundred." I pull off the stocking and gasp for air. I hand the money to Lori, who greedily counts it.

"Nice job, Cheerleader!" She hands me a beer.

I take a swig, and the girls cheer. I have officially committed my first armed robbery. Although it isn't quite armed. What Lori, Ronnie, and Cracker don't know, and what Brent and his girlfriend didn't know, is that the gun wasn't loaded. While I sat in the dark waiting for their car to arrive at the ATM, I discreetly ejected the magazine and gave it to Natice for safekeeping.

Natice looks over at me with a smile, and when no one is looking, she slides the magazine back to me, and I lock it into place.

"Here you go." I hand Lori her loaded gun.

CHAPTER 48

POP FINALLY HAS ENOUGH OF Natice and me coming in late and calling out sick, and he fires the both of us the day after the ATM robbery. I don't mind because working at the pizzeria has already served its purpose. Not only am I friends with the girls, but I am a branded member of their Black Diamond gang. Natice doesn't care because she has saved a good amount of money, and next January, she is heading to California.

"Congratulations! This is awesome!" I tell Natice, admiring her acceptance letter to Loyola Marymount. She has it taped to the mirror in her bedroom.

"I can't believe I did it." Natice stares at it. "January can't come soon enough."

We celebrate by drinking beers and talking about what Natice thinks college is going to be like and who she might get roomed with. It's something I was never able to do with Lea or anyone else from my high school. The last thing I could do is get excited about anyone else's life. But right now, I'm riding Natice's high right along with her.

I end up spending the night at her house since her stepfather is not at home. I want to ask Natice about Cracker and who she shot, knowing that Cracker was not joking the other night when she said she had. But Natice is in such a good mood, and every other time I have brought up the subject of Cracker or Lori killing anyone, she's gotten angry. I don't want to push it. And it still bothers me that I have no idea how involved Natice was in the store robbery. *Not to mention all the crimes we committed together.* By the time I get what I need, will Natice even be able to go to college?

The next day is Sunday, and we are playing basketball. The game is especially rough, and the referees have to intervene a few times to prevent a fight from breaking out between our team and the girls we're playing. The game is almost finished when the girl who is guarding me grabs my shirt. She won't let go, and I feel her nails pinching my skin. "Ref!" I yell. He doesn't even turn his head, and I reel back hard with my elbow and knock her to the ground.

Another fight almost erupts, and Vince and his boys have to separate our two teams. There are threats of kicking one another's ass and tons of cursing, and the refs promptly call the game to an end. The one thing they do not tolerate is fighting.

As we walk off court, Lori compliments my rough play. "Nice job, Cheerleader!"

"Thanks." I see Glendon, the crackhead from the East Cantor game, watching me from the bleachers. I keep walking off court, hoping that maybe I'm wrong, but when I look back, he is still staring in my direction.

I try not to think about Glendon as we pack into my car and head over to Ronnie's house. Her mother has prepared an Argentinian meal for us. Both of Ronnie's parents were born and raised in a small town south of Buenos Aires.

Ronnie's house is tiny, but unlike Lori's and Cracker's, or even Natice's, it feels like a real home. It smells amazing, thanks to what Mrs. Rodriguez has been cooking all day, and there's an immediate sense of being welcomed when I walk through the door. Family photos, many of Ronnie's daughter, Keisha, cover every inch of the living room, along with a collection of Catholic artifacts. I count at least seven crucifixes.

Ronnie's mother has just put Keisha down for a nap, and I get the feeling that Ronnie's mother is raising her daughter more than Ronnie is. I like Mrs. Rodriguez immediately. She's a sweet woman who hugs each one of us as we enter her home. She grabs Lori's face and kisses her.

"So *guapa!*"

I wonder if Mrs. Rodriguez knew what Lori does outside her home, she would still call her beautiful. Then she notices me. "*¿Quien es ella?*"

"This is Cheerleader, Ma," Ronnie says.

"What is cheerleader?" she asks.

The girls laugh.

I introduce myself in Spanish. "I'm Ally. Thanks for having me over for lunch. It smells amazing."

Ronnie practically falls over. "Shit, this bitch speaks Spanish!"

Her mother gently smacks Ronnie on the head. "¡*Dios mio!* The mouth on my child!"

"Sorry, Ma." Ronnie walks straight toward the kitchen. "Where's the food?"

Moments later, we sit down at the kitchen table and dig into a plate of beef empanadas. I've never had an empanada before. It's a light pastry filled with spicy beef. "It's delicious," I say in Spanish.

Ronnie laughs, still amused by the fact that I speak Spanish.

"Where's your good-looking husband?" Natice asks.

"Ay, running around with other women." She turns to me, noticing I've taken a break from eating. "Eat, eat."

I smile and take another bite.

Ronnie inspects her mother's hair as her mother bends over the table to fill the plate with more empanadas. "Ma, you gotta let me give you a new haircut."

"What for?" her mother says.

"You been wearing this tired old style for years. Look at this. You got split ends. It's all dried out. Forget the haircut. You need to condition this head."

"It's fine."

Ronnie feels the ends of her mother's hair. "You can't be running around lookin' like this. Let me fix it."

"No. Another day." Her mother pushes Ronnie's hand away. "Last week, she wanted to dye my hair red."

We break out laughing.

"What's wrong with red hair?" Cracker is the only one not amused.

After lunch, we go back to Lori's house to celebrate Ronnie passing her beauty school exam. Ronnie received her license in the mail yesterday.

I crack open a forty and take turns with Natice. My drinking, I've noticed, has progressed to every day.

Cracker bounces a basketball as she reads Ronnie's test score off a piece of paper. "Eighty?" she says, unimpressed.

"Yeah, eighty," Ronnie answers. "What's wrong with that?"

"Shit, you better be scorin' a hundred if you want to cut my hair."
Cracker hands the paper back to Ronnie.

"Damn, Cracker, can't you never just say nice job or good work?"
Ronnie says.

"The day that happens, I'll blow crackhead Glendon," Natice replies.

"Nice job. Good work," Cracker says.

"You gotta mean it!" Natice swipes the ball from Cracker's hands.

A cell phone beeps. "That's my five o'clock. Be back in five, bitches!"
Ronnie says, reading a text message and then heading off toward the school.

"Better watch out. Fines are double in the schoolyard!" Natice jokes.

Twenty minutes later, we are talking about heading over to Vince's to
hang out while waiting for Ronnie.

"What the hell is taking her so long?" Lori looks toward the schoolyard.

"Probably haggling over prices," Cracker says.

"This ain't no Best Buy!" Natice yells, imitating Ronnie.

We laugh, and by now, even I know Ronnie well. She sells drugs like a
used car salesman. A noise grabs our attention—a *pop* or a *crack*.

"What was that?" Lori says.

The second time we hear it, it's clear—it's a gunshot. We all sprint
toward the schoolyard.

Natice arrives first. "Oh God! *No!*" She runs to Ronnie, who lies on the
ground, bleeding from her chest. Natice kneels down and lifts Ronnie onto
her lap. Ronnie's face is severely beaten, barely recognizable.

"Call 9-1-1!" Lori screams.

I dial in a nervous rush, and a female voice answers. "This is 9-1-1.
What is your emergency?"

"My friend has been shot!"

"What is your location?"

"I don't know. It's a school off Oak Street!"

Cracker looks up at me. "Tell them to hurry!"

"Hurry!" I yell, sick to my stomach. My throat is tight with tears.

Lori drops to the ground and takes hold of Ronnie, becoming covered
in her blood. She begs Ronnie, much the way I begged Jenny. "Hang in
there, Ronnie! Don't you fuckin' leave us!"

Natice is crying. "Ronnie, we're here, girl! We're here, baby girl!"

Tears fill my eyes. I stare at Ronnie, begging God, *Please do not let her die.*

Cracker walks in a circle, her hands pressed against her face, repeating "fuck" over and over. Suddenly, Cracker stops and picks something up off the ground. It's a thick gold necklace. "Lori!" Cracker yells.

Lori stares at the gold necklace and instantly knows who it belongs to. Even I know. It belongs to Tonya, the girl from the Locust Park gang.

"Keep it! Put it away!" Lori says, her face lined with rage.

"Ronnie's phone!" Natice says, pointing to a bedazzled iPhone lying on the ground, a few feet away from her.

Cracker grabs the iPhone and stuffs it and the gold necklace down her pants.

"No one says a word about Tonya!" Lori points a shaking finger at all of us. "Nothing about the text or necklace. We don't know shit!"

And that's when we hear an ambulance's siren.

Seconds later, a team of medics jumps out of an ambulance and quickly goes to work on Ronnie. She barely looks alive. Her normally tan arms are ashen and limp. Her hand is ghostly white, her fingers like pieces of chalk. They stop the bleeding and place her on a gurney. We have to restrain Lori while they lift Ronnie's unconscious body into the ambulance.

"Ronnie! Be careful with her!" Lori screams.

Three cop cars have also arrived as a handful of uniformed police officers swarm the scene. One of the cops is Moreno, Thoms's Latino partner. He tries to speak to Natice, but she is hysterical.

"We don't fuckin' know who shot her! We found her like this!"

Moreno starts asking Lori questions. I vaguely hear what they are. "What were you doing?"

"Do you know who did this?"

"Did you see anyone?"

I keep my distance from Moreno, telling my account of what happened to another officer. "She was walking through to meet us. There were gunshots. That's all I know."

"We don't fucking know!" Cracker keeps shouting.

Finally, Lori pulls away from the officer who is questioning her. "This is bullshit. I'm going to the fucking hospital! You can question me there!" She runs off.

"Fuck it!" Cracker says as she, Natice, and I quickly follow after Lori. The cops don't chase after us. They know where we will be.

When we arrive at the hospital's emergency room, we are told Ronnie is still alive but in critical condition. We sit and wait, and I hate every second being in this hospital. "She's gonna be all right. Ronnie's tough," Natice says.

It isn't long before Ronnie's parents show up at the hospital. Her mother, who served us lunch a few hours earlier, is hysterical. "Where's my daughter!" she yells in Spanish. "Where's my baby!"

Ronnie's father has his arm around her, trying to calm her down, despite that fact that his eyes frantically search the hall, and he grabs at his neck as if trying to help it swallow. A nurse tries to talks to them, but Ronnie's mother keeps asking in Spanish, "Where is my daughter? I want to see her!"

Lori walks over to them, and Ronnie's mother grabs Lori, crying and begging to know what happened. I think about Ronnie's baby girl. I think about her younger brother and sister. I think about the intense pain they all will feel if Ronnie does not make it. I need to get out of this hospital. I can't breathe.

An elevator door opens, and Detective Thoms and Moreno step out. Thoms spots Lori at the front desk, talking to Ronnie's parents, and immediately heads toward them. I stand up and abruptly walk away.

Cracker yells after me. "What the hell, Cheerleader! She's fucking dying!"

Natice doesn't say a word. She simply watches me walk away.

I get to the elevators and press the down button. I hit it several times as if forcing it to go faster. Thoms is less than twenty feet away. He stands in front of Ronnie's parents, asking Lori questions. Finally, Lori walks away from him.

"Lori!" Thoms turns and calls after her.

He looks directly at me. It is brief, but our eyes lock right before the elevator door opens, and I disappear inside. I hit the lobby button with a heavy thumb, back up hard against the elevator, and watch the door close, willing it to move faster.

I run to my car and hop in. My hand shakes as I insert the key into the ignition. It takes me a few times of hitting the gas pedal before the engine starts up, and I am able to speed away. I'm barely out of the hospital's parking lot when my phone rings. It's Natice. I can hardly understand a word she is saying. She's screaming and crying hysterically and not making any sense. Finally I hear, "Ronnie is dead! She's fucking dead!"

The impact of this hits me, and I break into tears. I picture the doctor leaving the emergency room. I picture him telling Ronnie's parents their daughter is dead. I hear Mrs. Rodriguez's horrific scream. I picture Ronnie's daughter without a mother. I can't believe Ronnie is dead. I hang up the phone and speed through a red light.

I explode into the motel room and collect my belongings. I need to get out of Cantor. I need to go home. I reach for my duffel bag, but my strength gives out. I collapse to my knees and press my hands into my face. I scream to God, who I am certain hates me. "Please, God! Help me!" I sit on the floor, wondering how all of this happened. How Ronnie is dead. How I came to be living in this motel room. Then I remember why I am there and what I still need to know. I leave my bag behind and sprint out the door.

CHAPTER 48

MARK'S MUSTANG IS IN THE driveway when I pull up to the front of his house. I bang on the door like a maniac. A minute later, it opens. Mark stands in the doorway, looking concerned. My face is streaked with tears.

"What's wrong?"

"Ronnie is dead."

"Oh shit."

Mark leads me into the kitchen and sits me down in a chair. "What happened?" He looks at me in shock.

"She went to the school to sell drugs, and then we heard gunshots…"

"I told Ronnie she needed to quit selling that shit!" Mark says angrily.

"It was Tonya."

Mark's expression changes. "Fuck!" He walks around the kitchen then stops and looks at me. "Do the cops know?"

I shake my head. "No." I force back tears.

Mark pauses then, in an unsteady voice, says, "Ally, Lori's gonna go after Tonya. Get out of this shit now while you can."

"I can't."

"Yes, you can. Just go home!"

"I can't go home!"

"Why not? Just get on a plane and leave!"

I stand and face him. "Tell me the worst lie you've ever told, Mark!"

"What? What'a you talkin' about?"

"This won't be the first time Lori's killed someone, will it? She killed a girl before. She was fifteen years old. They said they were here that night. But they weren't, were they?"

"Who told you that?"

"Is it true?"

"Who told you that?"

"*Did she kill her?*" I scream in Mark's face.

"I don't know, Ally! And I don't want to know! They were here that night. And then they weren't. Anything in between isn't my business. And it sure as fuck isn't yours!"

I hold his eyes and look at him as if he is pathetic. "You're so weak. You're so fucking weak!"

I turn to leave, and Mark grabs my arm. "She's my sister, Ally! My sister! What the hell would you do?" Then he looks down at my hand and sees my iPhone. On the screen is an icon of a tape recorder. "What's that?"

"Tell me the worst lie you ever told, Mark. Did Lori kill my sister?"

Mark looks at me in shock. "Oh my God," he says as it registers who I am. "You need to go home. Please. Just leave."

"I can't."

I walk out of his house, leaving Mark staring after me, knowing full well I'm the sister of the girl who was shot and killed in that convenience store robbery.

I know I should drive back to Middletown right then, but I don't. Natice calls me and begs me to come over to her house. "Ally, I don't want to be alone! I'm afraid of what I'll do! Please!"

When I arrive at Natice's house, she is a mess. She is high and drunk and out of her mind. "Fuck, Ally!" She paces back and forth across her bedroom carpet. "I can't believe Ronnie's dead! I can't believe it!" Then Natice's eyes land on the photo of her, Lori, Cracker, and Ronnie. She crumbles into tears, and I stand there watching her, too numb to do anything else.

CHAPTER 49

Ronnie's funeral is excruciatingly painful. I watch helplessly from the back of the room as Mrs. Rodriguez cries hysterically, begging Ronnie's lifeless body to wake up from the casket, while Mr. Rodriguez keeps her from collapsing onto it. She yells as if her heart is being ripped from her chest and she cannot breathe. I know the feeling well. Crying right along with Mrs. Rodriguez are Ronnie's younger brother and sister. Family members try to console them, but it is useless. Then I notice Ronnie's little girl, Keisha, being held in the arms of a weeping aunt. Even Keisha looks sad, as if aware her mother is dead and she will never see her again.

Despite Ronnie's illegal activities, which most people have no idea about, Ronnie was well loved. Along with the tons of relatives who pack the room, there are numerous high school friends and beauty school classmates who show up to pay their respects. Even some of Ronnie's schoolteachers are present. Everyone cries, me included.

———•••———

"We play for Ronnie today," Lori says, finishing off a forty before leading Natice, Cracker, and me onto the basketball court. It's Sunday and only a day after the funeral. Lori thought it would be a good idea if we played in Ronnie's honor, challenging another team in a game of four vs. four. But we play sloppily, and by the time the second half arrives, I have no idea what the score is other than we are getting our asses kicked.

I'm thankful when the game finally comes to an end. None of us says a word as we gather our stuff and head toward my car. I'm lagging behind when I hear a voice yell after me.

"Yo, Number 15! Number 15!"

I turn and see Glendon walking toward me, excited.

"Yeah. I know you! I know you!"

I freeze, hoping no one else heard.

Glendon quickly approaches me. "I knew it was you. You threw that elbow and bam! Number 15. Down by two!"

He spots Natice up ahead. "Yo, Natty! Natty, you know who this is?"

Natice glances back at us but keeps walking.

"Natty!" Glendon yells after her.

I take hold of Glendon's arm. "For sixty, we could be best friends." I pull out all the cash I have and slap it into the palm of his sweaty hand.

Glendon smiles greedily. "Yeah. Number 15." He crumbles the cash into a ball and runs off, eager to fill his addiction. I relax slightly, watching him go, until Cracker appears behind me.

"What was that about?" She is staring after Glendon.

I hadn't seen Cracker walk back to get her bag.

"What are you talkin' about?"

"Number fifteen? Why's he saying that? Your shirt says Number 2."

"Maybe the crackhead's number blind. Who gives a shit?" I walk away, but I feel Cracker's eyes on my back. I know right then my time is running out.

As I drive us back to Lori's house, I begin to have second thoughts about remaining with the girls, especially now since Cracker's suspicions are dangerously high. I see her studying me in the rearview mirror. *Not to mention Mark.* I still haven't heard from him since I tried to record a confession. I know I'm crazy to be showing up at his home with his sister, but if he hasn't told Lori who I am by now, then why not? Maybe he's carrying his own guilt and trying to decide what to do? Or he believes Lori would make sure I'm planted in the ground next to Ronnie if she knew my true identity. I hope that's it, and he's keeping quiet to protect me. At least I know he didn't lie about Tonya. Lori has every intention of getting even with her. While the cops think it was a drug deal gone bad, we know different, and now, Lori wants to give Tonya the kind of beating Tonya gave Ronnie. I'm the designated driver because I'm a Black Diamond. *If only I could give back my membership.*

"Where the fuck is he?" Lori checks her phone for the third time.

"When's Vince supposed to call?" Natice asks.

"After he finds out where Tonya's gonna be tonight. Bitch knows I'm gonna fuck her shit up. She's hiding."

"I can't wait," Cracker says.

"Yeah well, as long as that's all we're gonna do is hurt her," Natice says. "No guns?"

"Yeah, Natty, it is! Don't fuckin' worry," Lori says. "I jus' need Vince to set it up."

I take it as a blessing that Mark isn't home when I pull into the driveway.

We gather in the kitchen and wait for Vince to call. It isn't long before Lori's cell phone rings, and she steps outside to talk in private. I sit down at the kitchen table, and Cracker takes the seat opposite me. She's making me nervous, more so when she pulls her revolver out from her sweatshirt pocket and puts it on the table. She spins the gun, making it go fast.

I try to pretend it doesn't bother me.

"*Will you put that fucking thing away?*" Natice yells.

Cracker stops the gun from spinning, and the barrel is aimed directly at me. She holds my stare for a moment then picks up the gun and tucks it into her sweatshirt pocket.

Lori walks back into the kitchen. "It's going down tonight. Vince is gonna stop by Tonya's place around nine o'clock. Dickhead's still been seeing her, so she ain't gonna think any different when he jus' shows up. After like fifteen minutes, Tray's gonna call him and say they need him at the warehouse. Vince'll ask Tonya to go with him, and when she does, we'll be waiting in the dark for that bitch."

"We're only beating on her, right Lori?" Natice asks.

"Yes, Natice! I already told you! I ain't gonna fuckin' kill her! A'right? I'm just gonna make sure she wishes I did!" Lori reveals the one weapon she will be bringing: a pair of brass knuckles, what Tonya wore when she beat Ronnie's face beyond recognition.

Lori tosses the brass knuckles on the table and opens a cabinet door. Her eyes grow wet as she stares inside. "Ronnie was right. Never shit to eat." She slams the cabinet door.

CHAPTER 50

I T'S ALMOST NINE O'CLOCK WHEN Lori, Natice, Cracker, and I pack into the Olds. I'm about to reverse out of the driveway when Mark's Mustang pulls in behind me, blocking us in.

"What the fuck is he doing?" Lori says, looking back.

Mark gets out of the Mustang and walks up to our car. I start to panic.

"Move your car, Mark!" Lori screams.

Mark appears at her window. "I need to talk to you." He slurs his words, obviously drunk.

"I'll talk to you later!" Lori shouts.

"It's important."

"I don't care! *Move!*" She swipes an angry fist at the air.

Mark looks in at me with a drunken stare.

My eyes beg him not to say another word.

"Mark, move your fucking car! *Now!*" Lori demands.

But he doesn't move. He stands beside her door, perhaps thinking about what to say.

"You got two fuckin' seconds!"

"Or else what? You'll shoot me?" he says, almost laughing. He glances at all of us in the car, takes us in as one big group. He shakes his head in disbelief, looking as if he may actually cry. "Whatever." He walks off.

My heart settles back into my chest as I watch him get back in his car and speed away.

"What the hell..." Cracker stares after him.

"Shit, I've never seen Romeo so torn up over anyone. He really loved Ronnie," Natice says.

I'm not so sure. I have a feeling it's me as much as Ronnie.

I throw the car into reverse and back out of the driveway, grateful Mark didn't give me up. His weird behavior, though, has affected all of us and made Lori even angrier. She pulls out a vial of cocaine and snorts a blast.

"When someone takes out your girl, you gotta do her justice. Ain't that right, Ally?"

"Exactly," I say, wishing that she were dead—not my sister, not Ronnie.

We reach the warehouse buildings, and Lori tells me to take the Olds around to the back. I splash the car through water-filled potholes and past deserted loading docks until I reach the very last building.

"Park over there." Lori points to an industrial-sized dumpster. I back up behind the dumpster, turn off the engine, and we sit in the dark. Waiting.

Around ten o'clock, Vince's Mercedes shows up. I see Tonya riding shotgun as Vince parks facing a loading dock. He keeps the headlights on and the engine running. Nothing happens for a few minutes. Then Tonya climbs into Vince's lap. He adjusts himself, and within seconds, Tonya's body is moving up and down against the window. Her arm braces her with each violent thrust Vince makes.

Lori stoically watches, along with the rest of us, as they fuck for what seems like forever. Finally, the driver's-side door pops open, and Vince steps out of the car and takes a piss alongside the dock.

"Tonya, come here," Vince yells.

Tonya steps out of the car, her pants collected at her ankles. She laughs, trying to pull them up.

"Suck my dick," Vince says. Tonya ignores her pants and drops to her knees with a smile. Vince backs away from her and zips up his fly, revealing Lori wearing the brass knuckles.

"What up, ho?" Lori says.

Tonya tries to stand, but Lori's foot is on her pants.

"No, keep that shit down." Lori winds up like a prizefighter and delivers the brass knuckles savagely across Tonya's face, shifting her nose to the left with a sickening crunch. Blood pours out of twisted cartilage, and Tonya crumples to the ground, where she is kicked, punched, and stomped mercilessly by Lori, Cracker, and Natice. No one seems to notice me as I stand off to the side. Another car arrives, and Tray and another boy exit the vehicle. Vince lights up a cigarette and watches the attack on Tonya as if he were sitting in a cinema.

Even though I loved Ronnie and hate Tonya for murdering her, it's hard to witness a beating like this. I can't take it anymore, and afraid that Tonya may be killed, I yell, "*That's enough!*"

Lori finishes with a kick to Tonya's head.

Natice has already tired and stopped seconds ago.

Cracker stands, breathing heavily and staring evilly at me.

I step closer to Tonya's body and see that her face is covered in blood. I worry I was too late and Tonya is already dead until she moans. Blood bubbles as the air escapes her lips.

Lori takes off the bloody brass knuckles and tucks them into her jeans. She starts to walk away then stops, pulls out a gun, and fires four shots into Tonya's body. "*Fade out*, bitch!"

Natice stands in shock, staring at Tonya's dead body. She turns on Lori, crazed. "You lying motherfucker! You said *no* shooting!" She lunges at Lori.

Tray steps in and grabs hold of Natice.

"You said no *fucking guns*!" Natice screams, fighting to hit Lori.

Lori stands defiantly, without any remorse. "She got what she deserved, Natice."

"Natty, calm down!" Tray holds onto a hysterical Natice.

"Let go of me!" She fights like an animal to break free then finally falls limp in Tray's arms and crumbles to the ground in tears.

"Get her the fuck outta here!" Vince yells.

Tray picks Natice up off the ground and sits her in the front seat of the Oldsmobile. Lori and Cracker hop into the backseat. I drive off feeling sick to my stomach.

"You said no shooting!" Natice sobs.

I reach the end of the warehouse buildings, when I hit the brakes, open the door, and vomit.

Natice gets out and starts walking in the dark.

"Natice! Natice!" Lori yells, chasing after her.

Natice turns and yells in Lori's face. "You said no shooting!"

"She got what she deserved, Natty! She killed Ronnie!"

"I don't care! You blew her brains out right in front of us!"

"You don't care? Ronnie was your girl! Your sister! Maybe you could'a let Ronnie down, but I couldn't!"

I wipe spit from my mouth and watch Lori take the gun she has just killed Tonya with and hold it out for Natice. "You need to lock this up."

Natice shoves the gun away. "Get rid of it yourself!" Natice turns to walk away.

Lori grabs Natice's arm. "I ain't playin', Natice. Take the gun, and lock it up. We'll deal with it tomorrow. I'm not askin' you."

Natice weighs the decision, and just when it appears she is not going to do it, she takes the gun from Lori's hand. "This is the last time."

CHAPTER 51

WE ALL GET BACK IN the car, and Lori tells me to drive to Vince's house. When I get there, I learn that, as with all the robberies, Lori had Tonya's murder mapped out in advance.

"Anyone asks where we were tonight, we were at Vince's playing poker," Lori says. "Got that?"

"Shit, I won fifty bucks tonight." Cracker puffs out her chest and steps out of the car.

"Natty, you gonna be a'right?" Lori asks.

Natice shakes her head. "I'm done. I can't do this shit no more."

"We'll talk tomorrow." Lori looks at me, and I can see she is mad that I didn't join in on the beating. "You understand we were playing poker all night, right, Cheerleader?"

I nod my head. "From eight 'til now, right?" I hold her stare with pure hatred in my eyes.

Lori smiles. "Right. Now put the gun in the fuckin' glove compartment." Without thinking, I bend down, feel for the gun under Natice's seat, and toss it into the glove compartment.

Lori steps onto the curb. "Make sure Natice brings it inside her house. You got that?"

"Yeah."

"How do we know she's going to?" Cracker says. "She didn't do shit tonight! Jus' stood there and watched! For all we know she's gonna call the cops."

"Fuck you, Cracker."

"No. *Fuck you!* You're a sneaky, no-good bitch!" She turns to Lori. "I don't trust her! I'm telling you, not one fuckin' bit!"

"Shut the fuck up, Cracker!" Lori shouts. "I swear to God! I don't need this shit right now! Jus' shut the fuck up!"

"I'm telling you, don't trust her!" Cracker yells.

"Trust me with what? The gun? If I was gonna call the cops, they'd be here already, you dumb ugly bitch!"

"What'd you call me?" Cracker says. "Get the fuck outta the car! You're dead!"

"I'll do it!" Natice shouts. "I'll lock it up! I'll put it away! Just go!"

"I ain't going anywhere! Get outta the car, Cheerleader!"

"Everyone shut up!" Lori yells. "I swear to God! Not another fuckin' word, Cracker!" Lori's face is red, and she looks fit to kill again as Cracker finally silences. Lori takes a moment to calm down before leaning into the car. "Natice, make sure you do."

Natice simply stares out the window.

"Natty, you hear me?"

"Yeah, I heard you!"

Lori gives me another harsh glance. "I got two people who said you were in on the shooting, in case you're thinkin' otherwise. You got that, Cheerleader?"

"I thought we were playing poker?" I hate her even more.

"Exactly." Lori turns to Cracker. "Fuckin' move!"

Cracker shoots me a last lethal look before walking off with Lori. The two disappear inside Vince's house. I sit with the engine running in the driveway.

Natice looks over at me. "I wish I was like you, Ally. I wish I could put it to my head and just pull the trigger."

I was too much in shock back at the warehouse to have it register, but then it hits me—I've witnessed Lori commit first-degree murder, and I have the murder weapon, possibly the same one she used to kill my sister. *Lori's going away for the rest of her life.*

"Lori, fuckin' A! How do you do that and not care!" Natice cries.

"You act like it surprises you, like it's the first time Lori's ever killed someone," I say angrily.

"It is!" Natice shouts.

I don't believe Natice, but if I'm wrong and she is telling the truth, that leaves Cracker as the person who killed my sister. "I guess Lori was right then. Tonya got what she deserved."

"You took someone's life. Do you deserve to die? Maybe I should kill you! Drunk driving—that's murder!" Natice screams.

"Maybe you should," I say, unafraid.

Natice breaks into tears and throws her hands over her face. "Fuck! How do you sleep at night?"

"I don't."

I leave Lori's house and find a liquor store that is open twenty-four hours. I don't bother to ask Natice if she wants anything as I go inside the store and grab two forty-ouncers. I head to the checkout counter, and when the guy behind it asks for ID, I hand him a crisp hundred-dollar bill, and he lets me walk out with the beer.

I don't want to go to the motel, and Natice doesn't want to go home, so we drive around for hours. At one point, a police cruiser pulls up next to me. Two cops are sitting inside. I think about stepping out of the car and telling the officers about the murder I witnessed and the gun in my glove compartment. But I simply watch them drive off ahead of me.

From there, I drive to the place in Cantor that I hate the most: the convenience store where Jenny was shot and killed. Natice doesn't say a word as I park and stare at the store. The sun is beginning to rise, and a man has just arrived to open the store. I wonder if he knew Jose Gutierrez, the man who was shot and killed along with my sister.

"Nice summer vacation," Natice says, her eyes wet with tears. "When you go home, will you take me with you?"

"Who says it's any better where I'm from?"

Natice wipes at her tears and focuses on the store. "When I was little, my mom used to take me here once a week. She'd let me pick out one candy bar. One day, I got greedy and wanted two. So I stole one, slipped it right into my pocket. It was a Snickers bar. She caught me eating it later and made me go back to the store and pay the owner. I started crying when I handed him the empty wrapper and a dollar. For being honest, the man told me to keep my dollar." Tears well up in her eyes. "If you could be anywhere or doing anything, right now, Ally, what would it be?"

I remain silent and think about Jenny. It would be driving around in my Jeep with her, listening to music, not doing anything at all.

"Man, I'd be five years old. Five years old and sitting on my mom's lap. I'd stay there forever," Natice says.

I decide right then it is time for me to go home. I've been a witness to murder, and I have the murder weapon. Lori Silva will go to prison for the rest of her life.

CHAPTER 52

I T'S EIGHT-THIRTY IN THE MORNING when Natice and I arrive at her house—more than twelve hours since this night began.

Natice takes the gun out of the glove compartment and turns to me. "You comin'? I don't want to be alone. I'm afraid of what I'll do."

"Sure." I'm worried about Natice, but mostly I want that gun. And wherever Natice puts it, I hope more evidence will be found.

"I need to take a shower and wash these clothes," Natice tells me as we enter her bedroom.

I notice a speck of blood on her forearm. Her cell phone rings.

"Fuckin' Lori." Natice eyes the screen on her phone. "Dammit, go away!" She ignores the call. "Ally, help me move the desk."

I watch Natice set the gun down on her dresser and help her move the desk a foot away from the wall.

"That's good." Natice grabs a ballpoint pen off the desk, rolls up a corner of the rug, and uses the pen to pry up a loose floorboard. Underneath is a hole. "Gimme the gun."

I grab the gun off the dresser and hand it to Natice, who hides it deep inside the hole. She snaps the floorboard back into place, rolls the carpet over it, and we return the desk to its original position.

"You need the bathroom before I take a shower?"

I shake my head. "No." I just want the gun and to get the hell out of there.

Natice is about to leave when her phone rings again.

I think for sure she's going to ignore the call, but Natice picks up. "What? I just put it away!" She turns quiet, and her expression changes as she listens to Lori. "Uh-huh." She looks at me. "No... yeah, I'm sure. I gotta go. 'Cause I gotta take a shower! I'll call you after." She hangs up and stares down at the floor, grabbing at her hair. Her eyes shift to me, and it's eerily familiar. I've seen that look a thousand times before, etched on the faces of the kids in my high school, all of them staring at me, not knowing what to say, but their eyes spoke volumes. *A mixture of sadness and pity.* Natice has that same look in her eyes when she says in a broken voice, "Lori wants us to go over to her house."

I don't know exactly what Lori said to Natice, but something tells me if I go to Lori's house, I'm dead. Maybe Mark finally told Lori who I am.

"I won't be long." Natice leaves the room.

I notice her phone is still in her hand.

I quickly push the desk aside, move the carpet, grab the pen, and pry back the floorboard. It takes me longer than Natice to pop the piece of wood up, but when I do, I reach down and immediately find the gun. I put it down next to me and feel around some more, hoping to find something else that may be used against Lori. And that's when I hear a creak—Natice stands in the doorway watching me.

"You never killed anyone drunk driving, did you?"

I don't answer, but I don't need to. Natice knows the truth.

"Good, that's good. You never want that feeling inside you."

I stand up, holding the gun, wondering what Natice is thinking.

"I didn't mean for it to happen. I want you to know I never meant for it to happen."

"You didn't kill Tonya. Lori did."

"I ain't talking about that. Lori didn't... she didn't kill her... it was an accident. No one was supposed to get hurt..."

A tortured look fills Natice's face, and I slowly begin to understand what she is trying to tell me. "Who didn't she kill?" I know in my gut what she is about to say. Every muscle in my body tightens. Oxygen drains from my lungs. Gradually, I feel the weight of a hand pressing down on my heart, twisting it, turning it, yanking it from my chest, tearing the life out of me. I shake my head no, not wanting Natice to continue. My knees go weak. *Please, God, please don't let her say Jenny's name. Please, don't let it be Natice who killed her.*

"We were only supposed to use the guns to threaten him, but the dude wouldn't give Cracker the money. She just... shot him. Blew him away. And... and I heard a crash. I turned and... I was startled..."

Natice starts sobbing, and I can barely understand her.

"The gun went off... I didn't mean to shoot her, Alex!" she screams, saying my name for the first time. "I just... I just turned and..." She cries hysterically, and I can barely see her. My own tears blind me. "I'm sorry. I'm so sorry, Alex. I didn't mean to hurt her!"

Natice takes a step toward me, and I raise the gun and aim it at her. "You didn't hurt her, Natice! You killed her!"

Natice stands in front of me sobbing. "I know. Please... forgive me..."

But I can't. I suddenly hate Natice. My arm is shaking as I fight to see her through my tears.

"I'm so sorry!" Natice cries.

My finger tenses on the trigger. I so badly want to pull it. If it had been Cracker or Lori, I would have emptied the gun. But it's Natice, someone who became my friend, someone I love. The gun shakes in my hand.

"Why? Why did you have to kill her?" I yell, wishing for the millionth time I'd never sent Jenny into that store. Wishing she were alive today. Wishing I could do it over. Wishing I could be with her one more time. I want my sister back so badly it hurts.

"I'm so sorry! I'm so sorry!" Natice cries, waiting for me to pull the trigger.

But I can't shoot Natice.

I lower the gun and collapse onto the bed. I sit there crying, feeling alone, more alone than I have ever felt in my entire life. Natice sits down next to me. She stares at me and wipes the tears from her eyes. She looks scared.

"Alex, Lori knows who you are. You need to go home."

Mark, I think, must have finally turned over on me. But I am wrong.

"Cracker broke into your motel room an hour ago. She found your driver's license, a bunch of other shit, and showed it to Lori," Natice says.

I walk out of Natice's bedroom without saying goodbye or asking anything else. I simply leave her crying and numbly exit her house. This is not how this was meant to end. Natice Gentry was not supposed to have killed my sister. It was supposed to have been Lori or Cracker, not her. I had been looking for evidence in all the wrong places, when it was right at my feet the entire time: Natice's mood swings, her anger, drowning her feelings with cocaine, her wanting to escape. I should have seen the signs. She was carrying around a black hole of guilt. *Just like me.*

I have my evidence with Natice's confession, but it doesn't make me feel any better. It makes me feel worse.

CHAPTER 53

I WALK TO MY CAR, HEARING police sirens going off in the neighborhood, trying to make sense of everything that has happened, when Mark's Mustang comes racing down the street. I know one thing. Mark is not behind the wheel. I hurry into the Olds, throw it into reverse, and I'm struck hard from behind. My head slams into the steering wheel, and I sit there feeling dizzy as blood pours down my forehead. I reach for the door handle as it flies open.

"Hundred bucks I kick your ass!" Cracker says as she and Lori yank me out of the car.

They throw me to the ground. The police sirens grow even louder, sounding as if they are right on top of us.

"You ain't so smart now!" Cracker's sneaker connects with my face. Then Lori presses a revolver to my head. It's Cracker's gun. I lie motionless.

"Go ahead. Do it." I hold Lori's hateful stare.

Before she can respond, three police cruisers and an unmarked car pull up to Natice's house. Thoms and Moreno spring from the unmarked car as a team of cops jump out of the cruisers. They have their guns trained on Lori and Cracker.

"Drop it, Lori!" Thoms orders. But she doesn't. Lori turns and aims her gun on Thoms.

"*Drop it!*" a police officer shouts.

I watch from the ground as Lori stands, ready to pull the trigger. This is what she always wanted. This is what she said she would do if she ever got the chance: shoot and kill Detective Thoms.

"Hold your fire!" Thoms orders, holding up his hand, waiting for Lori to lower the gun.

"Fuck you!" Lori yells.

Another cop trains his Glock on Cracker, who stands beside her. "Step away! Hands up!"

Cracker raises her hands, walks away from Lori, and is promptly thrown to the ground by two cops. She is handcuffed as Lori remains standing, aiming the gun at Thoms.

"Don't do it, Lori! Put the gun down!" Thoms orders.

Lori takes a step toward him.

"Hold your fire!" Thoms yells.

He's dead. She's going to shoot him.

But Lori breaks into tears and drops the gun.

Cops swarm her and bring her to her knees. One of the officers seizes the gun. Cracker is dragged toward a cop car, fighting and kicking as they shove her into the backseat and slam the door closed. Today, she turned eighteen.

Thoms walks over to me. "Is anyone else in the house?"

I don't answer. I wonder why Natice hasn't come out yet. Then I remember what she said to me earlier: "*Don't leave me alone, Alex, I'm afraid of what I'll do.*" Natice has carried the guilt of killing my sister for eight months. She has been in as much pain as I have been in. And she is alone in the house with a loaded gun. "*I wish I was like you, Alex. I wish I could pull the trigger.*"

I turn and run toward the front door. Moreno sees me and raises his gun. "Stop! Stop!"

I hear Thoms yell, "Hold your fire!" He blocks Moreno's shot as I disappear inside the house.

I take the stairs two at a time until I reach the top. I'm out of breath when I arrive in the doorway of Natice's bedroom. She sits on the floor. Tears streak her face, and in her hand is the loaded gun. She looks up at me, begging. "Please tell your parents how sorry I am." She brings the gun to her temple.

"*No!*" I dive at Natice as the gun fires. The sound pierces my ears. I lie on the ground with the smell of burnt sulfur filling my nostrils.

The gun drops from Natice's limp hand, and she falls into my arms sobbing. There is a hole in the wall inches from our heads.

Thoms appears in the doorway and looks at me, relieved. I am holding Natice in my arms as she cries.

241

I figured Natice called the cops, but I am wrong again. It was Mark. After sharing my ID with Lori, Cracker also showed it to Mark as proof of my identity. He said nothing, but when Lori took the keys to his Mustang and drove off with Cracker—a loaded gun in her hand—Mark could no longer keep quiet. He dialed 9-1-1. Apparently, Mark cried as he told the dispatcher Natice's address and added that his sister, Lori Silva, was armed.

I am brought out of Natice's house in handcuffs. My description matches that of the armed ATM robber as well as the perpetrator of several other crimes I committed. Natice is placed in a separate car, and we are driven to a police station.

My fingerprints are taken, and I am placed up against a wall for my mug shot photo. I am questioned by Thoms and another detective for hours. I decline an attorney and confess to every crime I committed, as well as those I witnessed Lori, Cracker, Ronnie, and Natice commit.

I also learn that Officer Rawlings, the bald cop with the tattooed arms, who I first saw in Thoms's office and then later in the chop shop talking with Tray, has been working undercover for the Cantor narcotics division for over a year. The department has been trying to nail Vince on a major drug trafficking charge for a while.

They ask me all sorts of questions about Vince, most of which I cannot answer. Apparently, Rawlings, who has not been seen since our arrest, gave Thoms all sorts of information on what Lori and the girls were doing—Thoms's way of keeping an eye on them. But what Thoms learns from me, and also Natice when questioned, is that all the information he had been given was bogus. Rawlings is a dirty cop with a huge gambling problem, and Vince paid him handsomely to pass along bad information.

By the time I'm done answering their questions, I'm exhausted. A cop escorts me to a small cell that holds only a cot and a toilet.

Ten minutes later, the door opens, and Thoms walks in. "Your parents are on their way. You're facing some serious consequences." He stares at me like a disappointed father.

I stare back, stone-faced and unfazed.

"What you did was stupid and reckless. Not to mention, you're lucky to be alive." He wags his head condescendingly then turns to leave the room.

"Hey, Thoms!"

He stops and looks back at me.

"You're a real winner, you know that? What did you do, huh? Other than tell my mother to move on with her life. You were keeping a close eye on these girls? When? You're a fuckin' bully with a badge, who was absolutely *useless*. So if you're gonna walk in here and say anything to me, say thank you."

I hold his stare, wishing for a brief moment Lori would've pulled the trigger. When he walks out, I'm relieved.

Aside from the fear of what my incarceration will do to my parents, I don't care. I have done what Thoms couldn't. I have gotten the girls arrested for murdering my sister. I just never imagined I would become a criminal in the process.

When my parents get there, I am moved into a white-walled room that holds only a table, four steel chairs, and a large mirror. The door opens, and Detective Thoms appears. He stands to the side and allows my father and mother to enter the room. Then he closes the door, leaving us alone. My parents are silent for what feels like forever. Their expressions are a mixture of shock and relief—shock over what I have done, relief that I am alive.

My father sits down next to me, uncertain, I guess, what to even say. Finally he asks, "Alex... are you okay?"

I nod and start to cry.

He puts his arms around me. "Thank God you're all right. Thank God." He chokes back his own tears.

I look up and see my mother standing against the mirrored wall, her face streaming with tears. "Why?"

I hold her eyes and cry harder. The truth is, I did it for her. I needed her forgiveness. And out of guilt. Maybe she senses that.

"Oh God." She walks over to the table, kneels down beside me, and hugs me tightly.

That little five-year-old girl returns with a vengeance, but only this time, she's no longer lost or scared or abandoned.

"I'm so sorry. I'm sorry for everything I said. I love you, Alex," my mother says. "I love you."

I haven't heard those words from her in a very long time.

CHAPTER 54

THE FELONY CHARGES AGAINST ME are armed robbery, grand theft auto, breaking and entering, and failure to report a crime—Tonya's murder. Since I was not involved in her shooting, nor did I have any knowledge Lori was going to kill her, I am not charged with accessory to murder. Detective Thoms persuades the district attorney to ask for a lower bail. He states that I am not a flight risk. I am a former straight-A student, a former All-American Athlete. I have no prior arrests.

The district attorney and judge agree, and I'm released on a hundred thousand dollars bail. My parents put their house up as collateral for the bail bond, and after living in Cantor for three months, I finally go home to stay.

———— •••• ————

I eventually serve eight months of a five-year prison sentence in a low-security state prison in Connecticut. I visit Natice as soon as I get out. She is serving a fifteen-year sentence with the possibility of parole in a federal prison in upstate New York.

I sit in the visiting center, in jeans and a white T-shirt, amongst half a dozen white, black, and Latino families. A door opens, and Natice appears. She looks exactly the same, aside from the khaki jumpsuit. She smiles at the sight of me, and I stand to meet her. Before we can even get our arms around one another, we're crying.

"Lookin' sexy in that jumpsuit, Gentry." I hold her tightly.

"Stop wanting me, Campbell."

We burst into laughter, and at once it's clear that we only have love for one another.

"How you doing?" I ask.

"I'm a'right," Natice says with a nod.

We sit facing one another, and I can tell there's something different about Natice, a lightness. "You sleeping okay?"

"Girl, the messed up thing is, I've never slept so good in my life."

I nod. "I get it."

"How was your time? You get a girlfriend?"

"Shit. I got three." I smile. "Nah, but I made friends. Tiny, she was in for mail fraud or scamming insurance companies, and then there was Eloise, my favorite. She was in for cutting off her boyfriend's nuts after she found him with a hooker."

Natice cracks up. "You're kidding?"

"Nope. But she's innocent. Said his nuts fell on the blade."

We double over laughing, holding our sides, and it feels good. Then Natice's face changes, and she takes hold of my hand, wanting to say something. Before she can speak, I squeeze her hand. "It's okay, Natice."

She cries.

"I know if Jenny would've met you, she would've liked you."

I leave with the promise to keep in touch through phone calls and letters. The first letter I receive from Natice, she tells me she scored an A on a recent criminal law exam. She's finishing her college degree in prison and says when she gets out, she wants to work with young adult victims of crimes. I write back that same day. *That's awesome. You'll do a great job! And be a fantastic mentor.* ☺ *xo Alex.*

Natice sometimes mentions Ronnie in her letters or in our phone conversations, but rarely, if ever, does she bring up Lori and Cracker, or anybody else from Cantor.

Cracker is currently serving two twenty-five-year sentences and one fifteen-year sentence for the murder of the clerk in the convenience store and various other offenses. She will be eighty-three years old by the time she is eligible for parole. Lori was convicted of first-degree murder and will spend the rest of her life in prison. Vince was shot and killed at his house while resisting arrest. He opened fire on police officers with a semiautomatic rifle. Tray and the rest of Vince's crew were eventually prosecuted and are currently serving time in various federal prisons.

Rawlings, the dirty cop, however, was never arrested. A day after the papers made news of all of our arrests and what I had done, his girlfriend found him dead in his apartment from a self-inflicted gunshot wound.

Mark, per his plea deal with the district attorney's office, moved out of Cantor and is living in Philadelphia. During his sister's trial, he testified against her, admitting that Lori was not at home the night of Jenny's shooting and that she was, in fact, part of the store robbery.

I palm the leather of a basketball and leap off the ground, hitting a three-point shot. My hair is tied back in a ponytail, and I'm wearing shorts and a tank top. I'm barely breaking a sweat, thanks to the unusually cool July night.

"Nice shot." Dr. Evans collects the ball and bounces it back to me.

"Your turn, Dr. E." I chuck the ball back to him. "Let's see a layup."

"All right." He gives the ball a couple hard bounces then goes in strong, laying the ball off the backboard and scoring easily.

I clap hard and loud. "You still got it!"

He catches the ball and pretends to limp off, one hand cradling his back. "I'm getting old, Campbell." He bounces the ball back to me.

"Nah, you're a young buck." I jump off the ground and hit another three pointer—this time, all net.

We play Horse for the next thirty minutes and then head over to Starbucks. Dr. Evans won't let me pay for my drink, and we find a quiet table outside to catch up.

"So how are your mom and dad doing?" He takes a sip of his iced coffee.

"They're good. Mom turned two years sober last week."

He smiles. "That's great. That's a big deal."

"Yeah, she's super involved, goes to like five AA meetings a week."

"Good for her." Dr. Evans nods. "Oh, I saw Jay last week in Red Bank, at McCloons."

"Yeah, he said he saw you. He's working there for the summer."

It's been over a year since I was released from prison, and a lot has changed. The year I got out, I turned twenty and enrolled in The College of New Jersey—the same college Jay goes to. We started dating again soon after, and it's been going great. Jay also went back to playing baseball and is the college team's starting second baseman. I'm proud to say I walked on to the basketball program's open tryouts and earned a starting spot. Jay and I are each other's biggest cheerleaders. I also started going to grief classes. They definitely help, and I have since had the black diamond tattoo lasered off the back of my hand.

My parents visited me every week when I was in prison. My mother and I have a very close relationship now. I can't remember the last time she criticized me. Most days, she tells me how beautiful I am, and I actually enjoy going to the movies and shopping with her. I've even discovered what a great sense of humor my mother has. My father and I continue to be best friends. The three of us often have dinner together and share stories about Jenny that are filled with love and laughter.

I see Dr. Evans strictly on a personal level now. He and his wife are expecting a baby in the fall. "Are you nervous to be a dad?"

"A little bit. Yes."

"You'll be a great dad. I'm not worried."

"We're pretty excited."

We share a smile, and Dr. Evans takes another sip of his coffee then places it down on the table. "So what else is going on with you?"

"I go to camp in five weeks. For real."

He shakes his head.

"Too soon?"

"Yes. Too soon."

When Dr. Evans first learned what I had done in Cantor, it was as much of a shock to him as it had been for my parents and everyone else in Middletown who knew me. But what was different about Dr. Evans is that when he visited me in prison, he confessed that, on the day I had met him at Starbucks, he swore he saw a black diamond tattoo under my Band-Aid. He said he almost called his friend at the University of Delaware's basketball camp to see if I had actually enrolled in the summer session. Something in his gut told him I was lying. He blamed himself for never having followed up. I understood the feeling.

We say goodbye and make a plan to meet up next week, this time with Jay. "Bye, Dr. E. Good job today."

He laughs. "Good seeing you, Alex." He gives me a hug and pats me warmly on the back. "Tell your parents I say hi."

"I will." I watch him walk off to his car. Then I slide behind the wheel of my dad's Audi and head home.

I have finally forgiven myself for sending Jenny into that store. I have also forgiven Cracker and Lori for their part in that robbery. When I was in prison, I often thought about them. I thought about how they were raised and where they grew up, about how we don't get to choose the parenting we receive or the environment we are raised in. If I had been given Cracker or Lori's mother as my own and been raised as brutally as they were, would I have turned out differently? Or if they had been raised in a quiet suburban town with two loving parents, or even one, would they be spending the rest of their lives in prison? I don't think they would, and I am grateful I am not.

I think back to what that woman in the grocery store said to me when I was fifteen years old. "*No. It gets harder.*" My life, for certain, has gotten harder. I will never be the same Alex I was before Jenny's death. I carry inside me a sadness that will never go away. But I do my best to enjoy my life. I do my best to have fun, even with the sadness. I know Jenny would want that.

Jay talks about getting married and starting a family. I feel too young to get married. But one thing is for certain: if and when I do have children, I will name my first child after Jenny. Hopefully it will be a girl. "Love ya, mean it."

ABOUT THE AUTHOR

Cheryl Guerriero was born and raised in Middletown, New Jersey, and she currently lives in Los Angeles, California. She began her writing career as a screenwriter. She wrote the screenplays for *Ghost in the Ring*, *Hunting Season*, and many more.

Cheryl wrote, directed, and produced the documentary short *My Best Kept Secret*. In 2004, Cheryl was invited to the Oprah Winfrey show to discuss the work.

When she's not writing and reading, Cheryl likes to hike and play competitive dodgeball in leagues and tournaments all over Los Angeles.

CPSIA information can be obtained
at www.ICGtesting.com
Printed in the USA
FSHW010749180421
80590FS

9 781940 215969